Praise for Raymo

T0023299

"Raymond Queneau's *The Blue Flo*[ ]
wildest rides in literature. With as much colloquial language as Joyce and Pound, as much bawdy humor as Shakespeare and Chaucer, and as much puzzle-like wordplay as any of his fellow Oulipo brethren, Queneau gives us an idiosyncratic masterpiece to enjoy, to study, to wrestle with for the ages."

—*Literary Hub*

"Queneau's role of combined scientist and pataphysician makes him seem more clearly than ever the forerunner of those other disintegrators of language: Ionesco and Beckett."

—*The New York Times*

"When it came to the novel, Raymond Queneau imagined a kind that would advance along strict compositional lines, like poetry or architecture, yet upset all expectation."

—*The New Yorker*

"In our century Queneau is a unique example of a wise and intelligent writer, who always goes against the grain of the dominant tendencies of his age and of French culture in particular--and he combines this with an endless need to invent and test possibilities. *The Blue Flowers* makes fun of history, denying its progress and reducing it to the substance of daily existence."

—Italo Calvino

"We always feel good reading a Queneau novel; he is the least depressing of the moderns, the least heavy, with something Mozartian about the easy, self-pleasing flow of his absurd plots."

—John Updike

"Raymond Queneau's books are ambiguous fairylands in which scenes of everyday life are mingled with a melancholy that is ageless."

—Albert Camus

Other Books By Raymond Queneau in English Translation

Witch Grass

The Blue Flowers

Children of Clay

Exercises in Style

The Flight of Icarus

A Hard Winter

The Last Days

Odile

Pierrot Mon Ami

Saint Glinglin

The Skin of Dreams

The Sunday of Life

We Always Treat Women Too Well

Zazie in the Metro

Raymond Queneau

SALLY MARA'S
INTIMATE DIARY

Translation and supporting texts: James Patrick Gosling

DALKEY ARCHIVE PRESS
Dallas / Rochester

Originally published in French as *Le Journal Intime de Sally Mara* by Éditions du Scorpion
Copyright © 1950 by Raymond Queneau
Translation © 2023 by James Gosling

First edition

All rights reserved

Paprback: 978-1-628974-60-7
Ebook: 978-1-628974-87-4

Library of Congress Cataloging-in-Publication Data: Available.

Cover design by Kit Schluter
Interior design by Anuj Mathur

Dalkey Archive Press
Dallas, TX / Rochester, NY
www.dalkeyarchive.com

Printed on permanent/durable acid-free paper.

Contents

PREFACE

First published by Éditions du Scorpion over seventy years ago, *Journal intime* (de Sally Mara, 1950)—now available in English for the first time as *Sally Mara's Intimate Diary*—has a unique combination of linguistic gymnastics, bizarre behavior, restrained explicitness, horror, and innocence. It's that rare thing, a darkly humorous and salacious story by a skillful and erudite writer. Raymond Queneau imagines Sally Mara, 17 ¾ years old in a nineteen thirties Joycean Dublin, beginning her diary in newly-learned French in memory of her beloved and just departed French tutor and polyglot linguist Michel Presle. She is also learning Irish with the poet Padraic Baoghal in order to write a novel in that language, but seems to spend much of her time, painstakingly and haltingly, struggling to unravel the mysteries of reproduction and sexuality.

Initially published anonymously but later republished under his own name as the largest component of *Les Œuvres complétes de Sally Mara* (1962), *Journal intime* was long regarded as just a piece of ineffectual erotica written in a hurry, just to gain some ready cash. However, since the early 1980s, appreciation of its complexity and finesse has grown. In fact, it is the product of substantial research and reflection as testified by its detailed awareness of the life, politics and streets of Dublin at that time as well as of the collection of the

National Gallery; and by a familiarity with the Irish language that allowed Queneau to seed it with many Irish words and phrases and even to exploit Irish humorously. There is also a fine understanding of publications for women, of fashion, and of perfumes in 1930s France. It has many facets:

Sally Mara's Intimate Diary is an erotic novel, revealing the supposed sexual thoughts, feelings, and clumsy initiatives of a naive young woman, but an erotic novel with a strong, combative, independent-minded heroine and mostly weak ineffectual men.

But it is a subversive erotic novel that would have left many early readers with mixed feelings, especially when their prurient tendencies were wickedly toyed with. Its humor undermines reactionary attitudes to women and especially to sex education, and the minimization by criminals and their families of their crimes is satirized.

In some ways it is also be a proto feminist tract. Sally labors to overcome the ignorance of sex and reproduction society has imposed on her, is subjected to regular petty sexual harassment, and rejects with skillful and sometimes bloody violence overt sexual attacks.

Reflecting very well Queneau's preoccupation, it is fundamentally about language and languages; the humor is largely linguistic, words are misused and misunderstood, and fun is made of how they are spelled in French, English, or Irish.

In all it is a Bildungsroman, the story of a young woman's crucial formative years and her becoming aware of the complexities of the human condition, how even others close to her are largely unknowable, but also with the challenges facing an aspiring writer.

Sally Mara's Intimate Diary

1934

He is gone.

The boat leaves, puffing its colorless smoke across the screen of the sky. It whistles. It chokes. It goes. And it carries away Monsieur Presle, my French tutor.

I waved my handkerchief, now, this night, I soak it with tears, before gripping it between my legs, on my heart Oh! God, who will ever know of my torment? Who will ever know that this Monsieur Presle takes with him my entire soul, which is most certainly immortal? He, Michel, never did anything to me. Monsieur Presle, I mean to say. I know that men of his age do things to silly young girls of mine. What things and why? I do not know. I myself am virgin, that is to say "I have never been exploited" ("virgin land: land that has never been exploited," according to my dictionary). Monsieur Presle, he never touched me. Nothing, except his hand on mine. Sometimes it slid along and down my back, to tap lightly on my bum. Simple gestures of politeness. He taught me French. With determination! He taught it to me not too badly, so that, in his honor, as a souvenir of his leaving I mean to say, I am going to, from today, from now on, write my diary in his mother tongue. These will be my French writings. And

3

the others, my diaries in English, I am going to fuck them into the fire.

"Fuck," he told me, "is one of the most beautiful words in the French language." It means: to throw, but with extra vigorosity. I repeat here his teachings, and what titillating pleasure it is to repeat them, a soft warmth filling my thoracic cavity from my shoulder blades to my young chest, which is not like a blade (i.e. flat), so for example: "you throw a glass of beer behind the necktie," but "a diamond dazzles by fucking light into your eyes." He, Monsieur Presle, greatly loved helping me understand the subtleties of the French language, and it is for that reason that now, in his memory, and one day to fuck over his idea of me, I will continue to write my diary in his native idiom.

I have kept a diary since I was ten years old. Mammy would say to me: "A good practice for little girls, it develops their conscience, they become more holy, and, in the end, that fucks up the impressions of the priest to the extent that he promotes their consecration as nuns—until they die." That is not my opinion at all. It is not that I think badly of nuns, but there are other things to do on earth for people of the feminine sex. On this I am of the same opinion as Michel, my dear French teacher, ah! if he had known how I repeated his name during the night until falling into a kind of anguish. It is curious how I have, at times during the night, some kinds of fits while thinking of him. Afterwards, I sleep marvelously.

Yes, off he is gone, on his boat and on the St. George Channel at the same time. What don't I owe him? Being able to write my *journal intime* in French for one, having a languid heart for two, and the excitations mentioned above for three.

Feeling so alone on the quayside, I made two solemn resolutions on this day of days, as the night-time moon was hanging moon-like and still under the canopy of the moonlit sky, lighting with its pale moonlight the ship on which Michel was floating off towards his future, academic but not Irish. So I made a double resolution, firstly, to keep my diary, no longer in English, the language of insular sailors—although it's not silly to be a sailor when living on an island—but definitely in French, as they—the French—live some in mountains and some even in the middle of plains; and also, secondly, to write a novel. But a novel that is something solid and rounded, that doesn't feel like it was written by a young woman who has not yet been exploited; on top of all that, in Irish, a language that I do not know. It will be necessary, therefore, that I learn it, and why do I want to learn it? To do as Monsieur Presle does. Monsieur Presle is a linguist: he knows all sorts of languages. He has even taken lessons on Laz and Ingush with Monsieur Dumézil. He learned Irish in no time: his stay in Dublin was like a lightning flash through the muscle of my heart. But it was mainly in French that he used to play around. And what a good teacher he was! The proof: I am writing fluently my intimacies in this language with ease and aptitude. If sometimes I am missing a word, I don't give a fuck. I go straight ahead.

And so he was going away. The wind started to blow across the harbor and the blotting mist blotted out the ship. I stayed for a time looking towards the movements of Saint George's Channel, along the granite line of the quay, the taut riggings, the stiffness of the *bittes*—one of the first French words that Monsieur Presle explained to me, because of its Scandinavian origins: "*biti*: cross beam on a ship." And the Vikings, did they not conquer our green Erin?

He was gone.

The wind began to blow with force. I turned towards the tram. I went along the quay. Other people—shadows—were following the same path, their goodbyes or their work done. The dense night was being shaken by a real storm. I heard again the siren of the ferry.

To reach the terminus, it was necessary to cross a small

footbridge over a lock. On the other side, I saw a vehicle, lit up as it maneuvered. With a heart full of the memory of Michel Presle, I began to cross the little footbridge, but halfway across I had to stop. I felt that the wind was going to carry me off and to fuck me down below, into the dock, into the middle of a pool of oil that was radiating iridescently in the light of the moon. I was gripping the balustrade, and, with the other hand, was trying, without thinking, to seize another point of support. I then, suddenly, became aware of the presence of a man behind me. I guessed that it was a gentleman: not a woman or a sailor. And I heard a voice, soft and polite, whisper into my ear these reassuring words.

—Hold tight the rail, miss.

At the same time, into my still free hand, was carefully placed, an object that had, all at once, the rigidity of a bar of steel and the softness of velvet. I gripped it convulsively and, full of surprise that this handrail stayed warm in spite of the north wind that was still blowing with a wintery chill, I could, with its help, make it to the other bank.

The friendly gentleman who had accompanied me readjusted his mackintosh (if it was not a raglan or a ouaterproufe; it was night, I could not be sure. Moreover, I had timidly lowered my eyes). I could not see his face, I could just make out the shadow of his mackintosh (or raglan) (or ouaterproufe) traced on the uneven paving stones of the quay, which, distended at first, regained slowly and curiously a vertical line, or slightly rounded at least. We had remained silent; then, although I knew well that one should not speak to a man to whom one has not been introduced, I said, with all of the gentility of which I am capable:

—Thank you, sir.

But he did not reply, and walked off.

Alone again, again the harbor, the night, the sirens. The

tram had finished its manoeuvre and was getting ready to fuck off. I ran after it. I sat down out of breath. There were only, as other passengers, two dozing dockers and a young man whom I had seen accompanying an old lady (his mother?) to the ferry. As I was smiling vaguely, he blushed crimson and let on to be reading a newspaper, his hands shaking a little. The tram started. I paid for a ticket and abandoned myself to my thoughts.

O tender emotions of a young girl's heart, o alluring excitements of the springtime of a soul, o innocent curiosities of a blossoming maiden. A charming exaltation was filling my being and I did not know what to think. A thousand contradictory ideas were clashing under my hair (which is beautiful . . . a little auburn . . . dark auburn . . . very dark auburn, to be exact) and a gentle warmth rose and fell the length of my back in the elevator of my spinal marrow, from the ground floor of my posterior to the sixth floor of my hair roots. I say sixth even though in Dublin the houses rarely have more than four floors, but then again I am quite tall.

I realize that I have not yet introduced myself and that the copybook that I use for my intimate diary is impatient at not knowing better the girl who scribbles on its pages. And so here it goes—Dear confidant: my name is Mara, the first name is Sally. I have been periodic since the age of thirteen and a half, a little late, but I must confess that in that respect I am a veritable little clock. I no longer have my father: ten years ago he went out to buy a box of matches and never returned, he was not nationalist, but never told anyone of that. I was eight years old then. I remember it well. He was there, in slippers and a dressing gown of yellows and violets. He was reading the newspaper while smoking his pipe. He had won the Sweepstakes and had given all the money to Mammy. Mammy said suddenly, just like that:

—Look, there are no matches in the house.

—I will go out and buy a box, answered Daddy, calmly without raising his head.

—You will go out like that? asked Mammy, quietly.

—Yes, answered Daddy, calmly.

That was the last word I heard him say. We never saw him again.

He used to spank my bottom regularly, twice a day, to practice, he said, his belief in the educational methods recommended by the English crown.

Anyhow, my mother, with her own small endowment and the remainder of the Sweepstake, made sure that we had good educations, myself, my sister, and my brother: for myself I do nothing, but I could be a student if I wanted. My sister, who is two years younger than me, wants to be a post office assistant: she wants to earn a living and be independent, an idea of her own. She studies geography a lot so as to achieve it one day. Joël, my brother, he's the eldest. He drinks not a little, mainly ouisqui and Guinness stout, the source for which we have here. He also likes Ricard pastis. But it's difficult to find it. Monsieur Presle procured him a bottle. We had a great laugh that day; we emptied it the same evening. For myself, I like herring with ginger, boiled leeks, and rollmops. I measure 1 m 68 in height and weigh 63 kilos. I am 88 cm around the bust, 65 around the waist and 92 around the hips. I wear very short skirts, knickers, and low heel shoes. My hair also, I wear very short, and I put on neither lipstick nor powder. I am a member of a sports club. I run the 100 meters in 10 seconds 2/10. I jump 1 m 71 in height and put the shot 14 m 38.18 But recently I have neglected the athletics. I like to cross my legs, I think this is modest and at the same time sophisticated: this is also, without doubt, what the young man in the tram was thinking, because from time to time he lowered his newspaper, raised his eyes to sneak a look, then quickly let them, his eyes, fall again. For myself, I thought about him who was now sailing on the waves of the Saint George Channel. We arrived in the city. And we—the young man and I—by chance of course, we got up at the same time to get off at the same station. I had never seen him in the neighborhood. I noticed that his legs trembled. For a moment I asked myself if he was not the man who had so graciously helped me to cross the footbridge. But no, it was impossible: the young man was already seated in the tram when I got on and the gallant gentleman had headed off in another direction.

As the tram jolted, the young man stepped onto the platform to get off before the car came to a complete stop. I feared for him and I almost cried out: "Hold tight the rail, mister!" but he had already jumped, run off, and disappeared into the night.

I, in turn, gripped the handrail and found it damp and ice-cold, it had neither the softness nor the warmth, nor the vigor, of that from a little while before.

At home, I found Mary in the process of learning by heart the sub-prefectures of the French departments, as always for the examination for post office assistants. Joël, distracted and with glazed eyes, was sitting in front of seven bottles of Guinness, five empty and two to be emptied. He giggled when he saw me. He was thinking that I was sad because of the departure of Monsieur Presle.

Mammy talked a lot about Monsieur Presle with Mrs. Killarney. From time to time Joël hiccupped stupidly. But, for me, I was smiling. Mary noticed it. After dinner she wanted to make me talk, but I was cautious: I went on at length about the handrail and said almost nothing about Monsieur Presle.

14 JANUARY

Last night I dreamt that I was in a kind of amusement park, like Coney Island, that you see in American films. A very friendly gentleman bought me a barley sugar stick but this delicacy was so large that I had great difficulty putting it into my mouth and sucking it. Dreams are stupid . . .

Monsieur Presle told me that on the continent, and even in England, there are charlatans who explain the meaning of dreams. This takes an hour and you have to lie back on a couch in front of them, which is not very respectable, it seems to me. In our country, the priests are completely against that.

I still intend to write a novel. But about what?

18 JANUARY

On re-reading the first pages of my diary, I ask myself if I correctly used the word "virgin." Because in the dictionary there is: "said of land that has never been exploited or cultivated." And, without flattering myself, I, for one, am quite cultivated. But I have to come to terms with my situation, there will be more than one mistake on these pages that are destined only for posteriority.

20 JANUARY

I am beginning Irish lessons, the young man of the tram is as well; it's remarkable. Our teacher's name is Padraic Baoghal. He is a poet. He has long flowing hair and a distinguished look. He wears a prominent black cravat like those that Frenchmen wear (not Monsieur Presle: just bow ties). His eyes are strikingly blue. I have not read what he has written because he writes only in Irish. He gives private lessons to put bread on the table. Mrs. Baoghal is there also, for mine at least. She sits in a corner and paints tiny miniature pictures, total concentration without ever raising her eyes. The young man of the tram arrives just after me. On leaving when I go through the entrance hallway, he is waiting there. Then he lowers his eyes.

25 JANUARY

Ah, Monsieur Presle has not written yet.

27 JANUARY

It's not very intimate, my diary. I, who wanted to lay out here all of my little (immortal) soul. But it's true that I spend long hours on Irish, which is a very difficult language. Padraic Baoghal thinks that I am making great progress. But where is my intimacy in all that?

29 JANUARY

Joël thinks of absolutely nothing except drinking. After dinner, while alone in my room studying the third declension (*ceacht* and *bádóir*), he came in very quietly and, without saying a word, sat on my bed. He looked at me benignly; he was not in a humor to break things, which happens sometimes. No, his bleary expression was that of a gentle calf. I found him hideous. We looked at each other silently for a few moments, then he lifted up his behind (there is another word in French, but I cannot think of it for the moment) and took out, from under his backside (ah, here it is! but no, there is yet another French word to indicate the rectal area, impossible for me to think of it for the moment), a book that he had concealed as he came in. He showed it to me:

—You recognize this book? he asked me.

Of course I recognized it. It was in a jacket of the colored paper that my dear French teacher was in the habit of using to cover his books. When he went out for a few moments, I used to seize them and turn them over in my hands without daring to open them (he had forbidden that). When I heard his steps returning, I would put them back, and, with a dry throat, I would put on the air of someone drumming into their brain "add -x in the plural—pou, chou, genou . . ."

—You stole it? I cried.

—He forgot it, answered Joël.

—What right had you to take it?

—So that you would not read it.

—And you, have you read it? He sighed.

I said:

—Well?

—Well, I've discovered something awful.

I did not dare to question him further, but he answered all the same.

—I have some.

—You have what?

—Complexes

—Whasit-thasit?

Monsieur Presle sometimes wrote French like this to demonstrate clearly to me the subtleties of French spelling. Naturally, as we were speaking in English, I just said:

—Ouatt?

Joël answered:

—Yes, complexes. I had them explained to me by an agricultural student who knows a lot about them. But I don't see how I can repeat such secret things to a young girl of your age. They're worse than the secrets of the confession box; there you can just tell your sins once and then they are gone, while with complexes you could talk about them for years without getting rid of them.

—I cannot understand a word of what you are saying.

—I hope not.

I began to feel a bit afraid that he would start coming out with strange unspeakable words, which, o fuck!, would make me blush.

He went on:

—The priests don't go along with this. They stick you with Our Fathers, Hail Marys, and rosaries, and afterwards you are done. The sins. Washed away. But as for complexes? They don't care about them! It would take them too long. They wouldn't have time to make their dough if they had to bother with the complexes of the whole country.

—Oh, you, you never liked priests much.

It's not that I myself like them a lot. In our family we are Catholic. But without excess: I believe firmly in the virginity of Mary, but as for God, the proofs for his existence that I have been given seem to me to be mainly inspired by superstition. I go to mass (in spite of having my bottom pinched, never less than three or four times a ceremony); I go to confession; I perform my Easter duties, but otherwise I'm not too bothered. As for priests, like Mammy says, they are just men like the others, simply those that you don't marry.

But Joël continued:

—Here, would you like me to explain?

I said neither yes nor no.

—So, take, for example, Mrs. Killarney . . .

(That's our housekeeper.)

He stopped.

—Well, what? I said.

I did not understand, truly, what he was getting at.

Joël still remained silent.

—Eh well, what? I continued. She has a moustache?

Joël's eyes brightened with a spark of life. It was a really long time since that happened to him, to this drunkard. But there was an eel under the rock—I am inspired by the chapter on French proverbs; my dear teacher had me learn piles of them by heart, like: "Of them he has two like the priest in Lisieux"; "For a wandering prick, nothing is impossible"; "Better to let the sheep piss than shit in the sauce"; "As for bordellos, I prefer the Metro, it's jollier and then it's warmer," etc. What a beautiful language all the same, French, and what a pleasure it is for me, alone in my dressing gown before an Irish turf fire, to be able to play with delicious, exotic phrases that are used on the other side of the sea by dockers in Le Havre, drivers of hackney cabs, mustard makers in Dijon and crooks in Marseilles. Aaah! I am melting, melting, so close my thoughts are to my tongue. But good God of good God, I am wandering off. Back to the brother. After his moment of lucidity, he rose thoughtfully and said softly:

—Yes, that's just what I was saying, that's just what I was saying.

And he went out.

Taking the book.

30 JANUARY

I searched his room. I found five bottles of ouisqui under his bed, but no book. He has hidden it terribly well.

31 JANUARY

No news from Monsieur Presle. He's not being very nice all the same; he who so definitely promised to write to me.

2 FEBRUARY

Still no way to put my hands on the book on complexes.

3 FEBRUARY

No letter from Monsieur Presle, again today. The fraud.

4 FEBRUARY

I took the tram today to Dunleary—Kingston that is, the port of Dublin. I pronounce it "Dimleary" in imitation of my master Padraic Baoghal. I must say that I find this kind of patriotic linguistics a little silly, but I suppose that I can permit myself that in intimate journalese. Night falls quite early still, and mist. I walked on the dock. I found it difficult to find my bearings. I hesitated between different footbridges.

Finally I recognized mine, dimly lit like on the day of Michel Presle's departure. My heart beat faster in my chest and I recalled clearly this other French proverb taught to me by him who has departed: "To innocents, full hands" But I did not find my gallant gentleman.

And on the tram, there was not even my classmate, the timid young Irishist. There was just a little less mist over Dublin, but the aroma of Guinness was stronger.

My sister Mary has just to learn the sub-prefectures of Tarn and Garonne and the Var. Joël has not sobered up for three days. I look at Mrs. Killarney without success in discovering what she could have by way of a complex.

Mrs. Baoghal has invited me to take tea at her home. I was terribly excited. Three times I made my little contribution before leaving, and in spite of that, in the tram while passing Cuffe Street I am struck by a great need. My God, my God, what was I going to do? My heart raced, a right panic. So intimidated. There would be other great poets and their wives who would examine me, and young men who would surely want to marry me, and among them, certainly, the young man of the tram who, like me, is learning Irish. And my need for release that kept growing and this jolting of the tram that only augmented my need and shot my bladder up to my eyeballs. I clenched my jaws, not moving my tongue. I clutched my knees. I looked around beyond everything, out the windows, without fixing my gaze on anything. I began to feel a little perspiration at the small of my back and under my arms. It even seemed to me that some drops were beginning to form between my young breasts. I told myself that I could hold out until I met Mrs. Baoghal, but clearly there would be stairs to climb and it's awful to have to climb stairs when one is tormented with such a necessary compulsion, and, clearly, the first thing that I would not dare to say to the hostess would be: "Where is the convenience." I would have to wait a while before putting the question, to have the reply, and to reach the requested location. My visceral torments grow with these worries, and then, who is this who joins the tram at the Dame Street stop? The young Irishist. Electric shivers run around my head, from chin to ears, from nape to occiput. And it was like as if a jar of hot water had been grafted into my belly, a tropical aquarium, a uric pot. I almost screamed; I could go on no longer. I saw that we were approaching Great Brunswick Street and I thought of my Aunt Cornelia. It has been two years since I have been to see her, but she would not refuse me this service. I stood up, and I noticed a look of alarm in the eyes of the young Irishist. He clearly believed that I would be travelling with him as far as Nelson's Pillar, that we would alight from the tram together, when he would talk to me, saying something like: "It seems to me, Miss, that we have already met . . ." Even if he were an awful nitwit, this fucked-up Irishist would have been obliged to say something to me. But then, I had remembered Aunt Cornelia and said to myself: "All the same, I am not going to suffer any longer; I only hope that it is modern." So I suddenly got off the tram.

Happily Aunt Cornelia was at home. And I remember it as being comfortable: it was English style.

7 FEBRUARY

It seems that in Paris France there have been ructions. Here, we have had some of the same. Hopefully, Monsieur Presle has not been injured, although he would not be a man to get into a fight. By the way, he totally turned me against the Blueshirts of our General O'Duffy, and, what's more, purged me of all patriotic sentiments by informing me that Ireland is an even smaller island than Newfoundland: a fact that is always kept from us.

An intimate diary is ok if it does not involve a lot of work. All these days, no desire, but a desire for what? . . . Certainly, I am becoming more and more intimate. All the same, it makes me sort of proud to think that, without a doubt, no other young girl, English, Scottish, Newfoundlandish, or from anywhere, is as intimate as I am.

On this subject, I notice that I did not finish my account of the afternoon tea at the Baoghal house. So, after my rapid visit to a surprised Aunt Cornelia, I took the tram again for Sackville Street. I was late and red-faced; actually lots of people were there: the master and mistress greeted me warmly and protectively, and introduced me to the intellectuals and intellectualesses present. The poet Connan O'Connan, his friend the poet Grégor Mac Connan and his brother-in-law the poet Mack O'Grégor Mac Connan as well as the bard-druid O'Cear and the primitivist philosopher Mac Adam, as well as their wives Mrs. Connan O'Connan, Mrs. Grégor Mac Connan, Mrs. Mack O'Gregor Mac Connan, Mrs. O'Cear and Mrs. Mac Adam and their sons George Connan O'Connan, Phil Mac Connan, Timoléon Mac Connan, Padraic O'Grégor Mac Connan, Arcadius O'Cear, Augustin O'Cear, Cesar O'Cear, Abel Mac Adam and Cain Mac Adam, and their daughters Irma Connan O'Connan, Sarah Mac Connan, Pelagia Mac Connan, Ignatia O'Gregor Mac Connan, Arcadia O'Cear, Beatitia Mac Adam and Eva Mac Adam, as well as the young Irishist of the tram: Barnabé Pudge. Thus I learned his name. And he reddened more than I did, as I managed to say something suitable for a well brought up girl, and pale.

—Come along my friends, said Padraic Baoghal, now that you all know each other and everyone is here, let us go . . .

—A cup of tea? suggested to me the wife of the master of the interior, while he himself tapped discreetly my posterior.

Never, is it to be permitted that I should be treated in that way, like a schoolgirl. I am a student I am. I did not believe my rump as this was going on.

—Thank you I replied, as I lightly shook myself like a mare shaking off clegs.

—She is charming, murmured Mrs. Baoghal.

As if she did not know me! She who does not budge, not an inch, during the whole duration of my lessons.

The cups of tea are passed around and everyone chats sophisticatedly around the sugar lumps.

— She is charming, confirmed the great poet.

A little bevy of admirers of several sexes took him away. Then Barnabé Pudge appeared suddenly in front of me, his face crimson red.

—But, he said,

—Eh? I asked

—. . . we not? . . . he continued.

—. . . would it not . . . be? I replied.

—. . . have we not? . . . not?

—. . .it seems to me . . .

—. . . I . . .

—. . . you . . .

—. . . tram . . .

—. . . yea . . .

Beads of sweat began to run down his fine forehead of a linguist.

—. . . I that you not? . . . he asked.

—. . . aps that that I can again. . . , I replied.

     —. . .so you you you yes yes . . . , he insisted.

—. . . but if you had had it there . . . , I replied.

—. . . ba la ble ble hihi . . . , he continued.

—. . . had had . . . had had . . .

He came back again to this point:

—. . . had had . . . had had . . .

During all this time I had only one thought: would my memory be exact enough for me to be able to scrupulously record this conversation in my intimate diary. And, eight days later, I was able to do it.

—. . . had had . . .

Padraic Baoghal passed us close by and said:

—Come now, come now, this is not the time for courting.

The séance, in fact, was about to start. I had arrived late. Everyone was getting ready.

Barnabé (I may as well immediately call him by his first name), Barnabé confided in me in a whisper:

—You are so mysterious, Miss.

I shivered with pleasure. It really was super, all the same, to intrigue a refined young man.

However, Mrs. Baoghal, who is an old woman in her thirties, had installed herself in an armchair and begun to gather her forces, while patting and pulling at her dress with one hand, both charmingly and unconsciously. The dress in question was everything that could be of the greatest taste: heavy aubergine crepe with a loosely draped collar, sleeves of canary yellow very full and loose above the elbow, and a large sash of light blue satin tied cleverly to one side.

Everyone finished up by being seated; the lights were extinguished. Immediately, without exception, a man's hand placed itself on my right thigh, and another on the left. That on the left (a right hand, consequently) was inquisitive and mobile, that on the right possessive and massive: the claw of a lion.

The séance began; from Mrs. Baoghal's ear a whitish slimy-looking substance began to emerge that little by little assumed a vaguely ovoid form. I observed the thing closely (I did not believe in it) and, to avoid being distracted, I took the hand on the right and put it in contact with the hand on the left: they felt each other for a moment then withdrew speedily.

The ovoid form changed gradually to resemble a head that was vaguely human; then contracted and withdrew into the ejaculatory ear (ejaculatory, what a learned word, and perhaps it should not be used in this sense, but it is late and I cannot be bothered to look it up in the dictionary). Then Mrs. Baoghal began to speak in a strange, artificial voice, describing the inhabitants of Jupiter, who are trigamous, hermaphrodites and reproduce by budding. I found this discourse deadly boring and repugnant, and I asked myself if, to pass the time, I could not, myself, put my hands on the thighs of my neighbors to see what would happen, but I dared not.

At last, the verbiage finished, Mrs. Baoghal let out some groans and the lights were switched on.

My neighbor on the right (Padraic Baoghal) turned towards me and asked me with a silly look:

—So little girl, you were not very impressed?

—Oh no! sir, I replied.

My neighbor on the left (the bard-druid O'Cear) looked at Baoghal with an insolent look.

—Miss Mara does not easily loose her bearings, it seems to me. I heard a voice in my head that murmured:

—Hold tight the rail miss.

And I saw again the quayside with its soft contact.

My soul totally preoccupied with the memory of my "gentleman," I spent the rest of the time chatting with Arcadia and Pelagia, while my eye rested absent-mindedly here and there on the trousers of these men.

18 FEBRUARY

Time passes. I am bored and feel very strange. It is not, by the way, the onset of the monthly menopause (another word that I should confirm the meaning of in the dictionary) that torments me. On this matter I have no cause for complaint. But I have a feeling like a lump on my jejunum that oppresses me, to the extent that I would like to buy myself a new dress, a beautiful dress like Mrs. Baoghal's, a dress from France. By the way, Michel has not written to me yet: perhaps he perished at sea. It would not displease me to have held in esteem a man who had been annulled in the salty water of the oceans. Perhaps, at night or on days of great storms, I would see his ghost, all green like the fringe of an oyster.

19 FEBRUARY

To think that there are so many admirers who would like to know him, Padraic Baoghal, while, as for me, I see him, familiarly, three times a week, always very correctly (his aberration was just ephemeral) and always, I must say, in the presence of his wife who does not believe in ephemeral things (she has a very elevated spirit) and continues to paint, minutely, miniatures. She never shows them to me. I think that they represent scenes from the other world.

20 FEBRUARY

I let Mary know about the book. She often has quick ideas. And Joël is more affectionate, more of a fool with her than with me.

21 FEBRUARY

Irish spelling is unreasonable. If I did not have a very strong urge to write a novel in this Celtic language, I would not learn it at all. One writes *oidhce*, which is pronounced ee, and *cathughadh*, which is pronounced *cahu*. Padraic Baoghal finds that marvelous because it puts French spelling in the shade. As if that had anything to do with it.

23 FEBRUARY

In spite of my confidences, my sister Mary has not been able to get from our brother an admission as to where he stashed the book that intrigues me so. All she was able to achieve was a kick in the arse (ah, there is the word that I was looking for the other day). She is now learning the Swiss cantons, Argovie, Appenzell, Glarys, Schwyz, Untenwalden, Jug, but who could ever know such places? It's getting on my nerves.

24 FEBRUARY

At last he spoke to me. He was waiting for me in the street.

—Good day, Miss, he said as I came out. Good day, sir, I answered with modesty.

—My name is Barnabé Pudge, he added in a slightly nervous voice. We were introduced at Padraic Baoghal's house.

—Yes sir, I confirmed modestly.

That is awfully well written, that "I confirmed modestly."

Monsieur Presle, all the same, taught me the French language fucking well. Of course, I did repeat myself: a few lines higher I put "with modesty." All the same, I should not be too hard on myself, otherwise I would never manage. I have to admit, as well, that it stifles me, this account of Barnabé. O how he can bore me, this lad. But, anyhow, I am describing the meeting to keep up my diary. Perhaps one day it will amuse me to re-read this.

We went on together for a few steps, ah yes, I had forgotten, he asked me if I would mind if he accompanied me a bit of my way, and I answered: my faith no. We took them in silence, the few steps, as he sought a subject for conversation. Finally, he gave a little cough and said.

—It's a very difficult language, is it not miss, our Irish Celtic language.

He swallowed to clear his mouth, undoubtedly including half of his tongue, and repeated the same phrase in Irish:

—*Is an-deacar an teanga an Ghaedhilig.*

—*Tá*, I replied, *is an-deacar an teanga an Ghaeldhilig.*

—Particularly the spelling, he added.

—Yes for sure, I replied reddening with vexation.

I considered his comment to be banal, so it annoyed me to have written the same thing in this diary two or three days ago.

Then we fell silent and we arrived at the corner of O'Connell Street.

—Mister Pudge, I said to him, you are going to be late for your lesson.

—O no, he bleated, I have made arrangements not to be.

—Ah? I went interrogatively.

—I told Mr. Baoghal in advance that I could not come for my lesson today.

He lowered his long upper eyelashes onto his lower eyelids.

—I gave as an excuse the death of an old aunt. An imaginary death, he added with a chuckle.

—Oh! I went, scandalized.

He, no doubt, had believed that I was going to admire his schoolboy astuteness; he looked upset.

—Do you believe that that could bring her bad luck? he asked me in a quavering voice.

All the same, all the same, the conversation did not need to become unpleasant. I left him, for some moments, to marinade in his superstitious juices, then I answered brightly:

—Bad luck? You mean that she could die with her gob open, and no later than the present hour.

I turned to him and noticed that I had somehow caused his inner spring to unwind; he looked like a watch that pants and gasps trying to avoid its hands crossing at midnight.

—Youyou believebelieve?

—Yes in your place I would rush in double quick time to Mr. Baoghal's house to avoid having a death on my inconscience.

—Ah well, ah well!

He was as green as an apple with some quince yellow here and there. A little disgusting to see, this Barnabé. I noticed that his legs were shaking and it was almost as if he were about to lose their use, but all the same, it could hardly be up to me to offer him the rail; the situation was not the same, and as for my own little rail, one might say that it would have been of no assistance to him, even supposing I had offered it.

He ended up slipping away, without any of the formalities of politeness. And all of that without moonlight.

10 MARCH

Have not seen Barnabé again. I must be too mysterious for him.

11 MARCH

Joël came home again completely pissed. Without waiting on him, we imbibed the soup. As for him, on coming in he immediately began to unbutton his trousers. O, how that made us laugh; he ran to the kitchen and we could hear Mrs. Killarney as she let out peculiar sorts of groans.

On this subject, the other day, she scorched the back of her dress. I could not get her to explain how it happened.

12 MARCH

It was very late when Joël came down to breakfast. His pitiful state saddened me. Without looking at me, he sat down and stuck his knife into the butter in order, afterwards, to spread it over the palm of his hand. He had forgotten to pick up the toast. I pointed this out to him. He replied:

—Ah! at last you deign to speak to me. You know, I am your brother all the same and your elder, the head of the family as father is not here. I am it and continue to be it . . .

He interrupted his sentence in order to lick his palm.

—. . . even if I have climbed the cook.

—You climbed up on Mrs. Killarney! I cried. But what for?

He looked at me with an air of pity that profoundly irritated me.

—Yes, I continued, if you needed to get at something in the cupboard, you had only to get the stool, and not gotten up on Mrs. Killarney's shoulders.

He shrugged his shoulders, wiped the back of his thumb and blew on his cup of tepid tea.

—Pouah! he went. What a hole! As for you, he added, it is high time that you had yourself climbed on, even by a donkey.

—What's that for an idea! I can't see myself with an ass on my shoulders. I burst out laughing, but managed to add:

—I would have liked to see you riding on the shoulders of Mrs. Killarney to get at the pot of marmalade.

I was crying from laughing. Mary as well. Joël gave the table a big wallop with his fist. All the cups gave a little jump.

—Idiot! I will say it again. It is high time. You will understand one day what I mean to say. But by then you will be rotten with complexes. Like me! You know, like me!

The cups started to make little jumps again. As for me, I was incapacitated. I was chuckling. Mammy ran in.

—What's going on? What's going on? Why the noise? This hilarity?

—He climbed up on Mrs. Killarney, I spluttered pointing at Joël. He climbed on her! He climbed on her!

A gentle smile appeared on the Mammy's lips.

—That's not nice that, she said to him gently, you showed her a lack of respect. You may do that with the lads when playing, but with this good woman . . . What will she think of you?

—She likes it, objected Joël. Mammy sighed:

—Humanity is quite bizarre. But in the end, everything is necessary to make a world.

She went out.

—Me too, I am pulling out, said Joël. Goodbye my lovely.

—Goodbye.

— *Cuir amach do theanga!* he shouted.

And he disappeared.

As he does not know a word of Irish, I asked myself where he could possibly have learned this phrase, the sense of which I did not understand. And I dared not ask my master, the poet Padraic Baoghal, the meaning of these words, certainly choquinge. As all of these happenings had crumpled my composure, I drifted into melancholy.

I felt the need, first of all, to go to the little corner and then to make contact again with that which raises up the (immortal) soul: Art. So a few minutes later, I found myself in front of the National Art Gallery, West Merrion Square. It was not the first time that I fucked my feet down there, but, on this day, a very particular emotion gripped my (immortal) soul. I was close to tears, as usual, before the portrait of Stella, did not feel up to climbing to the first floor to see the pictures by Leslie, Maclise, Mulready, Landseer and others, including Wilkie, and went out to walk in the garden. I was alone, and with the trees, still without leaves, holding their harsh network of branches above my head, I observed, one-by-one, and at length, the antique-style statues that decorated, here and there, the pathways. They are not originals, they are casts, copies: some in bronze, others in plaster, others in marble or in granite. The one that attracted me at first, after my general walk around, was the Apollo discobolus. Like all the other gods he wore shorts (brief, but shorts all the same). It seems likely that in reality the gods had none, their statues that is. Why does the museum curator equip them so? It's a mystery. Something must be hidden inside them.

A narrow band of lawn separated me from this work of art. After having looked around me, but no, nobody there, I jumped over it and found myself with my nose up against the calves of the divine athlete. I began to lick them. But they were of plaster, and, after a little time, a taste of white cheese, too creamy and a little too dry, filled my mouth. I regained the gravel path, and a few steps further on, fixed on a Farnesian Hercules. This one had feet of marble. I stepped over the lawn again. A look all around. No, no one. Began to rain a little. Very small drops. I bend my head, I apply my lips to the big toe of the hero with my cheek resting on the metatarsus. A drop of water falls in front of my eyes, onto the semi-divine foot. I open my mouth, extend my tongue, spread its rosy benign influence over the divine undulations that form, at each toe, the base of the next. Other drops of water fall, I take them in. All this is cool and pleasing. I explore the inter-digital valleys and I polish with my saliva the nails—deliciously fashioned by Glycon—of this mass from mythology whose bulging musculature I admired from below. By now feet were no longer enough for me.

It was raining more and more. Still no one in the garden. At the windows of the Gallery, no watchers. A little pull-up (infantile), allowed me to hoist myself onto the plinth and I found myself nose to nose with the statue. I embraced it, pressing myself against it, but I felt nothing special. His eyes were empty and the rain made it seem like he was crying foolishly. I whispered into his ear.

—You are afraid of me, eh, my little Barnabé Pudge, you are afraid of me?

But it was really only marble in shorts. The furies of my imagination calmed down and I got ready to descend again when I heard a voice that said to me, without humor:

—Take care not to fall, Miss.

Frightened, I just held on more tightly to my Farnesian, and dared not turn my head.

—You have the intention to stay up there for long? resumed the voice. Would you like me to bring a chair to help you get down again?

As it quavered, this voice, which I suspected was that of an old man as it had nothing ironic about it; I supposed that this old fellow was sympathetic and I decided that I should reassure myself that I was not about to fall into the hands of a dirty old man who would profit from my illicit situation to take advantage of my charms and to inflict on me shameful acts like pulling my hair or smacking my bum.

So I turned around and saw what I had guessed, one of the Gallery attendants, that is a hoary old man (what does that mean, exactly, "hoary"? I really should look in the dictionary later), who, by the way, I knew by sight (and perhaps he me, since, obviously, it was not the first time that I had come to the Gallery, but until now I had never dared touch the sculptures) and who had white hair under his cap and decorations on his uniform coat. Whether these decorations had been won in the service of England or of our native Éire was a thing about which I could not give a fuck.

—Good day sir, I said to him in a tone that seemed to me to be most natural.

But at this moment I realized that I must have cut a delicate figure, hanging on in the rain, to this big marble brute. I blushed from vexation.

—Good day Miss, answered the ancient, very politely. How are you going to get down from there? Wait, I am going to look for a chair for you.

He was serious, the poof.

What does he take me for?

I dissociated myself from my Hercules and with a graceful bound landed in a little pool of mud in the middle of the path, splattering the old dodderer in the process. While wiping himself down he expressed to me his admiration.

—How well Miss can jump, he said. How well Miss can jump. Miss is clearly an athlete.

I did not know very well how to answer him.

After having wiped himself down, he put his handkerchief back in his pocket and, ceasing his hypocritical praise, he asked me coldly, looking me straight in the eyes.

—So this Hercules, is he much more handsome up close? Under a magnifying glass?

—It is, sir, that I am short-sighted, I thought it shrewd to answer.

Predictive shivers of a storm took hold of his hands, hairy and greying. It continued to rain and the attendant to interrogate me.

—Is it muscles that interest you?

—No, sir, mythology.

—Because, as for muscles, it's not worth the bother to climb up on the pedestal to feel them. See here, feel!

He bent his arm so that I could appreciate his biceps. But I did nothing.

—No interest, I murmured.

A touch of hate colored his countenance. He was beginning to get on my nerves, the mug, and even make me afraid. What if he starts to touch me. We were still alone in this garden, rendered leafless by the preceding autumn, and which the spring had not yet turned green. Did he truly make me afraid, this stupid fellow? I looked at him impartially. No. With a flick I could knock this ruin into the muck.

But he wanted to intimidate me.

—Miss, you should know that it is rigorously forbidden to spit on the parquet, to bring dogs into the room of the Dutch masters, to lean against the displays and to hoist oneself up onto the pedestals of statues. Everyone infringing these interdictions will be punished with a penalty of from five to twenty-five strokes of the cat-of-nine- tails.

Another one who thinks of nothing but that, I said to myself. He reminded me of my father. Well, what could have happened to him? Perhaps he still has not found his box of matches? But really, for everyone in the house, we are well rid of him. Of course, if he had been here, Joël, no doubt, would not have become a drunkard. But, since Daddy left, I have had, at least, a peaceful backside. That makes up for a lot.

While these thoughts (if I may say so) made their way through my little (immortal) soul with the speed of a pure-bred harassed by a pure cleg, the sex maniac of the fine arts

had dared to place his detrimental hands on different parts
of my raincoat. It's crazy how little effect that had on me. I
judged that it was not worthwhile that he continue; finally,
to persuade him, I put him in a rear arm-lock, followed by a
backwards kick to the left tibia and a stamping of the toes of
the right foot.

I left him on the ground in the throes of his meditations
and went out of the Gallery to go to the Baoghal's house. A
little disturbed in spite of everything, I felt the need to relieve
myself and made a very short visit to Aunt Cornelia, who
was even more surprised than the last time. This was going
to be a day of events: Mève, Mrs. Baoghal's little maid, told
me that the master and his wife had left for Sligo to bury a
great grand aunt. I stood there on the landing all at sea, not
knowing what to do.

—Come in so, all the same, for a little, Miss, said Mève.

She is very nice and very friendly, Mève. She comes from
Connemara and speaks Irish as well as she does English. She
knows it even better than Baoghal himself. She serves for him
a little like a dictionary. Often he goes to consult her secretly.
To find myself face to face with her caused to surge up in my
little (immortal) soul the idea (if I dare say) to ask her the
meaning of the sentence that my brother had said to me this
very morning, but fearing that it (the sentence) was very dirty,
I decided that it would be better, to first have a little chat with
the kid, especially since she gave the impression that she was
well disposed to that.

—Perhaps, I replied. Yes, I would like . . .

—Would you like to relax for a while in the office?

That's where I took my lessons.

We went in.

Everything was in order, every book in its place. The
armchair pushed up against the master's worktable seemed

strangely empty to me. The other worktable, that of Mrs.
Baoghal was draped with a sort of cover, a challenge to curiosity, a veritable provocation. I did not know Mrs. Baoghal's
works, and I was not dying from a desire to know them, but
constantly seeing her there, in her corner, manipulating her
brushes and her pots, I ended up being irritated by it.

Mève, who was observing me, directed me, all casually, in
that direction.

—The Missus is secretive, she said to me. She hides everything. Not only her colorings, but also the sugar and the
butter.

She laughed with a mocking and knowing air, which
annoyed me a little.

—You know Miss, it's me who prepares the kind of stuff
that comes out of the Missus' ear during the spiritual séances.
That's what amuses me the most here. It's certainly not the
Master.

She played casually with the patterned cloth that covered
Mrs. Baoghal's little painting materials.

—Perhaps Miss would like to see the works of the Missus,
she continued with a growing insolence that made me blush.
I am sure that Miss does not know them. Only the Master
has seen them—and me.

With a sudden movement she raised the covering.

—Come and look Miss.

She moved, without timidity, the objects placed on the
table and held out one of the miniatures to me.

—Take this one here, for example, she said to me. It's an
inhabitant of the planet Ceres, apparently. A pure spirit.

I approached to have a look at it, without touching it.

— Ah! I went, after having looked.

It represented a naked man with wings on his back and
bizarre attributes between his legs.

—It's well drawn, no? went Mève with the tone of a connoisseur.

—What a funny imagination, I murmured.

—What? that?

She pointed to the wings.

—No that, I answered.

—Oh, that! Whether the spirits come from Saturn or from Jupiter or from elsewhere, the Missus never forgets to stick a fine pair onto them. It's awfully well done, she added, while bringing the image close to her eyes, all the details are there.

She put down the miniature, and took up another.

—Ah! this one, it's Napoleon in exile on the planet Neptune. He's in exile because he allowed himself to be beaten by the English.

This time I took the object into my hands and examined it closely. One had, in fact, to admit that it was very well drawn. Napoleon was a perfect likeness, with his little hat; for the rest, he was, like the former one, entirely naked, with his lower attributes of a volume clearly much greater than those of the former. Without doubt, according to the thinking of Mrs. Baoghal, this was a mark of distinction, a rank undoubtedly, like epaulettes or stripes.

I was losing myself in dream-like considerations of human vanity when I felt Mève's body snuggle against mine.

—The Missus, that torments her, she said to me.

—What so?

—That.

While pointing at the thing with her finger, her other arm circled my waist. As she is much smaller than me, her cheek pressed against my breast. It was agreeable, but after all it was neither my mother nor my sister.

—All of that is really strange, I suggested gravely.

I returned the object to Mève and, although I was wary

of upsetting her, I disengaged myself gently. Silently, she put everything back in place.

—Mève, I asked her shyly, could you tell me the meaning of: *Cuir amach du theanga?*

—Put out your tongue, she answered without looking at me.

—Is that all?

—Yes. What more could you want?

She had adopted a stubborn air. We separated without any further words. After this truly eventful morning, I went back home for lunch.

18 MARCH

Padraic Baoghal is back from the funeral. During my lesson, I could not stop myself looking at his wife from time to time, too often even, as my teacher pointed out. She was concentrating, working methodically.

That left me wondering.

Mève is very polite with me. She lowers her eyes while opening the door for me.

19 MARCH

I just have three girlfriends: my sister Mary, Arcadia O'Cear and Pelagia Mac Connan. Arcadia and Pelagia came to the house for tea yesterday. We shared confidences: Arcadia says that she is in love with George Connan O'Connan and Pelagia says that she is with Padraic O'Gregor Mac Connan. As for me I said that I loved Baoghal. They believed me.

Afterwards we exchanged some words on womanly

matters: so, Arcadia has violent diarrhoea the day before her period, as for Pelagia she suffers rather from constipation. After that, we talked about the immortality of the soul and about ancient sculpture. We finished up by promising definitely to go together to Paris in order to visit the Galleries Lafayette and a nightclub with gypsies, where gentlemen with monocles and stiff white shirt-fronts debauch themselves.

21 MARCH

To celebrate Spring, Joël decided to go on an eight-day batter, that is to say, he locked himself in his room with twenty bottles of ouisqui and two small casks of Guinness of a bushel each, or, in the metric system, seventy two liters seven deciliters and two centiliters of beer. I supply these details because I do not know the equivalent term in French. Without doubt, in France, they do not have this custom? I would write to Monsieur Presle to ask his opinion on this subject, but I will not write to him so long as he has not written to me.

His negligence makes me indignant.

28 MARCH

Joël ended his batter today. Mammy was so happy that she prepared a great feast. Joël did not come down except for the dinner, unshaven but in great form. We ate herrings with ginger, bacon and cabbage, a ten-pound round of cheese, and a carageen tart. We drank sedately, we sang in unison; we put Mammy to bed towards midnight because her head was spinning, and we continued to laugh and recite limericks until three in the morning. As for limericks, the less I understand

them, the more I find them good. I remember this one that
Joël recited:

> Michael the grocer is not alone in saying
> That a melon for a man is divinely pleasing
> And a young boy is cause for jubilation
> As for a woman? Good for procreation.

It's incoherent but that's what pleases me about it.

29 MARCH

This morning I woke up very early and went down to the
kitchen to make myself a cup of coffee. Mary joined me
shortly afterwards.

—Up already? I said to her. You slept badly?

—Guess what I did?

—You learned by heart the list of the Soviet republics.

—No. Yesterday evening, did you not notice?

—You were a bit drunk.

—Not at all. You did not see that I went out for a few
minutes.

—What's surprising about that?

—It wasn't what you thought. I had an idea.

—You?

—Yes, me. I thought that after his batter, Joël might not
have hidden very well the book that you are interested in.

—That is true, I wasn't thinking about it any more.

—So well, I went at full speed up to his room and what
did I see on the floor between two bottles of stout? Your book!
Heh, not stupid, this chick?

—You took it?

—Yes, I even read it all night.

—So?

—So? It's amazingly interesting.

—Give it to me.

—I don't know that I should . . .

—Idiot. Give it to me.

—I don't know that . . .

—You are going to give it to me.

Mrs. Killarney came in.

—Oh, mistress Killarney, said Mary taking on a very serious air, tell us what happened the other day with the pots of marmalade?

—What pots of marmalade?

—O yes, And Joël.

—I do not understand, went Mrs. Killarney, dignified.

I gave Mary a kick under the table, I was sure that she was making a blunder, but what blunder.

Joël, in turn, arrived.

—You are making a racket, he said arrogantly.

He was staring at Mrs. Killarney who had her back to him, leaning over the toasts that were grilling.

—It's not the time to be getting up, he added in a lower tone.

I looked at him from his head to his feet. On the way, I was surprised to confirm that he was perhaps shaped like Mrs. Baoghal's spirits.

I have not got over it yet.

31 MARCH

Mary refuses to give me Monsieur Presle's book. We are having great screaming rows.

2 APRIL

There is nothing more that I can do. The little bitch. I searched her room. She is just as shrewd as Joël at thinking up hiding places, so I have not been able put my hand on it (on the book). What a horrible pest a child of sixteen can be. To think that I was once that age too. And that I am going to be eighteen in two weeks.

3 APRIL

And then, I really don't give a fuck about that stupid book.

5 APRIL

Met Barnabé. Just a few polite words were exchanged. Could it be that he still finds me mysterious?

Now, every time I look at a man I see some of the characteristics of a pure spirit. Not that he has wings. But the rest. Their spirituality can be seen in a way that is more or less clear, more or less unquestionable, when one pays attention. I go from discovery to discovery. A glance, a simple glance can even awaken in a gentleman a spirituality that is until then latent. It is even very interesting to see it happen. However, my eyes should not all the time be roaming over the trousers of citizens; that could become an obsession and I could drift into a kind of mysticism with phallucinations. I must also reflect on materials: on marble, on bronze, on all those materials that are hard and smooth and used to make works of art.

Hold on, that gives me the idea to go back to the Gallery. I have not dared to up until now. I will not lose heart because of an over-zealous attendant. Tomorrow I will go. Bet I will.

7 APRIL

When lunch was over, Mammy left the room and Joël evaporated. I remained alone with Mary, who, very shiftily, was pretending to learn the list of the various independent states of India. I have been slow to cop on: if Joël has not bellowed like an ass, it is because Mary has not pinched his book. She bluffed it, the little imp. I say nothing, I get up and leave her to her Hindu principalities.

So I headed in the direction of the Gallery, and I was so focused on it in my head that I did not hesitate for a moment when I found myself before the entrance. I went in. I crossed the hall. The attendants didn't even look at me, my persecutor was not there. I went into the garden. No one was there. The statues towered above, all in their places, in their plaster, in their bronze, in their marble, some in shorts, the others with immense fig leaves made from zinc. The trees looked less dead, the buds were turning green, the weather was beautiful.

I stopped dead, I sensed someone near me, I turned my head and I saw Barnabé Pudge who was smiling inanely, but full of boldness, as if, suddenly, I was no longer mysterious to him.

I started to laugh.

—Dear Miss, he said to me, I can see nothing here that is amusing.

—That, I replied to him.

I designated, by finger, a man whom I had just discovered, the tip of whose cap was showing behind the plinth of a statue. The attendant of the other day.

—I fail to see, said Barnabé, what is funny about that old man.

—Me neither, I replied.

I made a half-turn and went out, a little to the surprise of those who had seen me enter a minute beforehand.

All the same, I had come back to their museum.

I found myself on West Merrion Street with Barnabé on my heels.

—It was not me who caused you to leave? You had just arrived.

—And you?

—Me? Arrived? I . . . I . . .

He had followed me, the ninny.

What was I going to do now? I had indeed returned to the Gallery, but I had not had my statue. This time, I think that I would have chosen one with a zinc leaf. It is just as well that Barnabé turned up, because the other sod had seen me arriving. Barnabé did not suspect that he had done me a favor, he was all upset for having interrupted my visit, that was clear.

—Will you allow me to accompany you, Miss? I liked his turn of phrase. It was well found.

—But I am not going anywhere, I replied quite candidly.

—Ah! went the other.

I surveyed him from the corner of my eye. It's fascinating to consider a man (more like a boy) in the course of making a decision. At the entrance to the Gallery, on the step of the main door, attendants were looking at us attentively.

—What if we were to visit the Phoenix Park?

That did not appeal to me. An interminable trip by tramway. He was not going to pay for a taxi.

—Yes, I said.

—Do you not like Phoenix Park?

—Oh, yes.

—We could visit the Zoo.

—That's an idea.

—You do not like animals?

—Oh! yea.

We headed towards Grafton Street."

—I believe that you would prefer something else, said Barnabé.

—But no. but no.

While walking beside him, or, more like, while allowing him to walk alongside me, I thought of the attendant at the National Galley: he had me well spotted, the dirty old man. I was reflecting on a way to play a hoax, a game, or a dirty trick on him, when I realized that, after all, he should be the one to feel the need to seek revenge. I must have hurt him badly, the other day.

—You seem preoccupied? Really, I apologize again for having disturbed you during your visit. I was there and thought it permissible for me . . .

We arrived at Grafton Street. I would have liked to have stopped in front of the displays to do some window licking, but my companion would perhaps have thought that I was hinting at things that he might buy me, which would have put him in a delicate situation, seeing that he certainly does not have much pocket money: one only has to look at him.

—Phoenix Park is still a long way off, I said. I have a horror of long trips by tramway.

—I don't mind that method of transport . . .

I glanced at him: he had taken on an air that was both shrewd and bright. I understood immediately: he was going to pay me a compliment. I interrupted and asked him bluntly:

—You have a long journey to make to go to the Baoghal house?

—Not very, in any case I go on foot.

—You like to take walks?

—Enormously, Miss.

Was this son of a bitch going to tell me where he lived or not. I would like to know his situation in society and what kind of places one could go with him. Because my own social standing is quite mediocre: my mother is alone, abandoned by her husband, she has three children to raise and the Sweepstake has been largely used up. But I am not going to tell him all of that.

—You go often to the Phoenix Park?

—Yes, often, it is not very far from where I live.

—Ah yes, so where do you live?

Not too bad that, as a question, to know what I wanted. Quite discrete.

—Behind Saint Catherine's church. In Hambury Lane.

Like I suspected, a seedy area. But all the same he should have enough for an invitation to the cinema. So I suggested to him that we go into the Shamrock Palace, in front of which we were just passing, and where *Blonde Bombshell* with Jean Harlow was playing. There was a big photo of her at the door: What a beauty!

Barnabé looked to be trapped.

—You believe that I could bring you to see this production?

—Is it condemned by the church?

—I read the notice this week at Saint James: it is a film forbidden even for adults.

After clearing his mouth, he added:

—If we go in, we are going to look like Protestants.

—Big deal, I exclaimed.

I don't go to the cinema very often. The occasion had presented itself, the film promised to be amusing, the actress looked to be as beautiful as Vénus callipyge (I do not know why, but there is no copy of this statue at the Gallery) and I was going to have to renounce the opportunity because of a priest at Saint James? First of all, for myself, I don't go to mass at Saint James.

Meanwhile, Barnabé, somewhat shocked by my last remark, became more and more miserable looking. With distraught eyes, knit brows, he seemed to be searching for arguments in his little parishioner's head. Passersby turned towards us, mocking our hesitation.

—As for myself, I'm going in, I said.

And so, I directed myself towards the cashier, opening my bag and pretending to be looking in it for change. Barnabé jumped forward, took two tickets for orchestra seats, and a little light led us to our places. The newsreel: the 6th of February in Paris. What a beautiful city! I stared wide-eyed to see if Michel Presle might be among the protesters, but it went too fast. For what I know of him, I am sure that he would not have got mixed up in it. All the same it gave me pleasure to see Paris Lumière.

Barnabé bought me a choc-ice. One licks it. It's good. It is hard and ice-cold, like the toe of a marble statue on a winter's day in the rain.

—Would you not like to go to Paris?

It was I who asked him that.

—What a country! he replied. You saw that brawl?

—More happened here.

—That is the past! Now is a time of calm days. We have found our equilibrium.

As for me, I am not political and I would love to go to Paris. Oh! the Galleries Lafayette, the Bon Marché, the Printemps, the Chartier soups, the Wallace drinking fountains, the beggars under the bridges, the taxi cabs, the abattoirs, the Saint-Lazare railway station, the moat at Vincennes, the French-Cancan. Oh! Paris!

I shut up because *Blonde Bombshell* had just started. What a beautiful woman, that Jean Harlow! Just like I would like to be! Hips! Breasts! My God! She is so great!!! And with an amazing walk! What a look in her eyes! Her hair puffed out!!! Ah fuck! Michel Presle would say, she's ripe! that chick!! As well, the film was hilarious! I laughed all the time! and very loud!!! It really is a splendid invention, cinematography!!!

To thank Barnabé for having brought me—somewhat forced and under pressure, it must be said, but, all the same, it was he who paid, I surely owed him gratitude—I wanted to make a small friendly gesture to him, for example to softly touch his upper arm, that would be sweet. But I was awkward and my hand ended up on his thigh. I was not fully aware of this at first, and I moved it up towards what I believed to be his elbow. But instead of coming across what is curiously referred to as the "funny bone" I bumped against an additional limb: not a wing, but the tri-form ornament of Mrs. Baoghal's pure spirits. I then realized that spirituality was much more widespread among modern men than I had thought and (in spite of my tendency to atheism) that the soul is perhaps immortal, hardening at death in order to cross the heavens, or to enter hell as it stiffens in the grip of a carnal fist.

On the screen, Jean Harlow, in a bathing suit, was getting ready to dive. We saw her from the back, she bent forward slowly, arms stretched out towards the mirror-like water and, suddenly, her bottom filled the screen with its rounded duality. Barnabé let out a heart-rending sigh and, taking my hand, threw it back violently towards me. Behind us someone went: "Tsseh!"

I could not understand the irritation of my companion. I asked myself what could I have done to offend him? I was, all at the same time, embarrassed, anxious, and vexed. I took no pleasure as the film ended.

On leaving, Barnabé did not even suggest accompanying me home. He had his hat in his hand, held up against his groin; he politely wished me good day and went off. I looked after him as he moved away, still with his hat in his hand and held against his groin, walking awkwardly.

Truly, truly, I do not understand . . .

10 APRIL

Joël has left for two weeks, on the pillion of the motorcycle of Timoléon Mac Connan, the son of the poet. I hope that Joël will know how to keep his balance and not smash his face. They are going first to Cork and coming back through Limerick and Kildare. They left at six this morning. The doorbell rang; that woke me up. I went to open the door: It was Timoléon who had come looking for the brother; he was dressed in leather from boots to helmet, goggles on his forehead. The motorcycle, a very big one, was throwing out thousands of sparks in the twilight of the morning.

—Joël is ready? Timoléon asked me without even wishing me the time of day.

—I'll go and alert him. Would you not like to come in?

—Of course. And would you not have a little sup of ouisqui to offer me? It's brass monkey cold.

—But yes, but yes, do come in.

I set him up in front of a bottle of ouisqui and went to wake Joël.

—Oh! shit, he went, give me some feckin' peace. I poured a pitcher of water on his head.

—Timoléon is waiting for you.

—What time is it.

—Six o'clock.

—You should have said that earlier, he moaned.

I went down again to keep Timoléon company. He had already finished a third of the bottle. I asked him:

—Are you going to be able to drive in a straight line?

—I see, he went. You are one of those who preach at

people. A disciple of Father Mathew or of Matt Talbot?

—Oh, it just came out.

—We don't see you around very often.

—Where?

—You don't go to the stadium any more.

—No, I have given up sport.

—For Padraic Baoghal?

—Yes

—And for Barnabé?

I said nothing.

—That fool.

I shrugged my shoulders.

He shrugged his shoulders in turn and repeated:

—That fool.

Then he asked me why I never went dancing at the Mac Adam sisters' house. They have a party at home every Saturday. To tell the truth, I did not know that. Neither Pelagia Mac Connan nor Arcadia O'Cear had ever spoken of it. Nor Joël.

—I don't like to dance, I replied.

He shrugged his shoulders once more.

Timoléon is not bad in himself, but I do not like his kind. He poured himself a new shot of ouisqui. I remarked that he could well run into a tree if he continued to booze like that.

—You can rest assured that I would never marry a girl like you, he retorted. I pity the lad who will have you for a wife. How boring you will be.

Joël appeared.

—Say Tim, you have done with slagging my sister.

—A good glass of ouisqui? I suggested to him.

—No thanks, but I'm going to put the bottle in the saddlebag.

He took it with one hand and, with the other, threw a book on to the table.

By the way, he said to me, you can read it while I'm gone. I've decided, after all, that you are old enough to absorb it.

He hugged me and said to Timoléon: Are you coming? I accompanied them to the doorstep, they were not long in leaving with great noises and roars. The day was dawning. Timoléon made some exaggerated zigzags. I waved my hand once more and went back into the kitchen.

I grabbed the book.

Towards nine o'clock, Mrs. Killarney arrived to prepare breakfast. I did not budge. Towards ten o'clock, I heard Mary behind me saying:

—What are you doing here? Are you not going to have your breakfast?

I had almost finished.

—It seems fascinating what you are reading.

—Yes, I said, it's the book forgotten by Monsieur Presle. Mary did not answer.

I finished my book and went to join her at the table. Mammy was studying the small ads in the *Irish Stew Herald*, she examines them minutely, one by one just like she does the short news stories; she continues to hope to find news of Daddy.

I was hungry. I eat in silence, the book at my side. I keep an eye on Mary who makes all kinds of expressions and passes through every kind of color. She cannot see the title, the book is covered with flowery patterned wallpaper: a practice of Presle.

I feed myself a pile of marmalade and drink five cups of tea. Mammy folds the newspaper. Still nothing today.

—So, little ones, not yet finished?

—No, Mammy.

—For myself, I am going to do a little sewing. Poor Mammy.

She leaves us alone. I, immediately:

—Eh, what have you to say about it?

—About what?

—Little liar. Dirty little liar.

—Sally, don't say that.

—Do you want to read it, this book?

She paled.

—Seriously?

—Yes, of course.

She became more and more pale. She was trembling.

—Yes, she whispers.

I took the book and I tore out the flyleaf, which I crumpled into a ball. Then I pushed the book in front of her. I got up and left. Behind my back she shouted:

—What did you take out? I want to read everything!

In my room I reread what Michel Presle had written [in French] on the cover page: *O, what in the way of complexes must the Countess have had. But in comparison to those of the Mara children they would be nothing.* I tore it into little pieces with the intention of throwing them into the bog. But I preferred to swallow them: the indirect route seemed to me to be more respectful.

As I went out to go to my lesson, I noticed in the dining room, my sister, elbows on table, fists held up to her ears, deep into reading *Général Dourakine*.

12 APRIL

Pelagia and Arcadia came for tea in the house. Pelagia said to me:

—My brother asked that you come on a Saturday to the Mac Adam sisters' house? She added quickly:

—When he will have come back.

I answered casually:

—Ah, yes, it's true, I saw your brother yesterday morning.

And then, in turn, I asked a question:

—How could you know that?

—They came back to our house. Tim had forgotten to put on his socks.

You know, said Arcadia, if you were not invited it is because you do not dance.

—That is reasonable, I acknowledged.

After a silence, I continued:

—One of these days, I will learn.

Afterwards we chatted, but it was not hot hot.

17 APRIL

Yesterday was my birthday. Eighteen years I have now, eighteen springs without much to show for them, all my teeth, well-formed behind and in front, ah fuck, a great day.

Joël came back in the afternoon and Mammy had prepared a spread to boast of, herrings with ginger, bacon with cabbage, a round of cheese weighing twenty pounds and a carrageen tart in which were stuck eighteen mauve-colored Bengal flares.

And Monsieur Presle has not forgotten me. It was fantastically well arranged by him: the same day, we received, sent from Paris, six bottles of Ricard 45 per cent. Mammy wanted to keep one with which, eventually, to celebrate the return of Daddy. But, in God's name, the sixth was liquidated like the others.

It was a great family celebration. Mary recited by heart the names of the one thousand two hundred islands of the Philippine archipelago, Joël declaimed some of Cuculain's exploits, Mammy sang *Cherry Time*, a French song translated with an Irish accent and I nodded my head gently.

And I continue to do so this morning, because good God of the hangover, how I am in pain, good God of the hangover.

18 APRIL

That's not everything. Not only did Monsieur Presle send me a little case of aperitif, now liquidated— poor Mrs. Killarney, she barely had one glass of it—but, he sent me a French magazine as well with, written on it in his own hand: "For Sally, Michel." Nicely fucking familiar for a dedication. Happily, Mammy did not spot it. The magazine in question is called *Votre Beauté*. I read it from end to end, the small announcements and advertisements included. What a peculiar civilization. All those women who are preoccupied with their blackheads, with their dry patches and eyelashes that are too stiff, it's hilarious. Apart from that and without going to any trouble, I have none of these issues. There is one woman, for example, who is in a panic because she has goose bumps in winter and red patches on her skin when it is cold. She is given advice, I note:

Cod liver oil: 250 g.

Resorcinol: 15 g.

Phenyl salicylate: 5 g.

Tincture of quiliyala: q. s. pr. émuls

Essence of wintergreen: q. s.

Apply this three times per day with a pad of cotton wool. Taking such measures must be no bother for French women. There are also those with backsides that are too large, thighs that are too broad, breasts that are too big or a little wrinkled. There are those who don't want their eyebrows anymore and then there are those who want to make them regrow. That beats the band.

And they are responded to with patience, with kindness and forbearance.

Cellulite, it's the great issue: a real infirmity. There's a very learned article on the question. That should fuck the wind up French women when they read it.

And then also, which interested me, was a big spread: *Man and woman, aesthetic comparisons*, with a pile of parallel measurements. My own are not bad, the chest is not yet au point, but as for my hips, wow! They also have a survey: *From the point of the view of form, do you prefer a handsome man or a beautiful woman and why?* Answers should not exceed twenty lines. For myself, as for form I like better a fine man. Why? Because we have too much fat, the substance of our roundednesses. I prefer muscle and bone. No measurement was given for the spirituality of a man. Nevertheless, that would be very interesting.

And then other articles: on lipstick, on face powders, on diets, on perfumes, on hats. They can't have an instant to spare, French women.

Anyway, I find all that really comical and Monsieur Presle was very nice to send me this periodical. I really need to thank him.

19 APRIL

There are in this magazine sentences that I do not understand very well, like this one (also in the article *Man and woman, aesthetic comparisons*) which is on p. 23: "The crease of a man's bottom is to be found at the lower limit of the fourth spinous process while, in a woman, it descends notably further down."

No, I don't get it.

20 APRIL

There is no mention of love in this periodical.

21 APRIL

I am beginning to know it off by heart, this monthly magazine.

22 APRIL

Mary gave me back *Général Dourakine*. She finds it to be very good. But she will never know what Michel Presle wrote on the cover page. Never. Never. Never.

23 APRIL

I cannot say that it would please me very much to pluck my eyebrows, to wear a girdle or to put on lipstick. But it's attractive.

25 APRIL

There are so many things that now seem mysterious to me and that I never suspected in the past. But they are so diverse and so contradictory that I can see neither their head nor tail.

27 APRIL

It seems to me certain that men must not have monthly issues, like we other young girls. But why do they not? This appears to me to be strange and unjust. I know well that they have need of all their blood to defend their mother and fatherland, but really Adam had neither mother nor fatherland. And these phenomena must go back to those times long ago.

29 APRIL

Perhaps there is a connection with maternity? That would be strange.

3 MAY

Have not yet thanked Monsieur Presle.

4 MAY

Fundamentally, all these matters that seem so unclear to me must have a greater or lesser connection with . . . I dare not put down this word on paper. Go on, Sally, a bit of courage. I dare not. Yes, dare. And then, fuck it, is this an intimate diary, yes or no? Yes. Eh so . . . must have a greater or lesser connection with . . . nuptiality. I blush for having written this term.

5 MAY

In agreement with Joël and Mary, I sent *Général Dourakine* back to its owner. It was I who went with it to the post: I came back to the house for tea and I showed them the registered mail receipt. Joël was in the process of buttering a slice of toast with his finger (he gets drunk much less often at the moment, I think that he goes out sometimes with a girl. I forgot to note that. But I don't know if it's with Pelagia, with Arcadia, with Sarah, with Irma, with Eva, with Beatitia, with Ignatia or with another. In any case, he does not bother Mrs. Killarney any more). He asked Mary brusquely:

—What do you think of what he wrote on the first page?

—The title? answered the idiot.

—Idiot, no, that which Presle wrote

—I saw nothing, said Mary.

—Ah, you saw nothing? Sally, it's not worth the bother to blush like that.

—Why is she going red? Mammy asked without raising her eyes.

She was knitting socks for the day when Daddy would return.

—Just as dense the one as the other. Say, give me a glass of ouisqui.

Mammy got up to go to look for the bottle.

—You are such a blunderer, I said.

—What do you dare say to me?

He looked as if he might get up to throw a slap at me.

—I tore out that page so that she would not read it.

—Oh! went Mary. You cow!

She bent towards Joël and shook his arm.

—What was written there? What was written there? Tell me! Tell me!

Mammy brought the bottle and put it in front of Joël.

—Tell her so, she said with softness.

She did not like it when we argued.

Joël emptied his glass of ouisqui thoughtfully, then recited with eyes closed:

—*O, what in the way of complexes must the countess have had. But in comparison to those of the Mara children they would be nothing.*

Mary, who knew less French than Joël and me, asked him to repeat the sentence, which he did.

—Who wrote that? she asked.

—Presle. Michel Presle.

—I have no complexes, observed Mary greatly serious.

—You do not know what it is, I said.

—Me? I do not know what it is? A student of dental surgery told me about it the other day.

—And what is it then?

—Stuff in the subconscious . . .

—For example?

—O well, for example, for a son to want to marry his mother.

Mammy was gripped by giggles.

—I can just imagine Joël making me a declaration.

She spluttered at the idea. Mary and I burst out laughing.

—Eh so, what, went Joël vexed. I can make a declaration just as well as another.

—I cannot imagine it, said Mammy.

—Mammy, Mammy, he exclaimed suddenly in a whining voice. You don't love me any more? You don't love me any more?

—But yes, but yes, answered Mammy reassuringly and tenderly. It's just that if I were of an age to marry, it's not you that I would choose.

—Ah! And why's that?

—You drink too much.

—And Daddy did not drink, him?

—A normal amount. Never more than eight to ten binges a week. While you, you never stop. As a mother, that is not disagreeable to me, but as a wife, I would not like it.

—As a wife, as a wife. All the same, your husband, such a drunkard as he was not, he fecked off and he ditched you. No?

—He will come back, said Mammy with calm assurance.

Joël raised his arms to heaven, then slapped his thighs:

—Bloody hell! If he ever returns, I would want to have them cut off me!

—That you have what cut off you? I asked.

Joël got worked up:

—You would like me to make you a drawing?

—That's it, went Mary, very interested. Make us a drawing.

—Mammy, go and look for a pencil for me so that I can make them a drawing.

Mammy got up to find a pencil for him.

—And paper, shouted Joël.

Mary started again:

—What does it mean, exactly, that sentence?

—Nothing. It's to do with literature.

—Literature! Literature! bawled Joël as he poured himself a fresh glass of ouisqui. In my place you would understand. It's awful to have complexes. You only have to look at me.

—So it's true that you would like to marry Mammy! asked Mary.

—Peuh! That would be nothing. With me, it's much worse.

—What then? we whispered in harmony.

—It's grandmother, that I, that I want to marry.

—But she is dead!

—Exactly. So, you must understand, you fools, that my life is fecked.

—You have a funny way of talking nonsense, I remarked completely impartially.

—You want my fist in your gob? I forbid that you devalue my complexes.

—What is it that they are, complexes? asked Mammy who was bringing the pencil and paper. You have been talking of nothing but that this evening.

—It's a French word, answered Mary. You would not understand it.

—It's nice, French, said Mammy. It has a nice sound to it. And, in the piece that Joël recited just now, I clearly recognized our family name. There is something to do with us in it.

—Isn't she smart, exclaimed Joël and Mary in harmony. Mammy smiled, quite flattered.

—But no I said. It is also French, marra is the third person singular of the past historic of the verb 'se marrer,' first declension, regular, to laugh.

—You can be such a pedant, observed Mary.

—And you, with your one thousand two hundred islands of the Philippine archipelago, I retorted.

—How you can be bloody fools, both of you, said Joël. Look, I am going to make the drawing I promised. Come over here.

We stood, each on one side, to see him do it.

In three seconds, he had finished his sketch.

—And how's that! he exclaimed with an extremely satisfied air.

It was completely comparable to the trinitary attributes of Mrs. Baoghal's spirits.

—One might say a bellows as used in a forge, remarked Mary.

—Well, I never! I said indignantly. I ask myself where you might well have seen a forge bellows.

—In the dictionary, answered Mary.

—Literature, so, I went.

—Ah! you, mind your words, she cried.

—Now there, now there, stop squabbling, said Mammy. Show me.

Joël held out the piece of paper.

—You draw not badly, she said. It's sad that you are such a drunkard, you could become a painter.

She gave him back the piece of paper.

—If not that, what are you going to do in your life?

—I can always join the French Foreign Legion.

—What prospects!

—But Mam, as long as you have the cash, I have nothing to fear.

We stayed quiet.

—Eh so! he asked us, as he held out the drawing before him, what do you think, little ones?

We stood in a trance, both of us. As for me, multitudes of things, facts, acts, words suddenly became clear, some, then others slowly. Associations became established between movements, phrases, objects . . .

—That needs reflection, I said slowly.

—And one might ask oneself what it can be used for, added Mary, no less thoughtfully.

—Ah! that's it, responded Joël boastfully.

—For not much, went Mammy disenchantedly.

—Everything has a purpose, said Mary decidedly.

—The tail of a dog, it's hard to see what use that has, I remarked.

—To show their joy as they agitate it.

—And you think that that too could serve the same purpose?

Joël and Mammy burst out laughing.

—It's not worth the bother for you to mock, said Mary going totally red. The solutions to problems are not always found immediately.

—Now there, now there, don't get upset said Mammy, still shaking with laughter. We examined the drawing more attentively.

—It has a hole, remarked Mary.

It was my turn to be vexed and jealous of Mary's gifts of observation. How can I ever become a woman of letters and a novelist if I do not develop mine? *True*, as Montaigne said; *let's roll up our sleeves*, as Buffon said; and *Peace to syntax*, as Victor Hugo said.

—That's right, approved Joël.

—She's not stupid, this little one, said Mammy. She will surely pass her examinations.

—And then afterwards?

At this moment, the doorbell rang.

—It's Tim said Joël. He is collecting me to play billiards.

He grabbed the paper and crumpled it to stuff it into his pocket. He rushed out to his pal.

—Don't get drunk, son! Mammy shouted after him.

—No, Mam! less than tomorrow.

The door closed after him.

—Maybe they use it for a special kind of billiards, suggested Mary.

—But then, why would it have a hole? I objected.

—Now there, now there, my little ones, went Mammy. Let that drop, you will end up knowing it well one day.

—O how she can annoy me, with her superior airs, murmured Mary.

We got up from the table.

For dinner, Joël did not come home drunk. He did not come home at all.

8 MAY

My issue of Votre Beauté has been pinched. It's not Mary, of that I'm sure. Mammy, little likelihood. Mrs. Killarney? one never knows!

Mary and I continue to have long conversations on the subject that interests us. Mary, who has method and a logical mind, has come to two conclusions: the first is, that that object, having an orifice for one thing and the form of a tube for another, serves for the discharge of a liquid, excreted, without doubt, by the two adjacent spheres. But what liquid? Milk, probably. Second conclusion: certain animals being equipped with an analogous appendage, we can arrive at a conclusion as to its purpose by the observation of the aforesaid beasts, namely horses and dogs. This is what we have decided to do tomorrow.

9 MAY

We, Mary and I, passed the whole day going around the town, with the objective of accumulating information. In the evening we brought our observations together and we arrived at the same conclusion: that it is, in all simplicity, just a very practical, and even astute, mechanism for satisfying one's little needs. We are disappointed and a little sad in thinking that nature did not favor us in this respect.

11 MAY

But why have Mrs. Baoghal's pure spirits the need for this adjunction?

12 MAY

Barnabé no longer speaks to me since the day in the cinema. Perhaps I have apologies to make to him?

13 MAY

After having reflected at length, I made a decision. I waited for him as he left his lesson and I just let on to bump into him. It was very well played and seemed perfectly natural.

—Oh!, he went.

—Oh!, I went.

We squeezed fingers.

—Would it bother you if I went along for some steps with you? I asked him.

Euh . . . that is to say . . . I do not know if that would be very correct, he murmured lowering his eyes.

—I promise you that I will not take your arm . . .

—Let us turn in here then, he said leading me into Catalog Lane.

—Yes, there, it would be more discreet.

We went for some steps in silence. I started:

—Barnabé . . .

—Miss . . .

—You are not annoyed with me, are you not?

—Oh, no, Miss.

—Barnabé, I apologize for the other day.

—What other day?

—At the cinema.

—And so?

—I apologize.

—But why, why so?

—Don't you remember?

—Euh . . .

—Oh come on, Barnabé.

—Ah! because we went to see a film banned by our Saintly Mother Church? But I confessed that the same day . . .

—No, it's not that.

—Nevertheless, that was serious.

—Oh! Barnabé, if you like. I apologize also for that. But there was . . .

—I don't know Miss. I know nothing. I have forgotten.

I looked at him: he was completely red. I began to be annoyed:

—But for me, I insist on apologizing, Barnabé. I should not have done what I did in the dark when I put my hand between your legs. An accident that happened quickly, and I understand really well that you could not hold yourself back. I apologize most sincerely with all my heart, Barnabé, and I promise to not do it again.

—Is that true, Sally? he asked me anxiously. Is that true?

—I swear it to you.

He let out a big sigh of relief. Or of satisfaction? I asked myself.

—All the better, because my confessor advised me not to let it be done to me again.

He remained silent for a moment and added:

—But it was very nice.

—You do not know what you want, I exclaimed, annoyed.

It's true, he can be so irritating.

—No, no, I said nothing, he stuttered so quickly that he pronounced these words without hesitation. It is just a little phrase that just came out, a tiny little phrase about nothing at all. That I take back, that I take back. No, no, no. I stand by what my confessor said and by what you promised me just

now. That's, that's it, that's it: we will go to the cinema again
and you will abstain from putting your hand on my tool.
That's it: we will go again together into the dark. Tomorrow,
for example? Would you like to? We will go to see a Tarzan.
That's it: a Tarzan. Goodbye, Miss, I have to go home now.
Goodbye . . . Sally.

—Goodbye, Barnabé.

We shook hands and he left.

I find it to be very cute and very appropriate to call that a
"tool." Could it be his invention? Barnabé, could he be a poet?

14 MAY

We went to see a Tarzan. All went well. But, how peculiar it
is: as he found that nice, why should I not give him this little
pleasure? It's a real pity that I had promised him not to do it.
I even swore it. All the same . . .

All the same, I resisted. And nevertheless.

The Tarzan films are approved by our Saintly Mother the
Church, as Barnabé says. And nevertheless, the Tarzan in
question, he is as handsome a lad as an Apollo or Hermes or
Hercules. A real statue this Tarzan: the shoulders, the muscles,
the face, he is a real god. The pure spirit of the jungle. As for
his tool, with the sort of loincloth that he wears all of the
time, one can distinguish nothing at all. Nevertheless, I paid
good attention. I kept my eye on that place, always, to stay
informed. And what thighs he has, this Tarzan, what calves.
All the same, it's beautiful the anatomy of the bearers of tools.
I would have been happy to concentrate on this study immediately. I had one at hand, but that which has been promised
is promised, that which is sworn is sworn.

I came back home, arriving in bad humor. Or more like,
with a good humor renounced (which I would have been

in if . . .) that came out in the form of bitter and disgusted comments.

All of which seemed to interest Mary.

15 MAY

It bothers me to have lost my *Votre Beauté*. I know now that it is Joël that pinched it from me. This morning he asked me if Presle had not sent me another issue. Bloody obvious, he couldn't stop himself. But what could possibly interest him in it? To compare his measurements with those of the French prototype?

And Presle, that fellow. Have not written yet to thank him. So, I am going to do it immediately, incognito, as is said in French.

17 MAY

Wrote yesterday to Monsieur Presle. I thank him, give him my news, news of the family, news of Baoghal et cetera et cetera and finish by asking for his, the news, for news of himself what (it seems to me that I am forgetting my French a little at the moment) and also for news of his tool.

I do not know if he will spot the allusion, but if he does understand, that really will make him laugh.

19 MAY

Padraic Baoghal stops giving lessons from next week. He is going to spend six months in Italy, the lucky fool. Mrs. Baoghal is going to invite friends and acquaintances to the last tea of the season. She will not demonstrate ectoplasm this time, that whitish substance that emerges from her ear, from where children are told that they are born.

By the way, from where are they born?

20 MAY

I have made notable progress in Irish, but really I am still far from being capable of writing a novel in that language. That will be for later. In any case, I have no ideas. But I do not lose sight of that project and I would like this future work—of which I still know nothing else—to be enjoyable while at the same time having a certain usefulness, for example for the education of young girls; in short, in homage to Barnabé, my motto will be: "Combine utility with pleasure," no! "Combine the tool with pleasure."

21 MAY

Met my Aunt Patricia in Sackville Street. I felt a little guilty with respect to her because I had not gone to thank her after my two hurried and selfish visits. What I had feared happened.

—Good day, Aunt Patricia, I said politely.

—Good day, my fine Sally, answered my Aunt. So? It is indeed a long time since you needed to use the facilities of my flat!

—But, Aunt Patricia . . . I would not impose . . .

—But do, but do, my fine Sally. I like very much to put people at their ease. Particularly when they are related to me, she added.

—So well, Aunt Patricia, I thank you . . . when . . .

—And so, I hope that that will be soon.

—Perhaps not, Aunt Patricia. I am not going to be passing by your area during the summer; I am stopping taking lessons.

—So, lessons for what, my child?

I had forgotten to tell her.

—For Irish.

—Very good, very good, and with whom?

—Padraic Baoghal.

—The poet?

—Yes, Aunt Patricia.

—That living heap of muck?

—Oh! I went.

Aunt Patricia seemed very agitated.

—Yes, a living heap of muck. You do not know, perhaps, that I was to marry him.

—You, Aunt Patricia?

—That surprises you, silly goose.

—But . . . Aunt Patricia . . .

—Exactly. He wanted to marry me. He loved me, that big lump, and then bang, he makes a barmaid pregnant. Wham, he is obliged to marry her and whack, he drops me. A poet, him? A lecherous boor.

—But, Aunt Patricia, how could he have made a girl pregnant if he was not married to her?

She looked at me with eyes that were wide-open and haughty. Then she smiled:

—He's a crafty one. He has his own tricks. Beware.

I cannot see what it is I should be wary of. Babies, they are a product of the sacrament of marriage, a gentleman and a lady who have not been blessed by the priest could kiss each other day and night for weeks, that could not make a baby, which is the blessing brought about during the ceremony by God or by one of his angels, generated I know not how, and

which comes out into the light, in what way, one might ask. I
say that now but at the time I was thinking of something else.

—But the present Mrs. Baoghal, she is the barmaid in
question?

—Of course.

—She paints really well.

—Her? She paints? . . .

—Yes, Aunt Patricia, Adorable little miniatures of celestial
spirits, with all their attributes.

—You have seen that, have you?

—She is there, at each of my lessons.

—Ah, she is present at all the lessons. With the poet?

—Yes, Aunt Patricia.

—Not stupid, the bitch.

—And I see her working.

—Ah well, never would I have thought that she could
have any talent.

—It's delightful and very realistic.

I ask myself how I could know that it's very realistic.

—I mean to say, one could say real men.

—Ah! went Aunt Patricia looking at me curiously with
her wide eyes.

—But, Aunt Patricia, and the baby?

—What baby?

—Well, Mr. and Mrs. Baoghal do not have a child, to my
knowledge. What became of it?

—Nothing.

—No? Nothing? How is that?

—It never existed.

I felt that Aunt Patricia was beginning to talk nonsense. I
had really suspected that Aunt Patricia was telling fibs about
this girl who could have had a baby without being married.

There was an awkward moment and we stopped talking.

Aunt Patricia took up again first.

—And your mother, she is still well?

—Oh, yes, Aunt Patricia.

—Still knitting stockings for the husband?

—Yes, Aunt Patricia.

—And Joël, always drunk?

—Always, Aunt Patricia.

—And Mary, always working?

—She will sit her examination next year.

—Eh, eh. I see that all is going well. So, goodbye, my fine Sally.

—Goodbye, Aunt Patricia.

—And, I say it to you again, my convenience is always at your disposal.

—I thank you Aunt Patricia.

—And don't forget to say to your Baoghal that I consider him to be a concoction of stinking nanny-goat shit.

—I won't say that to him, Aunt Patricia.

—I see. He has designs on you. You poor silly goose. That big serpent left over from the last Saint Patrick, that big-arsed, fiftyish bollox, is surely taken with you, given the sex maniac's lure that you are. My niece, beware, my niece.

And off she went.

Poor Aunt Patricia.

It must be good to be married, given that those who are do not have such crises.

I shed a tear and dampened my copybook.

And I, who did not want to marry. What an affair that must be. With one's husband, one should be intimate, more again than with one's diary. Talking with him one can use words that are exhilarating and forbidden like: shorts, devil, bloomers, aubergine, box, arsehole.

Me, I would never dare.

By the way, Monsieur Presle, he has not yet replied.

22 MAY

Well, contrary to what I believed, a lady can have a baby with a gentleman without them having been married. Oh, it's a real story, a real story. From it, I am like two rounds of sponge. From it I am a trifle. From it I am whipped. From it I am a mousse. From it I'm chocolate. Now, I must recount it all.

So today, for dinner, we were all four at the table. Mrs. Killarney prepares the dinner, and she leaves immediately afterwards, she does not serve it, Mammy does. So we were all four at the table, it was a small dinner, a cabbage soup, some meters of black pudding with potatoes and bacon, a ten kilo round of cheese, and a carrageen and margarine tart, when—let's see where was I?—Oh, I am disturbed, so moved that I no longer know where I'm at, let's see, let's see. So, we absorbed our cabbage soup with good appetite, faith. Joël was not too drunk. Now and again he poured the contents of his spoon into his socks but not too often; that was tolerable.

We had just about finished, the bottoms of our plates were being scraped, when Mrs. Killarney, who we believed had left, came in and said to Mammy:

—Mrs., I would have two words with you.

—I'm listening to you, Mammy answered, while licking her spoon and passing her tongue around her mouth (oh how she loves cabbage soup).

—I would like to explain to you in private, said Mrs. Killarney.

—Why so, said Mammy. I have nothing hidden from my children.

—It's in front of these young ladies that it would bother me.

—Say now Mammy, Joël intervened, you should go for the pudding and the potatoes with bacon, they're going to get stuck.

—I am going, I am going, said Mammy; your plates my children.

When Mammy was gone. Joël said to Mrs. Killarney:

—Two words will be sufficient to say what you have to say to Mammy?

Mrs. Killarney, very dignified, did not respond.

—You could have chosen another moment to tell her your stuff, Joël continued. I hope that the potatoes have not stuck to the bottom. I hate that. That smells worse than actual burning.

—The master is particular.

And Mrs. Killarney sniggered

—Oh, you, shut up, you old tart!

—Oh! I exclaimed, stupefied.

—I know what I say, You will see! You will see!

And he too started to snigger while spreading butter on a toast with his nose. Normally he does it skillfully, but, without a doubt, this quarrel had disturbed him, because he filled his ears with it.

At this, Mammy came back, and the great main course was attacked.

—Well, Mrs. Killarney, said Mammy as she sectioned the pudding with her butcher's scissors, we're listening to you, we're listening to you.

—In front of these young ladies?

—Why not? They are my daughters just as much as Joël.

—I am not your daughter, said Joël.

—Isn't he clever, said Mary.

—Would you like my piece of pudding across your gob? Joël asked her.

—And his tool as a bonus, I added, guffawing.

Mammy, Joël, and Mary joined in and we rolled about, all four, for five minutes without being able to stop ourselves laughing. We even cried from it. During this time, the potatoes with bacon went cold and Mrs. Killarney remained just as dignified.

—But, Mammy cried suddenly as she calmed down, sit with us Mrs. Killarney. You'll share our meal. But yes! but yes! Hold on I am going to set a place for you. But yes! but yes! There it is. And a good piece of pudding. And some of these excellent potatoes with bacon that you prepared, Mrs. Killarney.

She gave in and, being five, we quickly emptied the dish. Then the ten kilos of cheese followed, as well as the carrageen and margarine tart, in the preparation of which our cook had surpassed herself. On top of that, coffee and a round of ouisqui. Joël puts his feet up on the table and lights his pipe, Mammy recommences her knitting, Mary and I smoke a cigarette while gently caressing our bellies, Mrs. Killarney unthinkingly pours herself a new ration of alcohol.

—By the way, Mammy asks her, without raising her eyes, well concentrated on her work, what did you want to say to me just then?

—Me? said Mrs. Killarney, startled. That's true. I must not leave before having said that to you.

She hiccupped quite resoundingly.

—Pardon me if I excuse myself, she continued. This is what I have to explain to you, straight out: that scoundrel (she designated Joël with a finger) has put me in the situation of a woman in expectation of posterity.

—That's very interesting, says Mammy continuing with her work, but what do you mean by that, exactly?

—Must I put dots on the 'i's for you?

—In Irish one does not put them on, I remarked. On the contrary one puts them on the letters b, c, d, f, g, m, p, s, and t to indicate aspiration.

—You are well educated, Miss, but that does not rule out that your brother, here present, has made a baby with me.

—You must be joking, said Mammy who seemed fascinated by the construction of her sock.

—But, I cried out, how can you have a baby as you are not married?

—You see, said Joël to Mrs. Killarney, there is no answer to that.

—It is not difficult, however, to find the answer.

—And what is it?

—It's a fact.

—What's a fact?

—That I am big.

—Not so much, I said.

—There are women of your age who are much more obese than you, added Mary.

—In any case, said Mrs. Killarney, I know who it was who obesed me.

—Who so? murmured Mammy, at last raising her eyes towards her.

—I say it again: this young man has put a puppet in my drawer.

—I don't believe a bit of it, that game is over at your age, remarked Mammy.

Then, Mrs. Killarney came out with such a terrible horror that I barely dare to transcribe it in this dairy, but in the end I must, because I swore always to say the truth, fully raw. So Mrs. Killarney said:

—I am pregnant.

And she repeated:

—Like I have the honor to say it to you, Mrs. Mara. I am pregnant through the works of your son!

Mary and I marked our extreme surprise by each letting out a whistle of admiration. Joël did not move a muscle.

—You would never have me believe that, said Mammy.

—It's like I said it to you, replied Mrs. Killarney.

—You're coming on strong, said Mammy.

—Not as much as him, replied Mrs. Killarney.

—And how do you know it? demanded Mammy.

—It is now two months that I have not been wasteful, responded Mrs. Killarney.

—It's the change of life, replied Mammy.

This left Mrs. Killarney silent, still and at a loss.

Thus, in five minutes, what am I saying, in ninety seconds, I came to learn that a woman can have a child without being married (what use is it then, the sacrament?) and what's more, that the begetting of a baby has to do with the phases of the moon.

Mammy followed up her advantage.

—How did you not think of it, Mrs. Killarney. It's obvious, come on now. It's obvious.

—You believe so Mrs. Mara?

—For sure, for sure.

—But, Mrs. Mara, there are women who . . .

—But no, but no.

—And all the same, Mrs. Mara, Master Joël, however, he me . . .

—That's nothing, that's nothing. The japes of a big baby. So go home, Mrs. Killarney and sleep on both your ears.

—You believe so Mrs. Mara?

—But yes, but yes, said Mammy. Come on, all is well that ends well. I am going to make a big bowl of punch flambé to celebrate.

—Don't forget to put cloves in it, said Joël.

Mammy put the stockings on the table and disappeared in the direction of the kitchen.

—What are you making tomorrow for lunch, Joël asked Mrs. Killarney.

23 MAY

No time to go on about my discoveries of yesterday, in any case I have not had the time to reflect on them. I got up at mid-day (we drank punch flambé until four o'clock in the morning) and I got ready to go for tea at Mrs. Baoghal's.

I was less nervous than the first time, but all the same, passing by my Aunt Patricia's apartment, I went to pay a little visit.

—I say it to you again, beware, beware, she said to me on the doorstep.

—Yes, Aunt Patricia.

I said that to her from politeness, so as not to vex her, but since the session of last evening, and well, like I wrote above, not having the time to reflect on it, I am more and more persuaded that it is the ceremony that makes the baby.

I was met at the door by Mève, who is quite cold with me. I ask myself why. "Good day Mève." "Good day miss," that was all that was said.

Mrs. Baoghal greeted me affably, she was magnificently done up with a pistachio-colored dress with yellow and mauve stripes, plus a clever bodice wrap in wine colored taffeta. Sleeves wide and open. Mr. Baoghal, in a grey frock coat and flower-patterned waistcoat, addressed some friendly words to me in Irish:

Conas tá tú?

There was Connan O'Connan, the poet, with his wife,

his son and his daughter Irma. There also was Sarah with her
two brothers Phil and Tim, her mother and her father Grégor
Mac Connan the poet. Equally, there was Padraic O'Grégor
Mac Connan with his father Mark the poet, his mother and
his sister Ignatia. There was in addition Mrs. O'Cear, her
husband, the bard-druid, her three sons Arcadius, Augustin,
and Cesar and her daughter Arcadia. Finally, there was Mac
Adam, the primitivist philosopher, with his wife and his children Abel, Beatitia, Cain, and Eva. And I will not forget to
cite Barnabé, who came with neither mother nor father, nor
brothers nor sisters.

—So are you an orphan? I asked him.

—My parents live in Cork, he confessed.

—I do not know Cork, I confessed, but my brother went
there last month with Tim Mac Connan.

—My humble respects, Miss, said Tim, who was listening
behind my back. Charming town Cork, he said to Barnabé
with an offhand air.

—Ah good, there you are, cried Pelagia. There is Ignatia
who's looking for you, Barnabé.

She led him away.

—They met at one of our Saturday parties, he said. You
still do not come.

—I do not know how to dance, I replied, and I am not
invited.

—Oh, if you do not like to, I won't insist. Apart from that,
how is Joël? Is it working out with the cook?

—Of course.

—No joke, she's keeping the kid?

—But there is none.

—No?

—It's just the change of life. Tim looked at me, astounded,
I ask myself why.

Then quite seriously.

—Sally, would you not like for us to go together one day to the cinema?

—Why not, I said.

—Do you like going to the pictures?

—Quite well. The last film that I saw was a Tarzan.

—A curious choice. You like Tarzan?

—It was Barnabé who took me.

—What! You went to the cinema with Barnabé?

He had an air of increasing surprise, but what was surprising about that?

—Barnabé, the chancer, he added.

At this moment Mrs. Baoghal popped up.

—Sally, Sally! I have been looking for you, there is a French gentleman, a friend of Monsieur Presle, who wishes to be introduced to you.

The friend of Monsieur Presle was a person of middle age, twenty-eight, thirty years perhaps, very well dressed with a stiff collar, his trousers sharply creased, a charming handlebar moustache and a lorgnette secured behind his ears by a wide ribbon of black silk. He made a bow to salute me by placing the point of his right shoe behind his left heel and making a small bending of the knees.

A true musketeer.

—How well you speak French, Miss, he exclaimed after I had said to him: "Bon jour, Monsieur."

—It is the fruit of the lessons of Monsieur Presle, I responded to him.

—Ah! dear Presle! He talked to me a lot about you. He did not spare his praise of you: on your gifts, your work, your intelligence . . .

I could not stop myself blushing.

He bowed once again.

—Oh, oh, I went, oh, oh, oh.

My face crimson, I swayed from one foot to the other, something that adds elasticity to the natural timidity of young girls.

—I can confirm, the French gentleman continued, that he did not exaggerate. I would even say that he was short of the truth, because I must confess that I have never met beauty comparable to yours.

He explained himself with large gestures.

—No, no, I stammered, you go too far.

—If we could talk in a small quiet corner? he suggested to me.

Taking a strong hold of my elbow, he led me out into the corridor, a dark place from where one could hear, as in a dream, the chatter of the those invited to the tea.

We sat down on embroidered cushions piled up on a Breton chest, souvenir of a voyage of exploration by Padraic Baoghal.

Immediately installed, the French gentleman grabbed my hand, holding and pressing it nervously. "Fuck I said to myself, how he goes at it." However, the sweet talk resumed:

—Sally, the French gentleman said to me, Sally, will you allow me to call you that?

—Of course.

—As for me, you may call me Athanase, he murmured into my ear.

I sniffed. He was fully perfumed. Was it *Scandal* from Lanvin, *Missive* from Roger and Gallet, *Zieline* from Weil, or *Vol de Nuit* from Guerlain, every one of them odoriferous substances advertised in the last issue of *Votre Beauté*? I was not able to say which, but, all the same, I was just a little interested to know.

—How nice you smell, I whispered to him.

—Is that so, my little chicken? It's the good air of France.

—What perfume is it?

—Chhtt! he went, while putting a finger to his mouth. Chhtt! It is a surprise.

He looked around him, then being assured no one could see us, he unbuttoned his trousers and took out something that I, at first, took to be his tool.

—Chhtt! he went again. Chhtt! I hid it there because of the customs, he explained as he handed me a small bottle of perfume. A present from our friend Presle, he commented.

I took it eagerly, pressing it in turn under my nose and on my heart.

—It's *Scandal*, I cried blissfully. How kind it is of him.

I filled my nostrils to the point of becoming breathless.

While I was thus absorbed by the pleasures of my sense of smell, the elegant Athanase, slipping an arm across the cushions, had gripped me by the waist, and slipping a hand under my green cretonne dress with red spots, orientated it in the direction of my knickers.

—The dear Michel, I sighed. He has not forgotten me, the darling!

Having well smelled it, I put the bottle into my bag, and put myself to realistically envisaging the situation. The gallant musketeer was becoming derailed.

—Oh, oh, oh! he went as he tickled my thighs. oh, oh, oh, she is so cute the beautiful little ggirrlie of green Erin, who is it who is going to take off her little nickickers? It is the best friend of her Mimi, of her Chechel, of her Préprèle.

I gripped his nose between two fingers and inflicted on this appendage a twist of a hundred and eighty degrees. Just like oil from the ground of Oklahoma, blood spurted from nostrils that were turned towards the ceiling.

—No nonsense, I said to him while he gave again a normal

inclination to his conk. And thank you all the same, I added.

I got up and left him to plug his gob.

As soon as I arrived in the saloon, Barnabé cornered me and moaned:

—You know, Sally, I was going to intervene.

—You spy on me?

—I confess, he groaned. With that Frenchman, I was afraid.

—Smell this for me, I said to him passing the bottle of *Scandal* under his beak.

—How horrible, he moaned. That stinks.

—A gift from Michel Presle!

—These Frenchmen! he groaned.

Mrs. Baoghal ran over, attracted by the smell.

—That's divine, she bleated as she let her nose wander over the stopper. A gift from Michel Presle, I explained.

—Where then is our visitor?

—He is buttoning up again, I explained.

Mrs. Baoghal had an air of surprise.

—In any case, here he is.

He approached: the center of his face glowed. He grimaced; that must still be painful. But he did not show it too much, faithful in this way to the courageous traditions of his nationality.

—Dear Sir? Is she not an exceptional young girl?

—Remarkable, he acquiesced as he bowed.

But when he spoke, that caused the vessels in his head to explode once more and the blood to piss out again. He mopped his snoot.

—My God, cried Mrs. Baoghal. What happened to you?

—I hit myself against the cistern, he gave as an excuse. But it's nothing, it's nothing.

—It still works? enquired the mistress of the house.

—Have no fears, dear madam.

—One of those little adventures that make travels charming, said Mrs. Baoghal.

—I wish you similar ones, replied the Frenchman, smiling.

—Isn't he astute, sympathized Mrs. Baoghal. Tell us, dear
Monsieur, how do you find our town?

—Just fine.

—Isn't he charming!

—Have you visited our Gallery? No? I am sure that Miss
Mara would be pleased to accompany you there.

—*Is cuma dhom*, I said in Irish, which is to say: it's not
my onions.

—*Ná bíodh eagla ort!* Mrs. Baoghal replied to me, which
is to say: don't be a coward.

— Good, good, I went.

24 MAY

And that is why, today, I took Athanase to the National
Gallery. We found each other again in front of that edifice.
We conscientiously admired the two views of Dresden by
Canaletto, the *Saint Francis* by Greco, *Christ Bidding Farewell
to the Virgin* by Gerard David, the *Portrait of a Woman* by
Goya, and some Gainsboroughs. Athanase behaved correctly
during the whole visit, barely attempting a bottom pinch from
time to time. His moustache was waxed, his shoes brushed,
his lorgnette shone with a thousand lights: a real musketeer.
He must have believed that I was wary of him but, to tell the
truth, what gave my comportment an appearance that was
possibly a little embarrassed was that all the time I expected
the appearance of the attendant I had knocked into the mud.
Of course it was not part of my plan to show Athanase the
sculptures in the garden. I feared too much encountering my

enemy there; also, I think that in Paris there must be much better. Putting myself in his place, I could only think of an Aphrodite and a Diane with calves that he could have licked.

Crossing the room of the Pre-Raphaelites, I made the mistake of letting him lag behind. Neglecting the erstwhile princesses who concealed their lack of breasts in the sepia-colored mists of immortal masterpieces, didn't he take it into his head to look out through the window, and I heard him behind me, guffawing.

—It's so hilarious, he said not too loudly. It's so hilarious.

—What so?

—Zinc fig leaves and shorts! Let's go to see them up close!

He led me along. I didn't know how to resist. We penetrated into the garden and Athanase, from the first statue, my Apollo in shorts, began to laugh inordinately. As I had, alas, anticipated, my attendant appeared.

—What is it that does not please you in our Gallery, sir? he asked coldly, letting on that he did not see me.

—What did he say?

Because the other one had expressed himself in Irish.

—The gentleman speaks only English, I said to the attendant.

—But he is not an Englishman, he replied, still in Irish.

However, Athanase, disdainful of the attendant, had planted himself in front of the second statue—my Hercules—and let loose loud chuckles while holding his belly with both hands, with the authentic elegance of a marquis of the eighteenth century. Profiting from this separation, the attendant whispered into my ear the following little discourse that he had composed in the Irish language.

—Little bitch! Little whore! Not only do you come here to practice your hysterical crises on the bodies of these innocent, cold statues, but, as well, you bring here foreign yobbos who mock the healthy limitations that the conservators of this Gallery have seen fit to apply to the extensions of human flesh. Shameless girl! Lecherous child of Erin! I know a lot about you, I know your name, your first name, your address, your occupation. Be careful! Be careful! If you continue to discharge base acts in the bosom of municipal aesthetic foundations, if you persist in transforming sculptures into means of solitary satisfaction or collective fun, a charge will made against you. Yes, a charge will be made against you Sally Mara! A charge! A charge! A charge!

How come this big lump knew my name? It was unbelievable! But, instead of trembling, I felt more like joining the hilarity of Athanase. Why was I not afraid? I am still asking myself that now. Anyhow, I was not wrong.

Instead of falling down, terrorized before the guardian of zinc leaves and shorts of plaster, I called over my companion, who hurried to join me, and said to him:

—This man is a dirty pig, he made disgusting suggestions to me.

—Euh, went Athanase.

—He wanted me to run my hand through his hair.

—Fi! went Athanase, and he wanted to lead me away. I resisted.

—What? I cried, you don't want to break his gob?

—The poor man! I understand him.

—No? You don't want to?

The attendant who did not expect this reaction began to take on an anxious air. Athanase went up to him and in halting English asked him to apologize to me, all of which the other seemed not to want to understand. Then, pushing aside the Frenchman, with my right arm I seized my compatriot by the lapels of his uniform and I fucked him into the bushes where he sprawled.

—Eh well! said Athanase. What a move. Will that not get us into trouble?

—Fear not. Every time I come here, I thrash him.

—Oh! Green maiden, declaimed the musketeer.

Immediately after we had left the Gallery, he made haste to take leave of me. I would have liked to ask him for details of the life of Michel Presle, but I forgot. And all of that happened a little fast.

But I ask myself how the other lummox knows my name.

24 MAY

I met Athanase in the street, by chance. He saluted me very politely but without speaking to me. What a peculiar person. However, I would like to have charged him with several messages for Presle.

25 MAY

Wrote to Monsieur Presle to thank him for his perfume and to ask him (discreetly) for other issues of *Votre Beauté*, or publications of that kind. Part of my letter is written in Irish to show to him my progress. I speak to him also of Athanase, without great enthusiasm: as Athanase is his friend I do not want to upset him, so I end with some compliments on his social skills.

26 MAY

We are going to spend the summer at the home of Uncle Mac Cullogh, Mammy's brother. He lives at a farm, some miles from Cork going towards Macroon.

27 MAY

Mrs. Killarney often has fits of vomiting; Mammy says that it is the liver that torments her, that woman. She advised her to say some prayers to Saint Boldo, who is supreme for the ailments of that organ.

28 MAY

I found my copy of *Votre Beauté* and this is how.

Three days ago (I forgot to note it but I'm tired of writing about all the drunken bouts of the brother), Joël started a thundering batter. So, that evening, as we all three dined, Mammy, Mary, and I, Mammy started to think out loud—'to think' or that which she calls 'to think' about what would be necessary to bring for the holidays. She was making her inventory aloud, dreamy and distant, slightly romantic. As Joël is to accompany us, she remembered suddenly that there were two buttons to be sewn on his flies. I suggested that I go to look for the object (not to sew them on, because Mammy does that very well).

So I go up to Joël's bedroom, I rap to keep my conscience happy for I suspected that, sleeping off his ouisqui and his beer, he would not respond to me. So, not hearing any response I enter.

I find Joël stretched out on the bed. He must have undertaken some sort of work and, overcome with fatigue, fallen asleep without being able put away his tool, which he held in his hand. On the ground lay my number of *Votre Beauté*, fully open at a page on which a charming Parisian model, photographed from behind, exhibits the qualities of a girdle designated as *Scandale*. The woman is ravishing, she smiles.

Her stockings rise high along apolloniaque legs, or more likely aphrodisian legs—I mean to say, in any case, divine—attached at mid-thigh so that they stretch and mold her gams by means of suspenders attached to the girdle, the latex tissue of which allows to be seen the partition into two hemispheres of this delicious globe that we other women trail around as an arse.

The strange part of the story is that this illustration was covered with a sort of paste, the origin of which it was impossible for me to establish.

Giving up on the solution to this interesting problem, I take his trousers to pass on to Mammy; they did in fact lack two buttons.

14 JULY

Today is the national day of celebration of the French Republic. In Paris, it seems that it is stupendous. Michel Presle wrote to me of: dancing at street corners, bottles of beer, fireworks on the bridges. Ah! when then, when will I be able to see Paris? For the moment, I only have under my eyes the green valleys of Erin, because it is now a few days since we installed ourselves in the house of the Uncle Mac Cullogh. Joël and he get on very well: they are never sober. Mammy continues to knit stockings for the eventual return of Daddy. Mary and I occupy ourselves as we can.

It is the first time since the age of eight years—God it's a long time—that I am visiting the country. It's pretty, the countryside. It has its charm: it's green, it does not move, it transforms easily into a dunghill which is very useful for the man who works these fields, otherwise called the "farmer."

Mary and I, we ignore the plants, which seem to be totally deprived of toolness apart from that attributed to them in school: the pistil, the stamens and other twaddle—at best good enough to feature in the catechism. We both, i.e. Mary, despise them then, and fix our attention principally on the animals.

What we do not understand, neither Mary nor I, is their mania for climbing on top of each other, particularly the little creatures. For example, the flies, which are not rare at Uncle Mac Cullogh's, are often to be seen falling down in front of you, one on the back of the other. It is clear that this is a trick by the one that is on top, to stop the one underneath flying and to submit it to the laws of gravitation. Generally, I crush both of them with a good bang, which may be unfair to the one underneath. Mary would like us to trap the one on top and pull off its wings to teach it a lesson: but I do not favor this educational method.

In the henhouse, analogous incidents occur. The cock thinks of only one thing: perching on the hens, while these good birds only think of perching before going to sleep. Also, that does not please them at all, because they squawk. So, a rod in my hand, I impose order on this little world. As soon as I see a cock jumping on a hen, I dislodge him.

Only, each time I enter the hen house, the cock in question jumps up on me with a savage and vengeful air. He does not appear to appreciate my schemes. Is it my fault? But they say of cocks that they are not very intelligent.

3 AUGUST

I observed the tool of a donkey. That is something. But for what could that be of use? Not for cracking nuts, all the same. No specialized industry is attributed to this animal. It is not like the beaver that makes dams with its tail.

25 AUGUST

It is not just the small creatures that climb on top of each
other, the mid-sized ones also. The gallant doggies, for example, never stop trying to play leapfrog among themselves,
but never manage it. Five, six come together, there is one
that serves as a springboard (in general a bitch, it seems to
me), they go back on two legs as if sitting up to beg, lean on
the rump of the other, then make convulsive efforts to jump
over the partner, but these efforts are never rewarded. After
having struggled for some time, they fall again on their feet,
exhausted, panting. It's comical and pitiful. The kids form a
circle around them, which hampers us a lot, Mary and me, in
our observations. We dare not approach more closely, which
until now has meant that we have not been able to study this
game in detail.

26 AUGUST

The prevailing heat, the ardor of my zoological research and
the approach of my monthlies this night, prevented me sleeping. Towards three o'clock in the morning I got up, put on
a dressing gown, and went out into the yard of the farm. All
was calm. The moon rolled along majestically on the carpet
of the sky, smearing with its milkiness the property of Uncle
Mac Cullogh. Suddenly, a piercing cry rose up in in the silence
of the night and fucked me into a blue funk, the blonde hairs
of my strong young virgin body stood on end with horror.
I froze. The cry repeated, piercing, aggressive, disquieting. I
began to sweat, first my forehead, then my underarms, then
the small of my back. The lamentation stopped only to renew
with a new intensity. I imagined for a moment the presence

of some phantom in grief, but, as none had ever been cited in this locality, that quite quickly seemed to me to be most improbable. Anyhow, I believe very little of that stuff.

A delicious breeze, transportress of a lovely odor of turf, arrived to cool my forehead. I opened my dressing gown so that it could dry the rest. Although the moaning had not ceased, I began to take courage and decided to see what could really howl in such a way. Guiding my way by the sound, I approached the sonorous being with many hesitations, and made out two cats. One of them, the noisy one, held itself stretched out, head on the ground with its rear raised up. The other was prowling around. From time to time, it approached the first one, and blows with claws were exchanged, meowing exploded, then beaten, it moved away again to prowl and survey its adversary. I was not slow in predicting the defeat of this last one, having well considered its position and its method of combat. I can speak knowledgeably because I am a member of the C.A.C.C.F.A. (Catch-As-Catch-Can Feminine Association), of the F.I.F.A. (Full-in Feminine Association) and of G.R.W.F.A. (Greco-Roman Wrestling Feminine Association). It is true that I do not practice since a year ago. I have not even paid my dues. I must start again. It is the study of Irish that has taken all of my time, this year. And will take even more from me. That fucking language, as Presle used to say, how tough it can be. It's different from Mary's studies for the post office. But I persist in this decision: to write a novel in this strange language. I sense in myself a vocation both literary and bizarre. I could write in English (my native language) or even in French (like I do for this dairy), but no, I want this novel to be in Irish. And I do not even know what will happen in it! Is this not peculiar? But where was I? Ah! yes, my cats. Eh well, it went as expected. The prowler jumped on the back of the other and, aye, he gave it one great shaking.

What is it with all these creatures climbing like that onto each other's backs? One could say that they think of nothing else but that, and that there is only that in life.

27 AUGUST

This morning in contemplating the beautiful turnip fields of the Uncle Mac Cullogh, I brought to mind fragments of the school teaching of natural science. There was indeed some consideration of the reproduction of plants, but that of animals, zero. I am beginning to get it, that everything that has preoccupied me recently has something to do with this delicate question. However, I can't grasp the analogies: the male tool does indeed resemble the pistil, but is that its function? What then could the stamens be? The downy hairs that grow towards my privates?' Mystery. All of that is not coherent.

28 AUGUST

Despite my height, and Mary is not small either, Uncle Mac Cullogh calls us "little ones." This morning he said to us:

—Little ones, if that amuses you, we are going to bring the nanny goat to the buck goat.

We said yes, then he put a halter on Betty, a totally white little goat, and we left (when there are three females with one male, should the feminine form of "left" not be used?) in the direction of the farm of Fyve O'Clogh, two miles from uncle's.

We had walked for perhaps barely half an hour when Mary and I exclaimed together:

—Ah, by all the saints, what a smell!

In effect, as pongs go, that stunk to high heaven.

—I smell nothing, said the uncle. But that must be Barnabé.

—Barnabé, I cried out with a tightening of my heart.

Mary guffawed.

The uncle assumed a crafty air.

—You, my little Sally, you must be playing around with a Barnabé. Our Barnabé here is O'Clogh's buck.

—He should be given a good wash, remarked Mary.

—That would take away his charm, isn't that so, little nanny?

He gave her an affectionate blow with his stick.

—So, this Barnabé, went the uncle again, when is the marriage?

—It is not decided, said Mary.

—I am not near to getting married. Above all with Barnabé. Whom I barely know. I only spoke to him two or three times.

—What does he do?

—He is learning Irish.

—That is real work, said the uncle.

—You can say that, I approved.

—Why would you not get married?

—She knows nothing about it, said Mary.

—It's not part of my present thinking.

The more we advanced, the more it stunk. And I had to find other good reasons. I came up with this one, the least true of all:

—If you think the example of Mammy is encouraging.

—Eh, so what! She profited from the youth of her husband, she is well rid of him now.

—She's waiting for him, said Mary.

—That's a sham, replied the uncle.

—Stupidity, replied Mary.

—Little impudent brat, cried the uncle, insulting my sister!

He had the air of being truly indignant. But everybody knows that Mammy is somewhat weak in the loaf.

—Hold the nanny, the uncle ordered me.

I took the halter, and the uncle, taking Mary under his arm, gave her six slaps on the bum. Then he lets her go. He goes to take the halter. But he reconsiders. He grabs my sister again, and again warms up her backside. Mary, released, stays behind. She sulks. She looks not quite herself. The uncle also, who has taken the halter again. I examine him from the corner of my eye from toe to head. Towards the middle of his body, I confirm that his spirituality manifests itself to the extent that, for sure, he could use it as a stick for the little doe who is bleating constantly and seems nervous. The farm with the buck goat is at the bend of the road. We walk in silence.

—Come on, the uncle said at last, don't make that face, Mary.

That had never happened to us, not to one nor to the other since the departure of Daddy, ten years ago. Joël did try a few times, but he was less strong and, together, we gave him a good beating. A real wimp, the brother. But I remember well those given to me by the Fazeur. He was ceremonious and methodical. Rolling up his sleeve, pulling down my pants, putting me across his knees, all that took time, time. It was a real mass for him, a communion. And the brute, what a hard hand he had. But me, I was not humiliated at all. Punished even less. I had a great feeling of triumph. I felt that it was he who lowered himself in taking such an obstinate interest in that part of my body, which, for me, was just what I sat on. I thought of myself as a queen and of him as a slave to my bottom, just something to be slapped. When it was finished, I put on my pants again without a tear (sometimes, yes, all the same, when he had hurt me too much), and I went off, dignified and satisfied, because, after all, I like having a hot bottom.

Meanwhile, Mary had re-joined us and was walking alongside.

—You must understand, the uncle explained to her, I know well that your mother is a holy simpleton, but it is not for you to say it. Ah! All the same. Rrrh.

He spat, proudly.

—Here we are. A beautiful farm he has, O'Clogh. And a handsome buck as well. My little ones, you are going to see the beautiful marriage that it will make.

He guffawed.

—The beautiful marriage! The beautiful marriage!

Mary and I looked at each other: the same apprehensions must have galloped through our noggins.

—But why do you take the nanny goat to the buck? I asked the uncle in a halting voice.

—You are going to see, my little ones! You are going to see!

We enter, we see old O'Clogh, there are explications, bleatings from all sides, the buck is in the shack beyond, "you're going to see, my little ones, you're going to see," ouisqui is drunk, the price of the wedding is discussed, because wedding it is, very loud bleating, they drink ouisqui, they finally make a deal, you are going to see, my little ones, you are going to see, the doe is dragged in, the door is open, what smell, what smell, a bearded being stamps its feet with impatience, its eyes flash, he wants with all his force to walk on his hind legs, he places those in front on the back of the doe and see how he exerts himself like a real dog with a very satisfied air. In my head everything whirls, the pure spirits, the emotions of Barnabé, the monthlies of Mrs. Killarney, the climbings of Joël, the asinine tools, the shorts of statues, the reproduction of plants, animals, and humans, nuptiality. Everything links together, everything explains itself—or at least it seems to me. Flashes cut across my little (immortal) soul. I am dazzled. The buckish odor suffocates me. I faint. I'm going to fall backwards.

—Hold tight the rail, whispers uncle into the hole of my ear.

I stretch out my hand and grip his stick.

A vulgar wooden cudgel.

Uncle Mac Cullogh is not a gentleman. Like him of the harbor.

1935

13 JANUARY
(ANNIVERSARY OF THE DEPARTURE OF MICHEL
PRESLE AND OF MY ENCOUNTER WITH THE
GENTLEMAN)

Here we are, six months, no, a little more than four, during which I have written nothing in this copybook. I had fucked it to the back of a drawer, and did not touch it again; I did not know what to put in it. Nothing much has happened since the holidays. I have restarted my lessons with Baoghal, Barnabé also. I never go out with him, ah, but no. Nor with any other man. Mrs. Baoghal still makes her miniatures with the same application; that annoys me, that gives me a sort of malaise, I work less well. Joël bought himself a phonograph. While he is not here, Mary and I learn to dance. Now she goes to a dance at least once a week, sometimes two. She is going out with a certain John Thomas. Nevertheless, the evening of the buck goat, suddenly in her bed—we shared the same room—she began to cry while stammering: "Poor little little doe, poor little little doe." And this is how girls are. For myself, I go to no parties. What else has happened? Mammy let Mrs. Killarney go because of her increasing obesity. That caused a fuss. She said that she would come back, that it would not finish like that. Now we have a young girl of a sort similar to Mève. Joël leaves her alone. He's still just as alcoholic. I do not see him much. Mary on one side, Joël on the other, Mammy who knits stockings for Daddy, who will come back, perhaps, one of these days; I feel myself to be really alone. There is nothing I want to do. I am totally melancholic, nevertheless, my ovaries are doing well, thank you.

I took out this copybook again because it is one year since I began to keep an intimate diary, but I don't have much heart for it anymore.

Michel Presle wrote to me twice, he sent me other French magazines: *Vogue, Fémina,* etc. It gives me pleasure to go through them, I would like to wear the beautiful things one sees in them, but it is unlikely that will happen to me, ever, so I feel very nostalgic. But then to make oneself beautiful, to doll oneself up, to cosset oneself, to adulate oneself, to perfume oneself, and then afterwards to finish up by having oneself pierced by a smelly brute—after all that trouble!

16 JANUARY

On recommencing my diary, I was not thinking that I would have, so soon, the occasion to consign fantastic events to it. There have occurred unprecedented, tremendous, staggering things. Here they are:

We were at dinner. We had just finished the herrings with ginger, making way for the bacon and cabbage; by chance Joël and Mary were there, it is rare nowadays that we are all four together, either Joël or Mary is missing. Joël, not too drunk, was absentmindedly cleaning out his ears with a gherkin. Mammy was cutting up the bacon, the cabbage smelled good, outside it was cold, inside it was warm, we were at our ease, when suddenly there is a ring at the door: the young girl goes to it. We heard voices, whining, a commotion; the door opens violently and there is Mrs. Killarney, who, pushing aside Bess, enters. She was totally deflated and carried a bundle in her arms. It was the bundle that was whining. She placed it on Mammy's knees.

—Here now, grandmother, here, she said to her, it's for you to look after. As for me, I have something else to do, good night.

She went to leave.

—Ah, but no! cried Mammy, you're going to have to take this.

And she rose to give the kid back to the old one.

—I don't want it anymore, bawled Mrs. Killarney. I had it for nine months in my drawer, that is enough for now.

—Nothing doing, bellowed Mammy, it's nothing to do with us! In any case, how are we to know that you did not pick it out of a pram just to use it to play a dirty trick on us.

The intelligence of Mammy was becoming astounding.

Mary, under the table, threw a kick at Joël.

—You're saying nothing?

He, who was examining dreamily the earwax that was decorating the point of his gherkin, responded simply: "Ouch!" He had not yet raised his eyes.

Mammy was limitless in her strategies:

—Bess! Bess! Close the door!

Bess galloped to it, laughing.

—Mrs. Killarney, you will not leave here without taking this adorable baby with you.

—Eh, isn't it nice? said Mrs. Killarney.

—Delightful. It looks like you, added Mammy.

—You think so?

—A real doll. It has your eyes.

—You believe so?

—It has very beautiful eyes.

—I think that it has eyes more like its father's, said Mrs. Killarney.

—And who is its father? asked Mammy with a detached air.

—Ah well, your son, responded Mrs. Killarney.

—Come on now, went Mammy with indulgence, since he is a son, he is not a father; look Mrs. Killarney, one should not say things like that, you will make a mockery of yourself. Say, you will take a glass of ouisqui while we finish our dinner. You have not yet dined, perhaps? Bess! a place setting for Mrs. Killarney and another bottle of ouisqui.

Mrs. Killarney found herself at our table with the baby in her arms.

—You are going to tell us what you think of Bess's bacon and cabbage.

Mammy put a plateful onto her plate.

—Thank you, Mrs. Mara, said Mrs. Killarney. That smells good.

She fell on it.

And we started to devour the bacon and cabbage, then a twelve-pound round of cheese, finally a carrageen tart.

—She cooks well, the little one, said Mrs. Killarney as she wiped her moustache with the back of her hand. All the better for you, as I am not ready to come back.

—We miss you, we miss you, went Mammy.

The baby had remained tranquil until then. I looked at it from the corner of my eye with an ashamed curiosity. Mrs. Killarney was eating just above its head and some small pieces of food had been falling on it. No longer hearing the sound of chewing woke it up. It began to wail.

—It's hungry, the little one, suggested Mammy.

Mrs. Killarney agrees, undoes her corsage and brings out from it an enormous hemisphere squirting milk, on which the baby falls with as much ardor as we had fallen on the bacon and cabbage. That this soft voracious chrysalis was (perhaps) my nephew, filled me with as much amazement as the thought that one day, after having supported the buck, my little firm breasts could become as globular as those of Mrs. Killarney and that she must have, on a certain day, gotten down on all fours in front of my brother. I could imagine only poorly how that could have come to pass. I could not well envisage the scene. I did not believe it. And everything became mixed up and confounded, I could not work it all out. And the baby glutton continued to feed and Mammy had a tender air and Mary a disgusted one, and finally, in the silence, Joël raised his eyes and said:

—Mrs. Killarney, you should hide that.

—Why so? asked Mammy. She's doing nothing wrong.

—Ah! she herself cried out, Sir deigns at last to speak to me.

—Hide that, I say to you.

—Impolite!

—Hide that, hide that!

—Insolent!

—Come come, said Mammy, you are not going to argue over so little. Joël, if this view disgusts you, I ask myself why. You only have to turn your head. I think it has not long more to feed, the little fellow.

—It's a girl, said Mrs. Killarney with dignity.

—And what is her first name?

—Salomé.

—Oh! how cute that name is, clucked Mammy.

—I gave it that in memory of Master Joël. That is what he called me during our intimacies.

—He called you Salomé? Mary asked her while looking into her eyes.

—Yes, Miss. He would say it to me like this: "You will be my Salomé, but you will keep on your seven veils."

—There, Joël, said Mammy with pride, as for imagination, he does not lack it when he wants to.

And she joined in with our laughing. Mary and I were creased up with laughing, crying.

—Bloody hell, roared Joël without moving, with an uneasy smile at the corner of his mouth. Bloody hell, he growled, and then for a start, that's not true.

—What nerve.

—Feck off!

Joël tried to assume a dignified air.

—Kss, kss, went Mary.

We couldn't stop.

—I have been too good with you, declaimed Joël. Anyway, we always treat women too well.

I was laughing so much that it was necessary to go somewhere. My little need satisfied, I was going to return to the dining room where the racket seemed to be increasing, when the bell of the front door rang.

—I am going to it, I cried but, in any case, no one heard me.

I opened the door. A man was before me, hat low over his eyes, hands in his pockets. The sickly lamp that lights the street in front of our house, the feeble light that came from the hall did not allow me to see his face. The man was as tall as myself, and broad in the shoulders, which were a little stooped.

While still joyful as I came to open the door, I stood there stupefied. I ended by stammering:

—What do you want, Sir?

He asked me in a muted voice if Mrs. Mara still lived here. I answered yes.

—Good, he went.

He carefully wiped his feet on the doormat and took his hands from his pockets.

Pushing me aside with a determined arm, he entered.

—Mister! I cried stupidly while following him. Mister!

But having arrived at the end of the hall, he stopped.

—What a racket! he murmured.

—Mister, I went again.

He took off his hat and threw it assuredly in the direction of the coat stand. Then he took me by the chin.

—It's you, the maid?

I pushed him away. I was more or less sure of having recognized him.

—No. I am Sally.

—Eh well, he said calmly, you may kiss your father.

I had no inclination to do so. He grabbed me by the shoulders and kissed me. He was poorly shaven, his beard pricked. He had grey eyes, very cold, and an aspect that was quite misshapen. I realized that I had no real memory of him. I noticed that his jacket was covered with stains, and threadbare.

—What is this rumpus? he asked again.

He seemed to be, at the same time, curious and withdrawn from events.

—It's our former housekeeper who claims that Joël is the father of her baby. You arrived at just the right time.

—He reflected for a moment, then said quietly:

—Shit. This is starting well.

He scratched his head and took a step towards the coat stand.

—I really feel like fecking off again.

At that moment, the ruckus in the nearby room doubled in intensity: an incoherent mix of yelling, laughing, wailing, jostled furniture.

—All the same, I am going to see this, Daddy declared. It's amusing? he asked me.

—From time to time, I responded, embarrassed.

He softly opened the door of the dining room and we caught sight of Joël, his tool out of his trousers, and who was about to squeeze the end of it with a nutcracker.

Mammy was crying at him in a heart-rending voice:

—Don't do that, Joël. You'll break it.

Mrs. Killarney was shrieking, the baby was wailing, Mary was laughing insanely, her eyes rolled back.

—Charming, murmured Daddy.

Joël was the first to see him—and to recognize him.

—Father! he cried.

He let the nutcracker fall and re-did his trousers. Mammy, turning round, cheeped:

—John! and jumped into his arms. Mary did nothing.

—Hello everybody, said Daddy.

He distributed kisses all round and shook Mrs. Killarney's hand while bowing gravely. A little smile to the baby. Then he sat down, poured himself a glass of ouisqui that he emptied with little sips, his air thoughtful.

—You got the matches? Mammy asked him.

—Yes. Here they are.

He rummaged in his pocket, and took out a box, brand new, and threw it onto the table.

—Thanks, said Mammy.

—You should pick up the nutcracker, said Daddy to Joël. Joël gave a start, but he obeyed.

Daddy then addressed Mrs. Killarney.

—And you dear lady, what is it your intention to do?

—Ah, Sir, I am really happy to see you: I'll explain everything to you.

—Pointless. I know. I know. You claim that this kid is my grandchild? Eh well, true or not true, you are going to feck off, immediately.

—No, said Joël.

—What did you say?

—I said no; she stays or it is I who will leave.

—She is fecking off and you can feck off with her if you like.

—Good.

He got up and went towards Mrs. Killarney. He helped her get up out of her chair and declared:

—Mrs. Killarney, permit me to share your life. We will raise our child in honor and dignity!

Mary and I, we applauded vigorously this declaration. Mammy sobbed.

Tomorrow I will come to get my things, continued Joël. Goodbye mother, goodbye sisters, excuse my leaving you. Duty calls.

And taking Mrs. Killarney by the arm, he left while we redoubled our applause.

—Youse, Daddy said to us, if you want to stay here, you are going to dance straight, if not, beware of punishments.

We froze. One could hear the front door closing. Silence followed.

At last Mammy had an idea. She said with a tone of gentle reproach:

—John, you took your time finding a box of matches.

—The matches, that was nothing, responded Daddy, the most difficult, that was the box.

And he poured himself a new glass of ouisqui. That is how I lost a brother and gained a daddy.

25 JANUARY

Spineless and severe, he crystalizes the atmosphere into hard ice or else he thickens it into a sort of glue. He drinks almost as much as Joël (no, still not, by far) but it does not show. He does not go out much, to tell the truth he has not even gone out once since his return. Mammy is still radiant, but Bess is terrified. Mary has declared that she will leave as soon as she is a post office assistant.

Yes, life has really changed in the house.

30 JANUARY

We went to see Joël, Mary and I. He lives in the laneway with a right angle turn that leaves Cross Kevin Street at the corner of the Technical School to join up with New Street. On the ground floor, there is a dealer in offal and entrails. We stepped over some decomposing pig's heads, some cirrhotic calf gizzards, and some wizened beef testes, and we mounted the broken steps of a dark staircase, down the middle of which a stream of urine had cut a path.

—Fantastic, shouted Joël as he noticed us. I have not been drunk a single time since my leaving. Not true, my Salomé?

We greeted Mrs. Killarney and we went to have a look at our niece, who was snoozing in the bottom of a suitcase that had been adapted as a crib.

—Look, at this moment, Joël continued, I am only on my eighth ouisqui (it was six o'clock in the evening). And I am working, I'm working! Yesterday, I carried a suitcase to the Westland Row Station and the day before yesterday I pushed a barrow all the way along Cooks Lane. I am a man regenerated.

He let himself drop onto a stool while smiling with satisfaction.

—Say, my Salomé, what is there that we can offer them. Ouisqui?

—There's none left.

—You could go out and buy a bottle.

—No dough.

—O'Coghtail will give you credit.

—Won't anymore.

He rummaged in his pocket, he had nothing left but a raol. Mrs. Killarney still had three pingins. Mary had in her bag a flóirín, and myself about three punts, but I only showed two coróins.

—That will do, said Mrs. Killarney, who went out perkily to seek the drink.

—And father? asked Joël while scratching with his fingernails the dried mud that covered his shoes.

—Father, I am fed up with him, with father, said Mary. I'll split as soon as I have enough to live.

—You'll go live with John Thomas?

—Perhaps.

—They talk of me at the house?

—Mammy wishes you well.

—He only speaks to say nasty things, to give orders, or to utter balderdash. A pretentious bollox.

—And you, Sally, you're saying nothing?

—Oh me, I responded, I don't give a feck.

—Say, Sally, is it not going well? I find you totally changed since the holidays. What's up with you?

—Me? Nothing. Absolutely nothing.

—She is suffering from frustrated love.

—You're going to make me blush, stupid.

—She doesn't know where to hang it, her love. Her life is lacking a hanger.

—You don't see Barnabé anymore? Joël asked me.

—Say, you are very interested in me now that you no longer live at home.

—I tell you, I am a man regenerated.

—Mrs. Killarney came back with five bottles.

—Credit not dead, she said, giving a wink.

We installed ourselves as comfortably as possible on the debris of furniture that lay about the room, and we began talking of some things and others, the financial situation in Finland, of the levels of vitamins in bacon and cabbage, the existence of Homer and of Shakespeare, the gob of the Prince of Wales, etc. When we had finished the third bottle, Mary pointed out that it was perhaps time to go home. I responded to her that I could not give a royal shite. We agreed to stop at the fourth bottle. Joël recited limericks, which doubled us up; now I understood about one in five of them. Mary recited the list of the twelve hundred Philippine islands, and we finished up with some songs. After having met our needs on the stairs, one after the other, we made our goodbyes to Joël, to Mrs. Killarney, to Salomé, whom our departure had woken up and for whom we promised to club together for the purchase of a distracting toy, like a Meccano or a microscope.

The stairs showed themselves to be particularly steep, the pavement particularly slippery. The others said a last goodbye leaning from their window from which hung dirty washing that would never whiten. Mary vomited on a case of sow's ears that awaited collection and we headed towards our home, now not just maternal but once again paternal. Walking seemed to us to be a sport that was at the same time both difficult and hazardous, so we livened ourselves up by singing a few verses into which we strived to introduce the greatest possible number of words the exact meaning of which was unknown to us. Several passersby cheered us. Some even proposed that we share their beds, but we refused, because, as for myself at least, I love my own bed and I am accustomed to it. At uncle Mac Cullogh's, for example, I slept very badly.

At the corner of Long Lane and Heytesbury Street, we

bumped into a young man whom we believed we recognized:

—But it's Barnabé! I cried.

—You think that it is really Barnabé? Mary asked.

—It looks to me to be Barnabé, I responded.

—How is Barnabé doing? Mary asked me.

—Barnabé is not doing too badly for the times that are in it, I responded.

—I am truly delighted that Barnabé is truly doing very well in the times that are in it, declared Mary.

—It is a fact that Barnabé is truly doing very well in the times that are in it, I confirmed.

—Would you not like me to bring you home? asked Barnabé.

—I believe that Barnabé has the intention of bringing us home, said Mary.

—What if we asked Barnabé to have the intention of bringing us home? I proposed.

After having exchanged different remarks that struck monochord notes, two and a half hours later we found ourselves in front of our door.

—I'm going to speak to your mother, said Barnabé in a confidential tone.

—Not worth the bother, I said to him. We'll arrange all that ourselves.

Mary rang the bell. Barnabé went off.

—When is it you'll take me to the cinema? I shouted to him.

I didn't hear what he replied to me. The door opened and we continued with a little gallop to the dining room. To our great stupefaction, the table was cleared.

—What so! said Mary. No grub this evening?

—Chtt, went Mammy, chtt, chtt.

—It's true, I said. What's going on?

Daddy came into the room.

—So, here he is, that one, I went.

And to Mammy:

—What so? And the table? Not yet set?

—The dinner is over, responded Daddy with the tone of a Baobab.

—Not us, we haven't even started.

—Eh well, it's going to be like that this evening.

—But for myself I am hungry, said Mary.

—You are thirsty as well, perhaps?

—Naturally. What a question! You see that!

She got a heavy clout that left her speechless. This act of brutality pushed me to extreme acts: I headed toward Daddy in order to grab his jacket and to teach him how to behave. I did not foresee that he could have some knowledge of the art of family fighting, and the ouisqui that I had drunk had diluted somewhat my memories of past coaching.

A few seconds later, I found myself on the knees of my father, my skirt pulled up, my knickers pulled down, in the course of receiving an energetic spanking of my backside. I began at first by reflecting on the vanity of the things of this world, the highs and lows of existence, on good and bad luck, then, aided by fundamental heat, I came to thinking of the reproduction of vegetable and animal species, of the makeup of the clothes of men in general and of flies in particular, of the dew of menhirs, of the beards of buck goats, of the obscurity of cinema auditoriums. I began to become delirious and, as Daddy unrelentingly tried to render scarlet the ample surface that I had the honor of putting under his eyes, I fell into an extraordinary bliss, although I was trying to hold on, as to a lifebelt, to these words: "Hold tight the rail . . . Hold tight the rail . . ."

31 JANUARY

Barnabé was waiting for me as I left my lesson. He reminded me that I had asked him to bring me to the cinema. We went to see *New Work-Miami.* I took good care not to put my hand on his thigh. As for him, he sat bunched up, it seemed to me, in his seat. He conducted me back to the house. We did not say much. There was some talk on Celtic philology. I ask myself what he could be thinking about. Daddy was a little more talkative today. He told stories about Chicago to Mammy, the bootleggers, the bursts of machine gun fire, and how he had almost found a box of matches there, how then he would have immediately come home. It was fascinating. But it was to Mammy he was talking, addressing himself to neither of us. Neither does he pay any attention to Bess. She is very pretty, Bess, she resembles Mève, a little skinny. I believed that Daddy was going to buck her. Not at all. He doesn't even look at her. Which does not prevent Bess from living in terror.

1 FEBRUARY

He should not be allowed to imagine that he could start again every day. Today, under the pretext that he had pinched one of his fingers with the nutcracker (always this sacred nutcracker), he wanted to redden my botty. But now I knew his force and his style. I went up to him and when he tried to grab me, I put him into my own personal arm-lock from which he emerged stunned.

3 FEBRUARY

As he can do nothing with me, he fell back on Mary.

There was whiting for lunch. Mary had the whim to put a little salt on it (normally we put on some sugar as the English do). That put Daddy into a fury, he threw himself on her and severely thrashed her. I looked on with attention; what is most interesting is to observe the changes in the color of the skin. It is curious to observe how a backside that is generally very white, almost opalescent (I speak for myself and for Mary) can become as lobsterish as a tomato. What is strange also, is to see the face of the person being spanked. She had a curious expression, Mary. I ask myself if I had the same bright look the other day, when it was I who was being spanked.

When we were alone, she made a terrible scene. That I had not come to her rescue. That I was a false sister, a perfidious cow and an absolute bitch. Little by little she calmed down and declared:

—All the same, this here is not going to become the house of General Dourakine. If he starts that once more, I am fecking off, even if I have not yet sat my examination.

—How will you live?

—With John Thomas.

—You will have to marry.

—And then what?

—Yes and then what?

We remained, both of us, thoughtful. I examined her face.

—It's curious, eh, I said to her, the effect that that has.

—What so?

—Eh well, the slaps on the bottom.

—Yes, it's true. Say, you see, at this moment, I could do it with a fellow.

—What are you saying?

—It's true. You do not understand.

—What is it that I don't understand?

—All of that.

—All of that, what? Explain.

—Things to do with love.

—Oh là, là, I went. Oh là, là.

As if that could mean something "Oh là, là," but that was all I had as a reply. In fact, what did I know of things to do with love, only that they happen on all fours and have a connection with the reproduction of species, vegetable and animal?

Mary did not insist, strengthened no doubt by a hidden superiority of which I was unaware. She returned to her primary preoccupation.

—Say, Sally, promise me that you will act in my defense if he tries to touch me again.

—Count on me, Mary.

Mary reflected:

—And if we did it, both of us? So then, he would surely be the weak one.

—And it would be us that would wallop him.

This prospect made us smile.

4 FEBRUARY

Barnabé sent me flowers, artificial because of the winter, but flowers all the same. Attached was his card, a visiting card, on which he had calligraphed his name in Gaelic script.

It's fun to get flowers. The first time that's happened to me. It's nice, it's eloquent, it's allusive. One thinks straight away of the pistil, of the pollen, of fecundation. I held them for a long time by the stem before putting them in my vase.

6 FEBRUARY

I suspected it. Daddy is afraid. Just now, I suddenly raised my arm to get to a cup behind him, and he unconsciously went to protect himself with his elbow. Afterwards, he blushed. He does not say anything to Mary anymore. He must have heard our conversation the other evening.

He's a wimp.

12 FEBRUARY

Went out twice with Barnabé this week. We have long conversations on the future on the Irish language. We practice our lessons together. We are good comrades, our skins only come into contact for the hello and the goodbye.

13 FEBRUARY

Profiting from my absence, Daddy attacked Mary because the day before she had put too much jam on her trout, and he warmed her up so much that she could barely sit down.

She is furious.

15 FEBRUARY

It was a month that we had not gone to see Joël. We found everybody snoring: it was about three in the afternoon. While waiting for them to wake up, we rounded up the dregs in bottles and found sufficient to make two decent whiskies. We watched them sleeping: Joël had the air of an angel, but Mrs.

Killarney was not a pretty sight, her moustache blew up in the flow of her pallid breath, and a dribble of saliva ran along her chin and down her neck.

—How can he do it with that auld one, Mary asked herself. It really is something, all the same, a complex, they result in stuff that is not common.

However I manage, in my imagination, to put this old one on all fours, I cannot see my brother in the act of bucking her. He was handsome, like that, in his sleep, calm, ethereal, poetic. As for Salomé, she had shriveled up since the last time, she was ageing at top speed, one could give sixty years to that little baby.

Then, we looked through the window at the movement of the street. It stank really strongly. Porters of offal and entrails came and went, clients haggled, beggars begged. A gypsy passed, green, red, yellow. Two dogs fornicated under the attentive eyes of a band of kids: seeing them learning for themselves, I thought of my youth, of the time when I myself was painfully climbing the ladder of sexual studies.

Having, no doubt, changed their minds, the two dogs looked for a way to detach themselves. They did not succeed, one pulling one way, the other in the opposite direction. At first we joined our laughs with those of the kids, then I noticed Mary's face stiffen and become very grave. I guessed her anxious interrogation: what happens when, in the same circumstances, the wife wants to go one way and the husband another and they aren't able to? Could that ever have happened with Joël and Mrs. Killarney? With Padraic Baoghal and Mrs. Baoghal? With Marc Anthony and Cleopatra? With Adam and Eve? Mystery. A bucket of water thrown by the dealer in offal and entrails crowned the efforts of the two doggies and also dispersed the assembly of brats.

We abandoned our observation post. In the room, the

snoring continued. We emptied our glasses, we scrawled some friendly words on a scrap of paper and left.

We were walking in silence for some time when Mary said to me:

—You know, I'm no longer a virgin.

I had suspected it; although I would not have known exactly the meaning of this word, the theological use of it seemed to me to be indecent. The priests who perpetually go on about trifles, they should blush for all of the time emphasizing such an intimate detail of an historical figure that, even so, inspires respect. Like the Joan of Arc of the French, who is forever characterized as a maiden. That is not pure, that. Immediately, one thinks of the opposite.

—Eh well, you say nothing?

No, I said nothing. Between sisters, one can tell all but I am not going to ask her if, during her passage to her present state, she had had problems analogous to those of the two bow-wows of just then. The question could not be begged however. I just managed to stutter

—Euh . . . It was . . . how?

—Oh, you know, that is not easy to tell. When one does not know that; it's really not for publication.

—Really?

—Really. It resembles nothing else. It's unique. You will see yourself.

—But I do not want to see.

—People say that.

I answered nothing, but I put another question.

—And . . . is it long ago that you have . . . that you are not . . . that you have . . . that . . . you are not . . .

—Just after the holidays. The second of October, at about fourteen hours thirty in the afternoon.

—And you said nothing to me?

—At that time then, that would have disturbed you too much. You were so much not yourself after . . . the event with the nanny goat.

—Were you not disgusted?

—Immediately, you know, I saw that from a sentimental point of view . . . the pity you know . . . that poor little white doe, so pretty . . . that wild hairy villain . . . but, you know, I can say it to you now, in love, pity does not matter . . . Yes, it is pity at first . . . the sadness . . . the fear . . . and then afterwards I reflected . . . I told myself that it was like that since the beginning of the world . . .

She has a good head, my little sister, and not just to retain the names of the twelve hundred Philippine islands and the five thousand streets of Paris.

—Then, since John asked me to, I slept with him.

—You slept? in the same bed?

—No, the first time, in bushes in the Phoenix Park.

I tried to imagine the scene using the sparse information of my experience. There was a silence.

—I can guess what you are thinking, resumed Mary. But you know, men, they are not beasts. With them, love, it's more . . . varied.

And she added:

—I should not say this to you. But you know, it's also very nice.

We found ourselves in front of the door to our house.

16 FEBRUARY

All the same, all the same. The more I try to represent to myself the scene, the more it seems unbelievable to me. (By the way, it was to the Phoenix Park that Barnabé wanted to bring me the first day that we went out together.) And what does she mean by "varied"? Varied how? Why? And what is varied? Ah, like Hamlet said so well: "There are more things in Heaven and on the Earth than philosophy dreams of."

17 FEBRUARY

But thinking about it . . . she is going to have a baby.

18 FEBRUARY

No. I asked her. It appears to be no. There is a way to arrange oneself, she says. I no longer understand anything. If it's not for having a baby that it is done, it's for what then? I dare not ask her. Because it's "very nice"? Ah, just as I said so well the day before yesterday, there are more things in Heaven and on the Earth than philosophy dreams of.

20 FEBRUARY

How can one be, at the same time, so cold and so limp? Daddy keeps himself quiet for the moment, he still does not go out, he does not want to spank anyone (which does not prevent poor Bess being very afraid of him); but there is something slimy in his being. His glance cuts, carves, pierces, penetrates, but that does not prevent him from resembling a snail, a snail that hides its shell under a jacket, always with its head outside.

What intrigues me is that, for some days, he has been staring at me with irony.

24 FEBRUARY

It's a long time since I saw Barnabé. He was waiting for me today after my lesson. After we had enquired about our respective states of health, we made some steps in silence, then I remarked to him that the weather was superb, very cold but dry. A glorious sun. He could not disagree with that. I suggested a wander on foot. He was not at all against it. I allowed him to propose diverse destinations. Merrion Square? Not interesting. Saint Stephen's Green? I do not like it. Rutland Square? The nearness of the hospital makes me sad. Mountjoy Square? Too far away. The quays along the Liffey? Too much traffic. He looked despondent. He could think of nothing else. But happily, I had an idea:

—What if we went to the Phoenix Park? I cried out.

—But it is much further away than Mountjoy Square!

We were just opposite the tramway depot.

—But it is going to be beastly cold.

—I am not cold blooded.

So he paid the tramway for me to get there and, leaving the central avenue, we started to wander, whilst talking linguistics. Or more accurately, I allowed him to monologue. I had something completely different in mind. Finally, he became aware of it.

—Sally, you have the air of looking for something.

Of course, I acted surprised and denied it. In truth, I was asking myself which of these bushes had seen the conjugation of little sister and John Thomas. A totally pointless interrogation, because there was certainly no placard to indicate it, it could just as well have been this one as that.

—I see now that you came here with a precise intention, continued Barnabé. Oh! I am not asking you what it is.

—However, I could answer you. Do you remember our first meeting?

—In the tram? he murmured, reddening.

—No, I mean to say, the first time that we went out together.

—I remember it, he murmured.

—One year ago today.

He mumbled in surprise something like "You believe so" or "not possible."

—That's all the impression that it made on you?

—I . . . I have no memory for dates.

—But that one?

How he can be confused, the poor boy.

—You do not remember that you waited for me at the end of my lesson and that you had proposed that we go for a walk together to Phoenix Park.

—Yea, he acquiesced humbly.

—I refused but I thought that for this anniversary it would be nice for me to satisfy your desire.

He thanked me in a faltering voice and declared himself to the very touched. As the first shades of the night began to impregnate the sky, we made an about turn.

A little further on, he asked me in a timid voice:

—You're sure that it was the same day?

—How so?

—That I had waited for you and proposed to you to come here?

—Eh well yes.

—I believe that that was another time. The day when I met you at the Gallery.

I look at him coldly.

—The day of the cinema, was it not?

He sank again into mumbling.

—You are lacking tact, Barnabé, I said to him starchily.

In the tramway, he appeared low and with his tail between

his legs. I stupidly pitied him. On leaving him, I accorded him some friendly words. And that sufficed to give him a happy look.

On re-reading my diary, I noticed that he was correct. My error must be related to my not wanting to allude to that visit to the cinema. And I do not yet understand very well what happened on that day.

25 FEBRUARY

Why had he not led me behind a copse? If he had done that, what would I have done? And if I had done it, what would we have done?

Answer: that which everyone does in similar circumstances. That seems simple, but for me it is terribly obscure.

And then, it annoys me that I never think of anything else but that, and that I am perpetually asking myself questions.

If I were to have a good go at it?

With who?

With Barnabé?

But he is such a twit.

He is the only man that I know.

Daddy is forbidden. Joël also. Well, there is Padraic Baoghal. But does he self-reproduce at his age?

On reflection, Michel Presle would not have displeased me. Incidentally, that bastard never writes to me. Me neither, by the way.

There's also the milkman.

2 MARCH

I point out to Mary that there will be an examination for post office assistants in fifteen days. I believed that the news would give her pleasure, but she received it with a certain indifference.

5 MARCH

All the same, she is preparing seriously for her examination. Today I suggested going to see Joël. But she wanted to work. I decided to go there alone.

On our doorstep, I bumped into a young man who was getting ready to pull on the doorbell. It was Timoléon Mac Connan. He was coming to see Joël.

—That makes it more than a month that he has not shown himself. Is he sick?

I responded that he no longer lived with us. I should have told him something else. That he had a contagious disease, for example. Because, to be sure, he was asking questions.

—I don't know what I should say, I stammered.

—Well, the truth.

I was well embarrassed. The truth. The truth. It is really fine, but what was it for my brother, the truth.

—I will tell him that you came. I suggested.

—You're seeing him soon?

—I'm going there now.

That is not what I should have answered. Immediately, he said:

—I'll take you there.

His motorbike was opposite the door. I had a great desire to go on the pillion, and, it would not have been polite to refuse such a nice offer, also I was sure that it would please Joël to see Tim.

I accept, install myself on the pillion, and indicate the route to Tim.

—Hold on to me if you're not used to it.

It roared, we took off at full speed, I grabbed hold of him.

—Pass your arms under mine.

I am too afraid not to comply. I hug him, I flatten my nose against his leather. We go off, it's marvelous. It jolts all the time, eventually giving you an agreeable effect in the bottom, an undulating trembling rises up the length of your vertebral column to your brain where it explodes in original and fantastic ideas.

We are not long in arriving. I show him the house. Outside, as always, offal and entrails and other high stuff.

—What a horror! exclaims Tim. He is cracked to lodge in such a place.

I went in first. He followed me into the perfectly obscure corridor and we climbed the stairs, still quite broken, still as pissy. We had almost arrived at the landing, when I felt Tim's hand caressing my calf. A friendly gesture no doubt, or casual, or cordial. I stopped suddenly. Tim also stopped, but without taking away his hand. Without turning around, I descended a step and, as he had not moved, his hand went up just as much. I ended up by finding it between my thighs where I immobilized it. We stayed like that for a few moments, lightly oscillating then, briskly, I set it free and, with a jump, I found myself on the landing. I knocked violently on the door. It was Joël who opened to me, his hair tangled, yawning, his eyes swollen.

—Tim is here, I said to him.

And so, Tim appeared and, before shaking Joël's hand, gave me a look of amazement.

Joël was very content to see Tim, he asked him for news of these and those, he spoke to him of his present life, of how he earned some feoirlíns, sometimes hunting rats, sometimes delivering packages. He was thinking of going into the business of skins and rags. The business of old bones also offered possibilities and, with the dealer in offal downstairs, he would have the raw material at hand. If he were to succeed in putting some pingins aside, he would buy a set of small tools and would make buttons from these old bones, buttons that he would go and sell in the streets. Later, if his affairs were to go well, he would acquire brushes and indelible paints to decorate his merchandise.

Tim accompanied this discourse with polite monosyllables, but I could make out that he was increasingly horrified. From time to time, he looked at me, always with the same look of surprise. I didn't succeed in imagining what I could have done that was so remarkable. Because, the incident on the stairs, I had only intended to flirt, a little, that's all there was to it. Perhaps I had gone about it wrong. Yet what the little sister said had led me to the conclusion that such contacts were completely normal between young boys and young girls.

In any case, Tim cut short his visit. I had the impression that Joël, as much as me, disturbed him. I let him leave, because I had no inclination to find myself again alone with him on those dark stairs, where perhaps, the idea would come to him to jump on my back.

Joël continued his monologue. I listened distractedly while drinking my ouisqui, which he never seemed to be short of. Then Mrs. Killarney came back with Salomé. Joël was allowed to ramble on a bit more, then I took my leave.

On leaving, I noticed some crumpled papers lying on the bed. I recognized the writing of my brother. They looked to be poems.

7 MARCH

When something begins to happen, things happen. When nothing is happening, nothing more happens.

In this way, since the return of Daddy, things have hotted up. Events succeed each other, speed up, knock against one another. I go from discovery to discovery, from experience to experience. It is a set-dance that swells my diary and disturbs my little (immortal) soul, the pure little pool of my conscience that is agitated gently by the reddening breeze of chaste pansexual emotions. I have often asked myself what would happen if I found myself in a closed room, talking alone with Padraic Baoghal. Eh well, that is what happened today.

When Mève came to open the door for me, I immediately remarked her distressed face. For months, we hadn't spoken to each other. But as soon as I entered, she whispered:

—Attention . . . Beware . . .

I asked her in a voice not less quiet what was going on. She explained to me rapidly that Mrs. Baoghal was sick, that she had worms in her nose, that she had been brought to a specialized clinic to have them pulled out, that, consequently, she would not be present at my lesson today. So: "Beware . . . Attention . . ."

And what if it pleased me not to beware? I did not want to upset poor Mève and I thanked her. Then in a sudden movement, she threw her arms around me and hugged me. I was moved by this mark of affection, but the expression in her look staggered me. Without doubt, it was just like that, that yesterday I had so impressed Tim.

But it was not possible for me to think further about Mève. I now found myself alone opposite Padraic Baoghal. I installed myself, took up my textbook, opened a copybook. As for him, he coughed from time to time, less I think, because he was intimidated than to make me uncomfortable. I started by conjugating for him some prepositional pronouns. I knew my lesson very well, there was nothing to find fault with, so we took up again the analysis of a passage from *Fiche Blian ag Fás* by Ó Súilleabhàin[1]. I like a lot this book, which is a little masterpiece of fresh humor and naïve candour. However, with respect to Mrs. Baoghal, (who, when present, nevertheless obsessed me) her absence prevented me from following with the desired respect the philosophical, syntactical and stylistical remarks of my teacher. As for him, he had received me grumpily and seemed to be watching out for the smallest error on my part, with intentions that were not clear to me. So Padraic Baoghal, was not tardy in noticing my inattention. He brusquely interrupted himself.

—You are not listening to what I am saying.

—But I am, sir . . .

—No. I can see it clearly.

—But yes, sir. So, you just pointed out that . . .

—No. I say to you that you are not listening. How can you succeed in learning Irish if you come here to think of your loves?

—My loves!

He was beginning to annoy me, the dear poet. Is it that he was taking me for a little girl?

—I have the practice of punishing every distraction with the most extreme severity, he continued.

That's it, this big rascal was taking me to be a little girl. Another one who, under the pretext of discipline and ethics, wants to put his hand on my bum.

He pushed back his chair and ordered me to come close to him. The bastard, another tin-pot General Dourakine. And

---

[1] It was translated into French by Raymond Queneau (Gallimard, 1936). (Note by Michel Presle)

for all the patrioteen Irishman that he was, he was another fanatic for British education. Decidedly, I was firmly opposed to these Anglo-Russian practices, but what a pain it is always to have to defend oneself against the enterprises of men. Thinking about it, yes, that, during all the fine years of my youth, and even of my maturity, and who knows perhaps even afterwards—I have the good example of Mrs. Killarney, on reflection, yes, that for a long-time yet—I must constantly protect my backside against attacks by bucks. I was overtaken by a great lassitude and, for a moment, I could envisage myself going to lie over the knees of the poet and allowing myself to be punished.

However, my pride triumphed and I said to Baoghal:

—And to do what, sir?

—To punish you for your inattention.

—And how are you going to punish me? I asked him innocently but in a mocking tone.

—You are going to see. Come.

But he was beginning to be embarrassed and even slightly uneasy.

—You want to, I continued, pull up my skirt, pull down my knickers, and redden my arse?

—Oh! the horrible word! Sally, are you not ashamed. You will be doubly punished.

He wriggled about, all red, on his chair, but absolutely without a clue as to what to do.

—That's it, is it not? You want to spank my bottom?

—Yes, that's it, he murmured timidly.

—Eh well, I responded to him, you can run off with yourself.

He did not know at first what to reply, then in an equally timid tone:

—And if I employed force?

—Try it.

He evaluated me with a glance. Although he was a fine man, he was a big softie, and not sporty at all. He understood immediately that he would not succeed. In any case since the time he first examined me slyly, he must have suspected as much. Intimidation having yielded nothing, he suddenly tried another approach, he began to rave:

—Come on, little Sally, he went suavely, be nice, let me do it.

—Absolutely not.

—Little Sally, little Sally, be nice, look, just two little slaps.

—No.

—One on each side.

—No.

—Then just a look.

—No.

—I'm going to be angry.

—Go ahead.

—Sally, Sally, let me do it. Look: a free lesson for a good spanking.

—No.

—Two free lessons.

—Three.

—No.

—Think about it, Sally. With the money saved, you could buy silk stockings, a brassiere.

—I don't wear one.

—And then, you know, Sally, it doesn't really hurt.

—I know.

—Ah! how do you know that?

Zut, a gaffe.

—No, I do not know.

—There are lots of young girls who like it.

—Not I.

—And even married women . . .

—It's all the same to me.

—Mrs. Baoghal, for example. I spank her morning and evening.

Could there be anything more in the world to be found out! Was this possible? The stupefaction was stronger than the desire to laugh. I stayed dumbstruck. Baoghal immediately profited from this advantage:

—There, you see. Come on, Sally, little Sally, let me do it. Come on to my knees.

But I continued to reflect. So many things that one would not expect. So many mysteries. So many hidden activities. So many secrets. So many masks. I was overcome by a feeling of vertigo. Far away, I heard Baoghal murmur:

—Then, I must go to get you?

I heard then the sound of a chair being moved, I understood that Baoghal had got up, judging the moment favorable because of my agitation. Happily, reason awoke in me and advised me "Hold tight the rail." I got up in a bound and shouted in his face:

—No!

He did not take another step. As for me, I headed towards the door:

—Mister Baoghal, do not be surprised if I look for another teacher!

I had no real desire to change teachers, but it was very important that I react.

Actually, that completely terrified him.

—No, no, Sally. I beseech you, no scandal, say nothing, please, stay, I promise you that I will not recommence, that's a promise, it's promised, but all of this stays between us, Sally. Swear it to me and continue your studies with me, you are my best student, the jewel in my master's crown, I beg you, stay on as my student.

I did not look convinced. He exclaimed:

—In any case to whom would you go?

—To Grégor Mac Connan.

—Grégor Mac Connan!

He sniggered:

—All his students have to pass by the saucepan.

—What does that mean?

—That he's a sex maniac.

—A buck?

—Yes, that's it.

I would not have believed it. He was so dignified and his poetry so full of innocent ethereal virgins and of noble ladies who are never adulterous.

—His son could help me practice.

—Timoléon? Tim, He knows nothing but his motorcycle. He can barely speak a bit of it.

—There is O'Cear.

—Worse again.

I suspected it: a bard . . .

—Eh well! I will go to find O'Grégor Mac Connan.

—A pederast.

—What does that mean?

—It's difficult to explain.

—You have already told me about your conjugal life. I am ready to hear everything.

—Eh well, it is a man who does with men that which one should do with women.

Again something strange.

—A buck for bucks then?

—That's it.

I reflected and I decided:

—With him I would be really safe.

—But you will never manage to get away from his wife.

—Why so?

—A lesbian.

—What does that mean?

—A nanny goat for nanny goats, as you put it.

More and more curious.

Seeing my hesitation, Baoghal declared in a solemn voice:

—Sally, I promise to never importune you again.

—You swear that to me, Mister Baoghal?

—I swear it to you.

He had a sincere air about him.

—With all of that, I remarked to him, the hour is almost up.

—I will not count this as a lesson.

That would be normal.

Now we didn't know what more to say to each other.

It was fortunate that I had an idea. A strange idea, I admit, without false modesty. It passed over the barrier of my lips even before I was conscious of it.

—Mister Baoghal, could you show me Mrs. Baoghal's works.

—What works? he asked, taken aback.

—Those that she paints there, on that table, during my lessons.

As I had foreseen, he was completely discountenanced.

—Ah! the works that she paints there, on that table, during your lessons.

He was not escaping.

—Ah, yes, he continued, her miniatures, yes, her miniatures. Those that she paints, on that little table?

He was floundering.

—I may not look at them? I asked with my most innocent face.

—But yes, surely.

What could he say otherwise? He approached the little table with measured steps and solemnly raised the patterned cloth that covered the work of the mistress of the house.

I approached. There were three or four miniatures, finished or almost finished, and two or three sketches. It was still the same thing. They resembled exactly and scrupulously those that Mève had shown me. It's singular the way people who have obsessions persevere with them and cling to them. From whatever planet or nebula that they might come from, the celestial genies and pure spirits of Mrs. Baoghal, to every—even only a little—informed eye, like my own was now, revealed themselves, in spite of their little wings, as ordinary bucks.

With a finger, I indicated one of the images and I said:

—See here is one with a part of the body that seems to me to be of exaggerated proportions.

—Aoah . . .

—You don't think so, Mister Baoghal?

—Ooah . . .

—And this one seems to me to be much too favored by nature.

—Ooah . . .

—As for that one, he must get his legs tangled up with it, at least if he does not put it through a bandoleer.

—Aoooh . . .

—Here's one at last that seems to me to be well equilibrated, although, it must be admitted that he would not be able to pass it through the eye of a needle.

Baoghal's face delighted me. From so noble to become so idiotic, from so pompous to hypocritical, from so stable to fragile. He swallowed my words in a stupor as if, without my knowing it, they could have come from oracles.

—And that one there, has he not a fine pair, I declared designating the spread-out wings of a spirit that was possibly Uranian.

—Ououououpii! Padraic Baoghal, suddenly, passionately aroused, began to howl.

He began to bound across the room, jumping over the chairs (those that were not too tall) and tossing his flowing mane, already going a bit grey. After having made two or three circuits, he turned in my direction, manifesting intentions that were clearly satyric. I waited for him with a firm stance; an elementary trip allowed me to send him flying against the wall. His skull colliding with this obstacle, my attacker crumbled, completely out of it.

This last scene had made a little noise. A door opened slowly, timidly. Mève's little muzzle showed itself. After a circular glance around, she entered and approached the imitation cadaver.

—You have killed him? she asked me.

—But no, I responded to her. He will wake up in five minutes.

—That would have been great, she murmured, if you had killed him.

She hugged me and pressed herself closely against me. We regarded in silence the unconscious one, she with an intensity such that, as she opened her mouth a little, the tiny end of a pink tongue protruded. She became aware that I was staring at her and raised her eyes towards me. I discovered such tenderness and fervor in them that soon our lips met each other's and our tongues mixed themselves in a kiss that was full of restraint. Then with chaste hands we mutually estimated our respective charms. My knickers fell modestly to my feet, Mève's little energetic hand led me to a couch and there, eyes closed, I began to feel the effects of the most pure spirituality.

In the shady valley of the foaming brook, the little pussy came to slake her thirst, her rough tongue worked unrelentingly against a little outcrop as if she wanted it to release a spring. No matter how much I repeated to myself: "Hold tight the rail, hold tight the rail," I ended up letting myself go, because, I said to myself: "What rail, what rail?" and soon the miracle happened, I dissolved in stars and clouded the sky.

When I came down again to Dublin, to the house of Padraic Baoghal, a soft head rested between my thighs and its hairs mixed with those that, by a peculiar fantasy of nature, decorate the ultra-intimacies of women. I passed slowly my fingers though Mève's locks, and she quivered. She wanted to raise her head up again, but I urgently pushed it down and, again, I enjoyed the modest transports of my little (immortal) soul.

Then Mève asked me:

—You will never forget?

And I responded:

—No.

I put on my knickers again. While arranging her hair, Mève approached Baoghal, whose big (immortal) soul must have been wandering over by Tír na nÓg, the land of happiness

—We should, perhaps, wake him up, said Mève. You are sure that he is not dead?

I responded:

—Yes.

—She gave him a kick in the ribs. He groaned.

—The bastard, said Mève.

I responded:

—Sure.

I added:

—It's just a matter of throwing water onto his face.

—Legs apart, Mève placed herself above his head.

—No, I said, cold water would be preferable.

She went to look in the kitchen for a dirty floor cloth, with which she started to slap the physiognomy of her master. Two streams of mud ran along the creases of his forehead: a dormant nasal hemorrhage declared itself: the swine started to babble and to blink his eyes. We dragged him to the couch where Mève and I had confronted our sensibilities, and installed him there. He gradually quitted Tír na nÓg and reached the stage of being dazed. He appeared to recognize me.

—Will you permit me to leave, Mister Baoghal? I asked him respectfully.

He probably accorded me that authorization. Mève brought me as far as the door. We hugged each other a final time and, without exchanging phrases or words, our tongues, one to the other, communicated the angelic ardors of our little juvenile (immortal) souls.

During all of our evening meal, I thought of nothing, I smiled stupidly. Mary examined me with an inquisitor's eye. Mammy knitted stockings for Daddy who was now returned.

Daddy, in any case, did not delay in returning to his room (he had taken Joël's); he was still as bear-like and a little more serpent.

After having waited some moments to be sure that he was not listening behind the door, I recounted to Mary and Mammy Baoghal's adventures. We had a good crisis of mad laughing. Naturally, I did not say much about Mève, just to boast of the original fashion by which she had wanted to make our poet leave Limbo, which made Mammy double up to the extent that she nearly suffocated. But little sister displayed greater discretion; she had an air of surmising things.

8 MARCH

Am I virgin or am I it no longer?

It is necessary that I talk about it frankly to Mary, so as to have a clear mind.

I am inclined to believe that I still am.

9 MARCH

Effectively, I still am. Mary assured me in this respect, but she mocked me. I was furious. She has no need to put on airs because she has the superiority over me of not being it.

16 MARCH

All these days I have spent a good part of my time hearing Mary recite the names of the twenty-two Swiss Cantons, the forty-two English counties, the eighty quarters of Paris, and the twelve hundred Philippine islands.

I should not forget to note that I have returned to Padraic Baoghal's, twice even; Mrs. Baoghal was present for the lessons, her nose surrounded by bandages, the master was very calm and Mève was content just to say to me "Good day Miss . . . Good bye Miss."

17 MARCH

Mary today sat her examination to be a post office assistant.

While waiting for her to come home, Mammy and I, drank punch to pass the time. Daddy was cloistered in his room shaking I know not what.

—Let's hope that she will be accepted, Mammy repeated mechanically, let's hope that she will be accepted.

—Do not hope for it too much.

—Why do you say that?

Why would I not have said it?

—If she gets employment, she will leave.

Mammy did not respond.

—And you will be sad.

I added, for fear that she had not understood:

—She wants to leave as soon as she can earn her way. She does not want to stay here any longer. With that one.

He could be heard, he came and went above our heads in Joël's room. What could he be fiddling with?

—He was always like that?

Mammy hesitated, then:

—No, he's changed a lot. It's the story of the matches.

—Could he not go in search of another box of matches and relieve the floorboards?

—Be quiet, murmured Mammy.

I continued:

—Happily all the same, he has understood.

—What has he understood my child?

—It is undoubtedly that which has made him sad.

—But what so, Sally?

I got worked up:

—That he can no longer spank our bottoms as the fancy takes him.

—But he continues.

I said ironically:

—On yours?

—No, on Mary's.

I gaped from stupefaction.

—That surprises you, Mammy continued. As soon as you are not here, she arranges it so as to get her spanking. On that matter, Daddy and she, they understand each other like thieves at a fair.

She sighed:

—A peculiar girl. I do not understand her need for moral discipline. Anyway, I hope that she will be accepted.

Mary came home, very satisfied by the way. She would await the results with confidence. I dared not look at her. I didn't know what to say to her. The dinner was gloomy. Daddy, of course, posed no questions. He had the air of not giving a fuck as to what Mary would do if she became a post office assistant, or not.

When alone in our room, she asked what was up with me:

—You are making a strange puss.

—You're going to leave if you're working?

—Naturally.

—Why?

—I told you. I cannot put up with the pater. He gets on my nerves. It's no life here. He is a phantom, that man. He is not a human being.

She added:

—He's making me more and more afraid.

—And John Thomas? You're going to live with him?

—Yes. It's understood. We will marry. One day or another.

It's just that I no longer believed in the existence of John Thomas. You are content then, I said distractedly.

—I have time. For the moment, I await the results.

—Of course, I acquiesced, in a perfectly false tone.

—You, in any case, you do not look to be content.

—I am.

—No. You're hiding things from me.

—And you?

—Me? What is it that you think I'm hiding from you? She looked straight into my eyes.

—I don't know.

—I tell you everything. Of course, not the details that a young girl like you would not hear without embarrassment and that you would not know from experience. But of the rest, I say everything. You don't believe me?

—Since you're saying so.

—You don't seem sure.

I remained silent. She hid herself under the bed covers while shouting at me:

—Shut up, if your antics with Mève put you into this state, I don't care! Shut up and good night!

To my great surprise, I burst out in tears.

Mary immediately got up again and took me into her arms.

—Then, big goose, what's up? Tell me what it is?

I only managed to splutter.

—It's because you are still a virgin and that is making you sad?

—It's not that, I spluttered.

—It's because Mève is not being nice to you?

—It's not that, I spluttered.

—It's because you would prefer to have intimacies with a boy rather than with a girl?

—It's not that, I spluttered.

—It's because you are not it anymore and dare not tell me about it.

—It's not that, I spluttered.

—It's because I am going to go away?

—It's not that, I spluttered.

However, it did bother me to think that I was soon going to find myself alone in this sad house, between a brute and a simple mind.

—Then what? Mary asked me. Explain yourself. Barnabé perhaps? It is a long time since you talked to me about that. What has become of him?

—He has the mumps.

—It's not that, all the same that makes you cry.

I began to laugh through my tears.

—No, of course.

—Then, it's what?

—It's that you are a double-dealer.

—Me?

—Yes, you.

I was not crying anymore.

—Yes. You, you, you. You are a dirty little hypocrite. I will never again have confidence in you.

—But, great God, what is it that I have done.

—You are having your bottom spanked behind my back.

She released me and went to sit on her bed.

—Who said that to you?

—Mammy.

—So! She noticed.

—Don't snigger.

—If I please.

—And you wanted me to defend you. And just now you told me that you tell me everything.

—Yes, I told you everything, except for the details.

—And that's a detail.

—Yes. My pleasures, intimate and personal, they are separate. I do not have to give you details about them. I would not like to make a virgin blush.

—A wonderful excuse! As if you have always been so discreet.

—And say now, you, your little personal pleasures, you never forget them when you talk to me?

There, clearly, I had to lie a little.

—Never, I responded.

—Never?

—Never.

I looked at her straight in the eyes, it was not difficult, she had done as much.

—And the personal pleasures that consist of rubbing oneself against a statue, you have already spoken to me of them?

I choked.

—Tell me, resumed Mary softly, tell me, you have already spoken to me of the pleasure that one experiences while pressing against a male made of marble?

How could she have known that? I made my surprise clear as I asked her:

—How can you know that?

—Then, it's true?

—How can you know that?

—I was not completely sure. It's the father of John Thomas who told him it. His father is an attendant at the Gallery. He was walking with John when he saw you, you were with me, he told his son everything, who repeated it to me; naturally he did not know that John knew me. Curious, eh?

—Very curious.

How could I be able to deny that it was very curious?

—And, I added, it's a long time since you learned all of that? Maybe a little more than a month.

So, since a month ago, she knew this thing about me, and she had remained the same in my eyes. And likewise, for more than a month, she was taking pleasure from the exploits of our own General Dourakine, without my having perceived the least change in her.

—Then, it's exact? she resumed.

—Oh, you know, that only happened once.

—It must be bothering you.

—For me, it's an old story, I said distractedly.

—With Mève it's better, clearly.

I do not know if there was irony in that phrase, in any case, I did not react. I was there, stiff. Stiff like a statue of plaster.

—So, said Mary, you should go to bed and sleep.

I went to bed and slept.

18 MARCH

Mary's peculiar tastes, the old man Thomas's tattles, these mysteries, these coincidences, all of that is really unbelievable. I do not know anymore who said that, but life often shows itself to be much more bizarre than a novel. This is a problem that will present itself to me when I write mine: should it be more, or less, unbelievable than reality? Should it pour matters out in strong amounts or proceed only drop-by-drop? Should it speed along or go softly? Should one add or subtract? Ah! fuck! art is so difficult.

20 MARCH

I do not see Mève except for the very short times between the moment when she opens the door and when I penetrate Baoghal's office. In the corridor, today, I tried to grab her to press her against me. Gently. But she pushed me away.

25 MARCH

Barnabé still has the mumps. What a baby.

25 MARCH

Caught sight of Tim and his motorbike. On the pillion, there was Pelagia. So . . .

It's true that at the moment, I no longer meet anyone. Not Pelagia, nor anyone else. Perhaps the whole town knows that I have indulged in eccentricities in the Gallery garden.

2 APRIL

Yes. What if the whole town knew that? All the same, no one mocks me when I walk around. I meet rather with friendliness and the men still make attempts to demonstrate signs of it to me. At mass (I go there more and more rarely) or on the tramway, it's quite rare that my bottom is not pinched two or three times.

5 APRIL

I have discovered that I hate Mary.

It was during dinner. For once, Daddy was holding forth. He had read in the newspaper the report of the lynching of a negro, and that started him off. When it concerns atrocities, he's inexhaustible. They titillate him and he chatters like an old gossip. As for me, I don't give a fuck about those stories, if he thinks that they impress me he is quite wrong, the General O'Dourakine. I looked at Mary: she, neither, seemed to pay much attention to the ideas of the nutcase. Since the scene of the other day, we have barely exchanged confidences; more exactly, we have not. I looked at her and I asked myself if she continued to maintain with her father relations that are infantile and justificatory. Suddenly, the memory of Baoghal's revelations about his conjugal life came back to me, this comparison, this resemblance between Mrs. Baoghal and Mary scandalized me. I began to detest her.

Hopefully she will be successful in her competition and goes away. And that she goes away quickly.

8 APRIL

A short, but charming letter from Michel Presle. He tells me that, perhaps, he will come to Ireland this year. I am really excited. Now with all that I know, if I were to find myself alone with him, what would I do? What would he do? What would he do to me? And what would I do to him? What would we do to each other? Perhaps horrible things like kissing the tip of the nose or interlacing our hands.

But I am becoming delirious.

9 APRIL

He also sent me, a little in advance of my birthday, some French fashion magazines. I flicked through them with melancholy. How they seem strange to me, these French women with their multiple preoccupations: the blackheads, the periods, the permanents, the sweat under the arms, the shape of eyelashes, the bi-colored makeup for the tips of their breasts, the vitamins of carrots, morning gymnastiquettes; what do they not think of? That must take them some time, all of that!

I flick through, I flick through again, I muse, I am tempted and then I am not tempted. I do not see myself buying a girdle or having my hair curled. I stay as I am, natural: flat shoes, cotton socks or stockings rolled to above the knee, knickers, no brassiere (ah no, while writing this—with the right hand—I caress my little breasts—with my left hand); a very short skirt, a pullover (it's not really warm yet), very tight-fitting.

12 APRIL

Mary and I, we went to see Joël. He had moved house from above the dealer in offal and entrails; he is living somewhat further out, near Harberton Bridge, this time in a cul-de-sac, where there are no other dealers in anything. A mangy rat was grooming itself on the steps of a shack. We almost received the contents of a chamber pot on our heads; it was poorly aimed. At last we came to the hole in the bottom of the lane, a sort of workshop, slimy and worm-eaten, on which was written in chalk this note: *JOËL MARA, specializing in buttons without holes made from natural bones of your choice, from cats, rabbits or sparrows. Knife handles from the femur of pure calf. By order only: suspenders made from pig cartilage.*

We entered, lowering our heads. Amid skeletons, more or less disarticulated, of little animals, our brother was snoring. At the back a baby was whining gently and we made out Mrs. Killarney in the shadows, sleeping an almost silent sleep.

We had great difficulty waking Joël who took a good quarter of an hour before recognizing us. He designated crates that could serve as seats and immediately proposed some ouisqui.

We did not want to annoy him.

—Eh, Killarney, he howled, a bottle and glasses.

—Mrs. Killarney made a spasmodic jump and, her eyes barely open, directed herself towards the door with the precision of a sleepwalker. She disappeared like an arrow, a sure source of alcohol probably known to her.

Joël chatted:

—I said "glasses" because it's incredible how easily they break, glasses. I use the pieces to shape and polish my buttons, of course I do not have the funds necessary to buy myself little tools. But I don't complain, the business is not going badly, but I have a terrible task, it is above all buttons with holes that interest the clients, and boring holes, that's tricky, right, little sisters?

We acquiesced.

—And you, what are you up to?

—She continues learning Irish, said Mary, she has made serious progress.

—She has sat the examination, I added, now she is waiting for the results.

—They will be out on April 16, said Mary.

—Say, that's the day of your birthday, remarked Joël with a presence of spirit that I did not expect.

—We have just come to invite you for that day.

—That's nice, I thank you.

—With Mrs. Killarney and the little one naturally, I added.

—Thanks, I thank you, I am very touched.

He was beginning to have the hypocritically tender voice of drunkards.

—Must drink to that, he suggested. Killarney! A bottle and glasses!

—She has not yet come back, I reminded him.

—It's terrible how they break easily, glasses, it is fortunate that I use the pieces for my work . . .

At that moment, Mary, turning up her eyes, fainted. I caught her in my arms. Joël did not budge.

—She is pregnant? he asked indifferently.

—It's more the smell, I responded.

In one sense, it smelled less strongly than the entrails, but it was quite deceptive. Happily, Mrs. Killarney showed up with a bottle (full) and glasses. A good glassful reanimated Mary. Joël was holding on to his idea:

—You are pregnant?

—It's improbable, responded Mary.

—How do you manage? Mrs. Killarney asked her.

—Ah, you know, Joël said to her, discovering suddenly her existence, we are invited to my parents for Sally's birthday.

—I would never dare, said Mrs. Killarney.

—Please come, I said.

—Is your Daddy in accord?

—Who's that? asked Joël. Their daddy?

—Yes, you know well that Daddy has come back.

—It's true, good God. He is going to be there, the bastard.

—You're going to make up, said Mary.

—I'm not that keen, said Joël.

—To give us pleasure, I said.

He pretended to reflect.

—There will be a good dinner? he asked.

—Mammy will look after you, said Mary.

He turned to Mrs. Killarney.

—What do you think of it, my Salomé?

—It's been a long time since we got stuck into a good spread, Mrs. Killarney remarked objectively.

—And you are sure that the father is in accord?

—Sure.

—Eh well, we will come.

We emptied the bottle in honor of the future reconciliation. Salomé (the infant) had even the privilege of wetting her lips and we all separated joyously, although Joël was sad not to see us stay to liquidate other flagons that were to arrive thanks to the skillfulness of Mrs. Killarney.

On my turning around to give a last glance at the

disgusting hovel where Joël was lodging, I asked myself if he was still writing poems.

13 APRIL

I do not hate Mary as much as all that. But I wish that she will be successful and that she leaves. Or else that it will be me who leaves.

15 APRIL

Barnabé was waiting for me after my lesson at Baoghal's. Mève is still insensible to my friendly gestures; I don't understand it at all. Again, there this day— today—I had wanted to place a kiss on her ivory-colored forehead. She pushed me away with a hand that was delicate but firm. That irritated me. Because I dearly wanted to recommence with her the amiabilities that had terminated in such total bliss. Mève does not want to, without doubt she is afraid of Baoghal or his wife. Whatever might be in it, this refusal irritated me. Barnabé was waiting for me:

—So, I asked him, these mumps?

—I am cured, he responded with a stupid smile.

—They have not deformed too much your physiognomy, I remarked, while examining him with a critical eye.

He reddened.

—And you, Sally, how is it going.

—No, that did not deform your features too much. They are painful, those, the mumps?

—Euh . . . a little . . .

—What does it consist of, exactly?

—There is pain . . . in the ears . . .

—Nothing to boast of.

—No . . . obviously . . .

—And with the little tests?

—I don't understand. I didn't undergo any psychological examination.

—Me neither, I replied.

How he could get on my nerves, this admirer.

—By the way, I took up again, what then is this illness called, when the ears fall to pieces?

—I don't know . . .

—Your own look infected . . .

—You . . . you think so?

—I do not think it, I see it. In any case, I am very happy to have your news.

And I said goodbye to him.

16 APRIL

This morning, I wished very strongly that Mary would be rejected in her examination. Like that. An idea.

My wish was not realized. She is accepted.

O how satisfied she is. Naturally.

She will not continue to have her chastisement, paternal and daily, but her John Thomas for life.

That is what she says.

She will miss it, perhaps, her spanking, paternal and daily. That's her business.

I am nineteen years old today.

For nothing.

It is five o clock in the afternoon. Soon there will be a tremendous feast for my birthday.

I feel out of sorts.

Not because of the feast.

For no reason.

If any kind of guy fell under my hands, I really believe that I would pull his ears.

And his cock. No, his conk. O how difficult the French language is.

Mève's little rosy tongue. Tim's hand.

Barnabé's flies.

The rigidity of statues.

Ah, nostalgia, nostalgia!

Hold tight the rail, I say to myself. Hold tight the rail.

17 APRIL

We waited for some time for the brother, his concubine, and their offspring; finally they arrived enveloped in a sort of quasi-fluorescent, alcoholic halo. Joël and Daddy embraced drunkenly. Daddy had put on an amiable mug, a little like that of an inveterate traitor in a crummy melodrama. Mrs. Killarney was received royally, and we smiled at the wailing kid, politely. Mary was congratulated on her success. Mammy, radiant, unconsciously scoffed everybody's glasses. Few thoughts were given to my birthday.

After having thrown back a bottle of 45 per cent Ricard, sent by M. Presle and received exactly the same afternoon, we installed ourselves around the table and Bess commenced serving the dinner, which was to be composed of, I say it right now, herrings with ginger (I adore that), bacon with cabbage, a hundredweight round of cooked cheese, and a carrageen tart decorated with nineteen candles.

The conversation, at first, was particularly conventional and of a trying banality.

—Well, said Mammy to Mrs. Killarney, you are content with my little cock?

—Faith, responded Mrs. Killarney, it's that he's really ardent, really ardent. A woman of my age, that tires her, indeed!

Really ardent at what? At polishing buttons?

—And your fella, said Joël to Mary, you are content with his services?

—Go shake yourself in your corner, responded Mary with good humor, and let the kid's ribbons flutter.

Shake what? The handles of knives?

Daddy, very gay, tried to interest me in diverse matters, such as the classification of methods of capital punishment according to the degree of longitude, or the indifference of cooks to the sufferings of animals destined for their grill.

The evening, without doubt, would have passed normally, that is to say, that towards two in the morning Joël and Daddy, completely plastered, would have fallen with open arms, the one on the other, with cries of tenderness; so, I say that the evening would have passed normally if, at the stage of the bacon with cabbage, Joël had not remarked the existence of Bess.

—Well, you are still here, you? he said brusquely.

I do not know what fly, more or less Spanish, had stung him, because no one was paying any attention to Bess, it seemed, not even Daddy, and never Joël in his time. He accompanied the few words noted above with an affectionate whack on her rump. This familiar, and perhaps tender, gesture heightened the timidity of the youngster to such a point that she tipped what remained of the plate of cabbage onto Mammy's head. Mammy has the good character of a dimwit, and, that evening, was particularly euphoric by reason of the grrrreat familial reconciliation. She found the incident to be particularly comical and doubled up laughing as she collected, from the length of her face, little heaps of vegetable that had lodged there. We were loudly sharing her easily understandable hilarity, when Daddy, for what reason I do not know, got up calmly and headed towards Bess, who, letting out a cry of terror, bounded towards the kitchen, but Daddy, moving with precision, found himself already in front of the door when she arrived there: he had only to grab her. His intentions, everybody immediately understood, were clearly correctional. Joël intervened. In a melodramatic voice, saturated with booze, he declared that it is for the son to punish insults to his mother and, taking Bess by her arm, he pulls her from the paternal clutches. Daddy, grabbing the other arm, ripostes that it is for the husband to inflict abuse on anyone who covers his wife with sauce. Bess oscillates to the right and to the left. However, Mary gets up and declares that she is opposed to any chastisement; she takes hold of Bess by the waist and robs her from her persecutors. These, letting out cries of fury, recapture their prey. Mrs. Killarney starts to bawl that it is up to her darling to spank the bottom of the maid, while Mammy, suddenly becoming enraged, claims that no one other than her good man will raise his hand to this child, towards whom, in any case, she feels a moral responsibility. I admire the ease with which everybody takes a side and I ask myself with which camp I am going to align myself—if I do not discover a fourth one—when the hostilities commence.

It is the female auxiliaries who open the combat. Mammy smears the face of Mrs. Killarney with the recuperated cabbage, while Mrs. Killarney replies with a souigne that misses its target and goes on to smash a dirty plate. Mary, with a kick to the tibia, makes Joël let go, but Daddy, catching her by the hair, sends her sprawling against the sideboard, where some glasses shatter, Bess lets out lamentable cries and Mrs. Killarney, who slashed her hand attacking our crockery, hops

about from the pain while pouring out curses. Mammy, profiting from her advantage, whacks her belly with a bottle of
custard. Mrs. Killarney collapses. In order to commandeer Bess
again, Daddy tries to smash Joël's head with a beer bottle, but
he only succeeds in fucking pieces of glass onto the plate of
bacon. Mary takes up the assault again armed with our nutcracker and, caught between the two arms of this lever, Daddy's
nose begins to piss blood. Mammy, who has fallen on Mrs.
Killarney, is rhythmically banging her nut on the floor. Profiting
from how, to free himself, Daddy is tickling Mary under her
arms, Joël pulls Bess into the kitchen and locks himself in. The
door is flown at, it is shaken, it is given kicks. It is well secured.

Calm must return.

Mammy helps up Mrs. Killarney, installs her on a chair
and offers her a restorative. Then, things are more or less put
back in place, debris is fucked into a corner and seats at the
table are retaken while waiting for service to continue. Only
then is it realized that Salomé, fallen on the ground during the
ructions, has been trampled on a little: she too is fed a restorative. Daddy pours out, all around, the ouisqui necessary to
slow down beating hearts and to regulate breathing.

From the other side of the door, varied sounds are heard:
moans, panting, timid protestations followed by wild acqui-
escences. But now that I know approximately what it's all
about, I guess a little of what is happening, I am a big girl
almost fully informed. And I feel a great satisfaction in being
able to follow, more or less, the conversation that is going on.

—Hopefully he won't make a baby again, murmured
Mammy, who looks very worried.

—All the same, that does not work with every poke,
remarks Mrs. Killarney with a very pretentious air.

—They are making a commotion, sprouted Mary, who has
an air of being quite aroused.

—The little one will have, all the same, her punishment, declares Daddy with the air of not having an air.

The vocal manifestations of Bess and of Joël have taken on such intensity that the door is vibrating with them. Mary, who has crossed her legs, claws the table spasmodically, leans her head back and sighs. As for me, I had long been sharing the same emotions.

Then, suddenly, silence.

A great silence.

One could have heard a cat lapping milk.

—Ah, goes Mammy, we are going to be able to continue.

—Yes, says Daddy. I am beginning to feel peckish. The more so because the bacon is fecked.

—There is a hundredweight round of cooked cheese, says Mammy.

—You still buy it from the grocer in Hatch Street? asks Mrs. Killarney.

—Always, responds Mammy.

—Then I am going to treat myself, says Mrs. Killarney.

Mary, all red, is looking steadily at the little glow that floats on her ouisqui. As for myself, I am no less aroused. She raises her head and our eyes meet: they do not know very well what they have to say. But, together we give a start: in the kitchen, the animation starts up again.

—Ah, no! bawls Daddy, while banging his fist on the table, that is enough of that. Myself I want to eat.

—What do you expect to happen, says Mammy, they're young.

—With me, that has never happened, remarks Mrs. Killarney with a praiseworthy concern for objectivity.

But again I start. There is a ring at the door. General anxiety. A ring with greater urgency. I say:

—I am going to it.

And I made it.

It was two constables, one, Kirkgoe, well known in the area, the other I had never seen. It was that one who spoke:

—Well? he asked in an important tone.

—Well what?

—The neighbors are complaining.

The neighbors! It revolted me to hear that, they never stopped living it up from New Year's Day to New Year's Eve when things were going well and bickering from New Year's Eve to New Year's Day when things were going badly.

—What is it they want, the neighbors?

—Serious things were happening in your house.

—A sing song.

—A crime may even have been committed. From what has been claimed.

—Lies.

—You agree that we can go and see.

He pushed me aside and entered, followed by Kirkgoe whose expression led me to understand that, as for him, he would not have had these requirements. Obviously, I should have asked for his hunting license, as is done in detective novels, but he was already in the dining room. I trotted after him and found him there, interrogating, in similar fashion, Mammy, who radiated innocence as usual, Mrs. Killarney, who, to hide her hand, was holding Salomé tightly in her arms in a gesture that was tragic and offended, and Mary was chewing timidly the end of her skirt, allowing the cop to admire her legs as far up as her navel. The said cop, in any case, paid no attention, a homosexual no doubt, in any case a swine, because, in spite of our unanimous denials, the little heap of broken crockery and glass in a corner, and the stains of blood scattered on all sides—whether they belonged to Daddy (look! where was he?) or to Mrs. Killarney—served as a basis for a more strict inquiry. What a shit stirrer! One could have said that he wished, no matter what, that someone had been killed. Whatever was said to reassure him, nothing worked. Finally, perplexed, he was content to say nothing; as we others had no inclination to talk, all became silent.

Then, what was happening in the kitchen was to be heard.

—What is that, that is what, again? asked the policeman knitting his brows.

—It's our little maid who is skinning an eel, responded Mammy with the grin of a first communicant.

—Alive?

—It's better.

—But the Protective Society for Animals is against it.

At this moment the little voice of Bess quavered:

—Not like that, you're hurting me!

The important policeman looked Kirkgoe in the eyes with a severe air and said to him timidly:

—We must intervene.

As they had not brought with them their O.D.S.,[2] they were content to pepper the lock with revolver bullets and the latch fell apart. The door swung open and we made out Joël who was taking the carrageen tart from the oven and Bess, who was burning her fingers while trying to help him.

—Excuse us, say the cops, who recognized their mistake.

After a certain number of polite phrases and a number, even more certain, of goblets of ouisqui, the representatives of the law withdrew, and it was possible for us to install ourselves around the tart decorated with nineteen candles in my honor.

—With all of that, remarked Daddy, making his re-apparition, we did not eat the cheese!

—Don't piss us off, Mammy replied to him with lots of gentleness.

I blew out my candles with a single breath and the feast

---

[2] Obusier de siège (siege howitzer), currently in use with the Irish Police (Michel Presle).

was continued until six o'clock in the morning. I have just
written the account of it. And so to bed.

   Alone.

Mary is assigned to the post office of Gyleen. Gyleen is located
near the mouth of the Lee, at the entry to the port of Cork,
not very far from the lighthouse of Roche's Point. She had
hoped to be assigned in Dublin so as to be with her John,
but no matter, she prefers to clear out. I went with her to the
station. On returning, I learned that Bess has disappeared.

I was invited today to one of Mrs. Baoghal's annual teas.
Numerous preoccupations darkened my brow, therefore, I
had no need, like previously, to take a break at Aunt Patricia's,
to build up my courage. I found there—at Mrs. Baoghal's—
Padraic and Barnabé, naturally, and Mève, as always so ret-
icent, and the Mrs. herself, whose nose was beginning to
look like a sieve. I met there also—also at Mrs. Baoghal's—
Connan O'Connan, Grégor Mac Connan, Mack O'Gregor
Mac Connan, all poets with their wives, and their sons and
daughters, George, Phil, Irma, Sarah, Tim, Pelagia, Padraic,
Ignatia. There also, was O'Cear, the bard-druid and his wife
with their four children, as well as Mac Adam, the primitivist
philosopher, with Mrs. Mac Adam and their children: Abel
Mac Adam, Cain Mac Adam and the two sisters Mac Adam,
Beatia, and Eva, they who give parties to which, until now, I
have never been invited; although now I know, more or less

nearly, how to dance; but how could they have guessed that, because until now, I had concealed my new talents; and in any case, I would have been strongly disconcerted exhibiting them before an audience, even a limited one.

There was no French monsieur.

Barnabé approached me.

—Ah, you there, you, I said to him.

—How beautiful you are, Sally, he murmured in a voice, trembling but convinced.

—What's up with you?

—I find you to be ravishing, Sally. And your dress suits you so well.

It has to be admitted that it suits me not badly: straw yellow with a pattern of light green crayfish. I also wore stockings, my best ones, those of cotton that have only been mended twice.

—Would you not like us to go, one of these days, to the cinema? There is Greta Garbo at the Palladium.

—That will be expensive, the Palladium.

—I invite you, Sally, I invite you.

So, was he ready to commit indiscretions for me? I decided to encourage him a little, but not too strongly for a start. I said to him, lowering my eyes as much as I could:

—I am pleased that you are over the mumps . . . And then you know, there is nothing wrong with them, your ears . . . They are even very pretty.

He reddened, radiant, and took on the expression of one who is preparing a compliment. But I was suddenly interested by O'Grégor Mac Connan who was passing close by us; remembering what Baoghal had told me about him, I asked Barnabé via the canal of his ear (and my warm breath, penetrating this orifice, seemed to make him shiver with pleasure):

—Is it true that O'Grégor Mac Connan is a homosexual?

—Oh, went Barnabé.

He retreated a step in order to consider me attentively.

—Oh, he went again.

—I am asking you a question, I pointed out to him with a certain annoyance.

He continued to examine me with as much perplexity as if I had been an inscription in ogham characters. With the gravity of a druid collecting marshmallow, he raised a finger towards the ceiling and solemnly asked me:

—Sally! Do you know the meaning of the word that you have just employed?

—Which? Homosexual?

—Oh!

And the hand that had extended an index finger towards the sky came to rest on his forehead in a gesture of despair.

—Yes, that one, he repeated. You really know the meaning of it?

—Do you believe that I speak without knowing what I say?

That does happen sometimes, but this was not the moment to go into details.

—Do you know the meaning, yes or no?

—Yes.

—Then, he whispered, tell me what it means, exactly.

Did he not know or was it a challenge? This imbecile was disconcerting me.

—Tell it to me, Sally, he pleaded.

Was he mocking me? I would not have liked that much. After having again reflected some seconds, I gave him, at last, the explanation of the thing.

—A homosexual is a man who does to other men that which I did to you in the cinema, the day when we went to see the film with Jean Harlow.

Because I now could guess what had happened that

time, although some details appeared to me to still require clarification.

I had, all the same, lowered my eyes as I communicated to him the main element of my knowledge on the question of homosexuals. When I raised them again, Barnabé had disappeared. Some demanding obligation to do with hygiene or politeness had, without doubt, taken him away from me.

Then the spiritualist session was announced and everyone began to install themselves around Mrs. Baoghal. She was wearing a dress of red crepe romaine with inlays of violet lace. Its sleeves from the elbow were very tight. Each person took their place, and Baoghal asked for the lights to be extinguished and the blinds drawn. By now, the sly little minx that I had become well understood that this obscurity is nothing but a pretext for feeling the clothes of the neighbor and determining if the cloth is soft.

I found myself, by chance, between the poet Mac Connan and Abel Mac Adam, the son of the primitivist philosopher. I say "by chance" because I knew neither one nor the other, and neither one nor the other had ever seemed to pay attention to me. Nevertheless, as soon as they were assured of anonymity (an ostrich's anonymity), they planted their hands on my thighs. That did not at all correspond with my intentions; I had not come for futile trifles but really to elucidate two theoretical points that still seemed to me to be obscure. Using my habitual method I put the two hands into contact, which then withdrew with velocity, and I could follow up my studies.

At first I hesitated between Mac Connan and the Mac Adam son. Finally, I thought it preferable to choose a young and vigorous subject in whom the phenomena would present—probably—with more clarity and speed (this session would not go on forever), than in individuals somewhat worn out by age. I decided, therefore, to work on Abel.

With an unearthly voice, Mrs. Baoghal began to spurt out sounds with strange pretentions that were supposed to be those of a somewhat archaic Martian language, while a slim phantom materialized near her, its resemblance to Mève so obvious that none of the believers could suspect a hoax. As for myself, I confirmed that the material of Abel's trousers was quite rough, no doubt a local touide. I then made some observations of general relevance on the varied methods for fastening clothing among men and among women; it is evident men prefer the buttonhole and women the knot.

But that did not divert me from my essential preoccupations. I had fully decided to settle my ideas in a definitive fashion as to the different contradictory aspects of what I now held in my hand. I could first of all assure myself that certain natural objects exhibit modifications in volume and consistency that are infinitely more rapid than those that transform a cloth envelope into a dirigible. This example is badly chosen, because with respect to consistency, the object of my attentive studies was infinitely more rigid than that out-of-date method of transport, the balloon.

Thanks to a series of delicate pressings, I also verified that the rigidity was equivalent all over; then, on proceeding to a rhythmic rubbing, I tried to determine if it was at all possible to bring about an even greater extension to what I had first of all touched when it was a little grub. In spite of my efforts, I did not achieve any appreciable effect, although, to assure myself of that, I had neither ruler nor compass.

By now, I could not wait to test the second theoretical point which was still in abeyance, even though contact with that which I had in my fist, both warm and smooth, was quite comforting. In any case I would have been wrong to be impatient because I felt a torrent rush on to my palm, spurt out as a geyser and fall back on my fingers. At this point modifications in volume and consistency occurred in a sense that was diametrically opposed to that which had led to the eruption, and I abandoned, to its trouserly nest, a little not-much-of-a-thing, humid and trembling.

I passed on to the chemical study of the substance that I had just extracted, of course only by means of procedures of qualitative analysis that were quite basic; that is, I limited myself to examining the odor, the flavor, the fluidity, the solubility, etc. In spite of the darkness, the color appeared to me to be whitish, but, for all of that, it was not milk. As I had suspected, this product of human activity was radically different from all of those that I had known up until then, and of an absolutely original nature. I experienced such a joy at finding my hypotheses confirmed that I immediately thought of a new experiment to try out, this time concerning the possibility of revivification. So I set myself to the task, but, to my great disappointment, the light came on before I had obtained a result that was completely satisfactory. Our neighbors stood up, and I noticed that Padraic Baoghal, who was just in front of us, had been splattered by our initial researches. Abel Mac Adam jumped forward with his handkerchief to wipe his back. Baoghal turned around, furious, and grumbled: "What is up with you?" I began to laugh stupidly.

21 APRIL

There is a ring this morning. I go to open. Again cops. Yet it had been really quiet at home. One of them was no other than the newcomer of the other day, the second, even more unknown, wore, loosely, a civilian suit.

—That's his sister, the first said to the second.

—Your mother is there? that one asked me.

—Yes.

—We would like to see her.

They followed me. In the corridor, they were very correct with me. I opened the door of the dining room for them; Mammy was knitting socks there. She gave them a big smile. They installed themselves.

—Give these gentlemen a glass of ouisqui, said Mammy.

—There was another sister, remarked the first policeman.

—She lives in Gyleen now, said Mammy.

—You have had news from her recently?

—She sends us a telegram every day. You see, that costs her nothing, she is a post office assistant.

—And when did you receive the last one?

—This morning.

—Since when is she gone.

—The day before yesterday.

He looked at Mammy with a profound air. Then he continued:

—And your little maid?

—Bess?

—Yes, the little maid who was here the day you made all that racket.

—Oh, protests Mammy, barely a din of the third class.

—Eh well, where is she?

—The third class?

—Crap, cried the first inspector, it's really our luck come across a fool.

—That foolishness seems suspect to me.

—Interrogate the family.

—Where is Bess? the rozzer asked me. (Fuck! Where did I go to find that word? That, that's French.)

—Disappeared, I responded.

—Disappeared?

—She said "speared," confirmed Mammy.

—And you did not think to search for her?

—No.

—Neither to inform the police?

—Even less.

They sighed.

—And your brother, where is he?

—At his home.

Where is that, his home?

—Near Harberton Bridge.

—He is living there for a long time?

—Three months about.

—And he is not here?

—Since he is at home.

With a look, the rozzer (I like it, that word) consulted his boss.

—No use searching the house, that one said.

—It would be more sure.

—No. Of no use. It's clear to me.

He emptied his glass and stood up. The other imitated him.

—We should perhaps inform them? said the second.

—Choose the words spoken with the usual care.

—Oh, I am tactful.

He turned himself towards Mammy, and, after having coughed, said to her:

—Eh well, my good woman, we are going like this, in this way, to lock up your son Joël, who is horrible and evil, and who killed your maid Bess in order to drink her blood, whose corpse has been found in a barrel that he hid along by the East Wall.

As we remained wordless and dumbfounded, he added:

—I am quickly pouring for each of you a shot of ouisqui

to fortify you for having learned of this terrible crime, and we are dashing in a wild rush towards the arrest of the Vampire of Dublin.

And off they went, at a jog trot.

We had barely finished our fortifying glassful when Daddy, slowly pushing open the door, entered on tippy toes.

—What is happening? he whispered.

—The cops, I murmured.

—What did they want?

—To arrest Joël.

At these words, Mammy, who finally understood, began to utter a lamentation.

—Shut up you, Daddy said to her.

And she stopped.

—They are gone?

—I believe so.

He went out to be sure, then came back to install himself in front of a glass. Mammy had taken advantage of it to shed twelve to fifteen tears behind his back.

—What do they want with Joël?

—He killed Bess. He's a vampire. So they say. I don't believe them.

—You don't believe it? marvels Mammy. But seeing that they said it.

—Joël drink blood! But no, they have never seen him, the rozzers, my brother! As soon as they see him, they will be convinced that he is totally incapable of drinking it, blood, even with a straw, like correct vampires do. He is even incapable of drinking water.

—You underestimate him, said Mammy softly. His alcoholic diet is not so exclusive.

—I am certain, I replied, that blood would give him serious indigestion.

—Perhaps he did not think of that.

Daddy made a great bang with his fist on the table.

—That's enough, he shouted.

Then, calming himself:

—They are idiots, those lads.

—Who so? asked Mammy.

—The police, by God.

—Ah! I cried out, you also, you don't believe that Joël could be a vampire?

—They are idiots. Not to arrest anyone, I could understand, but to arrest an innocent.

—You are sure that he is innocent?

—Archi-sure.

Fragments of the *Odyssey*, of *Oedipus-Rex*, of the *Song of Roland*, and of other detective novels that I had read, arose as a crowd in my brain, and permitted me to raise myself to the level of the situation.

—Daddy, you will be able to provide him with an alibi.

—Faith no.

—How to prove his innocence?

—Ah, so, he responded, that is just what I ask myself.

—You know the culprit?

—Of course, it's me.

During some minutes, Mammy and I fought over the ouis-qui bottle in order to pour ourselves fortifying glassfuls.

I suspected that Daddy was a swine, but, as for this, it was a new record. I looked at him in consternation. I thought of the day his picture would appear in the newspapers, of how it would bring no honor to our family. Usually, criminals have faces that resemble something, with an air of injured dignity that, for the most handsome of them, gives them a Satanic aspect, for example Landru or Napoleon. While, as for him; never has the most snotty spinelessness been smeared with such effectiveness over a colorless head; never has the most perverse cowardice been spread with such sliminess on the mug of a rotter, never has the most cruel sluggishness been displayed with such baseness on an ashen puss.

He allowed us to calm ourselves a little. Then:

—Apart from that, you must not believe that I killed the little one.

—He didn't even kill her! whimpered Mammy.

—No. This is how it happened.

—Go on, tell us.

—Eh well, for a long time it bothered me that she was afraid of me, because, I don't know if you noticed, she trembled in my presence. So, the other day, to mollify her, I promised her a ride on a merry-go-round.

—That was nice, said Mammy.

—It's only that, I don't know how it happened, I swear, I did not mean to, we found ourselves out by the East Wall. The waste ground, wandering dogs, the dusk, the dead streetlights, the absence of a merry-go-round, caused her to get into such a state that she passed out.

—The poor child.

—She fell like that: plop! I bent over her. She was dead.

—Mercy me!

And Mammy made some pious gestures.

—I was in an awful state.

—I understand, went Mammy.

—I dragged her into a quiet corner, and then I . . . and then I . . .

He got worked up:

—If only you had been there, you! As for myself, I did not resist. It's not every day that there's such an opportunity.

—I understand, went Mammy again.

—Afterwards, I hid her in a barrel.

—Not so fast, said Mammy. Give us the details.

— All the same, simpered Daddy. All the same.

—But yes. It would not be nice of you not to give them to us.

—I swear to you, in any case that I showed her respect.

—Oh!

Mammy had an air that was totally incredulous.

—I promise it to you. I only indulged in the one vice of anthropophagy. And again. I ate nothing at all. I only drank.

And carrying on in the same voice:

—Afterwards, I hid her in a barrel. And that's it.

We pulled ourselves together in silence, which gave a certain grandeur to the atmosphere. I began to have a certain sympathy for him, he was not an evil guy after all, simply weak-willed, an impulsive. Joël took after him. Yes, Joël. By the way, Joël.

—What are we going to do for Joël, I asked.

—That one, said Daddy, if they catch him, he's in a right mess.

—My poor Joël, said Mammy, who had taken up her knitting again.

—Never could he prove that he didn't kill her, continued Daddy. An act of vampirism, that always incites the indignation of juries. I know from experience. So, he will cop the maximum, that is to say, to be hanged until death follows.

—Never would I have foreseen that end for him, said Mammy. That doesn't matter, I will take in Mrs. Killarney and Salomé.

—We'll see, said Daddy. In brief, he is caught up in a dirty business.

—He will have an alibi perhaps, I exclaimed full of hope.

—That would be awkward, said Daddy.

—Why so? said Mammy.

—Because they would come back here, and this time they would carry out a search, and I don't want that, you understand?

—I understand, said Mammy.

22 APRIL

This morning, our name was in big letters in the paper. I used to believe that that would only happen when I had published my novel, in a few years' time. What pride for us! I promised myself to cut out the article to send it to Michel Presle. Daddy read it to us in a loud voice. There was no doubt: it had started badly for Joël. He even had had the regrettable idea to resist when they came to arrest him. It was also insinuated that he fabricated his buttons from human bones; this made us laugh; aren't they stupid, journalists.

Later, the men neighbors and the women neighbors came to congratulate us. Daddy, naturally, hid himself. Mammy, delighted, held forth, poured drinks, cried.

Every moment, a bicycling courier brought me a message of sympathy: from Baoghal first of all, then from Barnabé, from Timoléon, from Pelagia, from Ignatia, from Arcadia, from yet others. Abel Mac Adam wrote to me:

Miss, the presence of your hand is still felt and revives, from quarter hour to quarter hour, the agreeable time passed near to you. Happy times, I will say, if I had not feared the consumption. I beg you to believe, Miss, in the respectful expressions of my aroused feelings. A.

Mr. Thomas, the attendant of the garden.

Miss, before the grandeur of the crime, pity is revealed. Fear no longer, Miss, to come to our public gardens if your melancholy attracts you to them. I will, myself, guard the entrance so that your little (immortal) soul may find its consolation there. I beg you to accept, Miss, the homage of your devoted servant. Thomas.

Post-scriptum: *My son, John, asks himself where your sister Mary could well be.*

Hold on, that one, she should be alerted; in Gyleen, she must not read the gazettes. I also received a telegram from Michel Presle:

Sincerely amazed and agreeably surprised by Joël. Stop. Kisses. Michel.

How nice he is, all the same. And then a little mysterious note:

Well done. M.

I asked myself for quite a long time; who well could have sent that to me, and I ended up by thinking of Mève.

Eventually, however, I had had enough of the men neighbors and of the women neighbors, and I went out. I took the tram, then changed to the connecting service. I got off at the King Street stop, then I walked. I passed in front of a barracks, three hospitals, a workhouse and two lunatic asylums before arriving at Richmond Prison. I asked to see Joël. I was received by the chief jailor with much consideration, but Joël's confinement is absolute: I endured a formal refusal, as well as a kiss offered by the administration, thanks to the intervention of the jailor. He even suggested that I share his bed. As the only kisses that would have interested me were the telegraphic ones of Michel Presle and that, in addition, I did not feel particularly tired, I made the chief jailor understand, by means of a lateral blow to the Adam's apple, that I desired none of what he was offering me. He let me out with signs of deep respect, a respect that was slightly distressed.

For some while, I walked up and down Grangegorman Lane. It's not at all funny, a prison. I had never paid it much attention until now, but to know that Joël was there upset me. I ended up moving away and I returned on foot to the house, but not without putting away some cakes on the journey. I also telegraphed Mève.

At the house it was bedlam. Mammy was completely drunk. However, the neighbors, having liquidated our provisions, were, I may add, beginning to leave. But, as more generous ones came to the rescue with bottles under their arms, it did not finish up before three o'clock in the morning.

23 APRIL

Today it was a little more calm. The newspapers are still talking about the Vampire of Dublin, but as Daddy cuts out the articles before me, I have to buy others for Michel Presle. I returned to the prison; still no authorization for a visit. Decidedly, this prison is sinister and I cannot relentlessly go at the Adam's apple of the chief jailor. We must end it by getting Joël out of there, all the same.

Mary arrived at the moment we were sitting down at table for the dinner. "So well, as she put it, what a carry-on," and she threw herself on the herrings with ginger because journeys, they make you peckish.

Afterwards there were bacon and cabbage, a round of

cheese of two kilos (all that remained) and a carrageen tart that Mammy had made quickly to treat Mary, but which was disgusting.

—Eh well, Mammy, said Mary, not meaning to flatter you, we haven't gained from the change.

—As for carrageen tarts, said Daddy, it must be recognized that she knew her stuff, Bess.

—What if we talk now about the poor kid. And about Joël. You believe that it was he who engaged himself in these eccentricities? I don't.

—We neither, said Mammy.

—We must find him a good lawyer, said Mary.

—That will be expensive, said Daddy. A defense for a vampire costs at least twice as much as one for a sex maniac or for a conscientious objector, and that's really saying something. We'll see if we can afford it.

—We can, all the same, make sacrifices, said Mary.

—All the more because he is innocent, said Mammy.

—I am not all that sure after all, said Mary.

—As for me, I am sure, said Mammy.

—How can you be sure of it? You know the culprit, perhaps?

—Yes, of course, it's him.

She looked in the direction of Daddy.

Mary slapped her thigh (a gesture that she had no doubt just learned in her occupation).

—That's hilarious, she said. I thought of that. No! don't you find that to be hilarious?

—You are sharp, said Mammy.

—And how do you know it, that it's him?

—He told us.

—Eh well . . .

She considered Daddy for some moments in silence.

—Eh well, she continued, addressing herself to him this

time, what are you waiting for before giving yourself up?

—Why do you want him to go and give himself up? asked Mammy dumbfounded.

—Because it's him, the culprit.

—Not all culprits give themselves up, said mammy. If they did, one couldn't read detective novels anymore.

—To have his son liberated, explained Mary. Yours.

—You believe that that would make something happen? asked Mammy.

—Wit-houta-dout, shouted Mary into her ears.

Mammy looked at her husband:

—Would you like me to prepare your things?

—So you as well! You are of this absurd idea! Since I tell you that I did not kill her.

—How so? asked Mary.

—But yes. She died from a blackout. She died all by herself, all by herself. I had nothing to do with it. I only drank her blood. And again, not all that much. I really only drank a little. That's all. I am not a criminal, me. That's not enough to risk the death penalty. I could never prove that I didn't kill her. I don't want to be condemned to death, me. I only drank, drank a little, that's all.

To say all this humbug, he took on his most cowardly air.

—All the same, said Mary, you cannot let Joël hang in your place?

—All the same no, I added.

—That would not be nice, said Mammy.

—But, since I tell you that I did not kill her.

—All the more reason, replied Mary.

—All the more reason, I added.

—That would not be nice, said Mammy.

—If you confess, said Mary, you'll have the sympathy of the court.

—The judge will congratulate you, I added.

—We will be viewed more and more favorably in the area, said Mammy.

—And you will have your photo on the first page, said Mary.

—We'll cut out the articles on you while you're in prison, I added.

—I would never have hoped for that said Mammy. My son and then my husband with their portraits in the newspapers. What joy!

—You see, said Mary.

—You see, I added.

—I ask myself, said Mammy, if I should put, with your belongings, some warm things for this summer. What do you think of that?

Daddy did not respond.

—What? went Mammy

Daddy let his arm fall on the table in a weary gesture.

—It's unfortunate all the same, he said. It's unfortunate, just the same. The one time that I allowed myself a pint of good blood.

He sighed:

—All the same . . .

He raised, with difficulty, his backside above the chair. He slowly left the room. We heard him climb the stairs, then come and go above our heads.

—What is he going to do in your room, remarked Mary.

—I don't know, said Mammy, placidly.

He came down again after a dozen minutes, perhaps less. He half opened the door, put in his head and said:

—I'm going to look for a box of matches.

Then his steps went further away in the hall. The door to the street opened gently, then closed without banging.

24 APRIL

Joël has moved to the third page. And in the evening papers his liberation had not yet been announced.

25 APRIL

Nothing.

It's obviously not by the prison that Daddy went to look for his box of matches.

26 APRIL

Nothing.

27 APRIL

Nothing.

28 APRIL

Nothing.

29 APRIL

Mary suggests denouncing Daddy, now that he has had time to get away. But we are not of the same opinion, Mammy and I.

2 MAY

We were right.

Joël's innocence is recognized. The culprit is a big man, stooped, in his forties, and on the run. An inspector came to the house to enquire. He left without having collected much information, except for the best kind concerning Joël, the poor lad.

3 MAY

Joël was freed this morning. Mrs. Killarney and Salomé were waiting for him at our house. It was a triumph. Drinking was continuous the whole day. The neighbors and friends rushed to congratulate him. An incalculable number of bottles were emptied. Towards six o'clock, Joël returned home with Mrs. Killarney and the kid. Mary again took the path to Gyleen; her train left at seven o'clock. We found ourselves alone, Mammy and I, for the dinner. It was lugubrious. I realized that I had forgotten to show the letter from the father Thomas to Mary.

4 MAY

Inspectors came again. They searched everywhere.

5 MAY

They ended up finding the answer: Daddy has his photo on the front page. It's him, the Vampire of Dublin. It even seems that he was guilty of similar ravages more or less everywhere over the surface of the globe. Mammy exults. Again, this was toasted with the neighbors and the friends.

I went to see Joël to find out what he thought of it all. There was a crowd in front of his workshop. He was being given an ovation. Climbing on a ladder, he was nailing above his door a notice: *At the Vampire's, better is sold.* When he had descended, he was acclaimed. There was no way to approach. Finally, he noticed me and made a way for me to enter his lair. Mrs. Killarney, banjaxed by the multiplication of parties, was sleeping in a corner, as well as Salomé, all wrinkles, insensitive to the clamor. Not without difficulty, he fecked everybody out the door, which he locked. Whiskey bottles littered the ground, full ones and empty ones. Joël grabbed a full one with a sure hand and pushed a box towards me so that I could sit on it

—It's booming, he said to me joyously as he filled my glass. Unlimited credit in all the shops in the area. Countless orders. I am also preparing new products: notably the square button with an internal spring of gut hair. I would even take on workers if I did not disapprove of the exploitation of the proletariat and of the growth of labor. In the end, I am not discontented.

—You were surprised to learn that it was Daddy?

—Not in the least. Say then, apart from that, the prison eh, I like it better not to think about it. It's awful. There's no drink in those places. I thought that I would go cracked.

—You believe that they are going to arrest him?

—Daddy, surely no. He has the air of knowing his way around. I regret now not having known him better.

—Anyway, he will not be seen again.

—We should not make ourselves sad over that. Another glass?

—Thanks, yes. If he did not really kill her, as he claims . . .

—Chtt. Don't spread that sort of talk; that would mess things up.

—I said it like it is.

—In any case, I well suspected that that wimp was well incapable of killing anyone at all.

—Did it make you sad to learn of her death?

—Why would that have made me sad? AH! because of what happened on the evening of your birthday? You know, it was just for a laugh. In fact, yes, that makes me sad. Now, that you have made me think about it.

—Don't think about it too much.

—Fear not. Say, I have news to tell you, but it embarrasses me to admit it to you. It will perhaps seem ridiculous to you.

—Go on.

—Eh well, the *Sunday Dubliner* has asked me, euh, for something written by me, to print it. So I gave them a poem.

—I did not know that you were writing poems.

—Indeed yes. And you, you have not a little idea, literature-wise?

—Yes, I want to write a novel.

—On what?

—I don't know.

—But you are sure that it will be a novel.

—That yes. And in Irish too.

—I will not read it, then.

—I think that I have the title.

It had just come to mind.

—Let's hear.

—*Women always treat men too well.*

—It's quite long.

—A sentence struck me, a sentence that you pronounced one day in my presence, yes, the evening when Daddy came back, when Mrs. Killarney brought in Salomé, and we did not want to hear about it.

—It was annoying, that evening. Things got pretty hot.

—You said like this: "We always treat women too well."

—I said that, me?

—Yes. But for me, I make a change, I put "men."

—And what will you recount in it?

—I have no idea.

—That will be hilarious, but in this case, if you put "women," that would be more original.

—You think?

—Of course.

There were knocks on the door, blows with fists, blows with feet.

—I must go and calm them down, said Joël. I am so popular that they would be capable of breaking everything.

I leave him to his admirers.

I walked at a pace, slow and meditative. There was nothing gay in finding oneself alone with Mammy. I had no real inclination to return to the house. At the corner of O'Connell Street, I met Barnabé. He didn't look like he knew if he should speak to me. Finally, he decided.

—You have become a person of distinction, Sally, he said to me, humbly.

—But no, but no.

—Yes, yes. I can assure you. There will be a celebration in your honor at the Mac Adam's.

—But I know nothing of it.

—It will be a surprise. They're going to invite you. The girls more likely, Beatia and Eva.

—You will come, of course.

—I don't think so. I will, no doubt, have left.

—You're leaving?

—Yes. I am going to live in Cork.

—And your lessons?

—I have to abandon them.

—What is happening?

—My father died.

—Sincere condolences, I said to him, with warmth.

—Thank you. Yes, he died, just the day after your brother was arrested. And I must go to Cork to help my mother run the shop.

—A shop for what? I asked politely.

—For hardware.

I almost laughed in his face. Hardware, there is nothing funny about that, nevertheless. And he had an air of being so troubled that I held myself back. He noticed it.

—I see well that you feel like mocking me.

—Not at all, I assure you.

—But, you know, it's an interesting occupation.

—I don't doubt it.

This time, I burst out laughing.

—Excuse me, I stuttered, it's idiotic, it's my nerves, you understand?

—I understand. All of the great emotions that you have had!

That was the last straw. I could hold out no longer. Even to wetting my knickers.

—Please, said Barnabé. Please.

I finally calmed myself down. There was nothing to laugh about, after all.

—I will come, from time to time, to Dublin, said Barnabé. I am hoping that I could meet you.

—By all means.

—You will remember me?

—Certainly.

—As for me, I will not forget you, Sally. Never.

He took my right hand and placed it on his left heart; he pressed down on it for a few instants while raising himself on his toes and looking up to the sky. Then letting my hand drop without precaution, he took some steps backwards, arm outstretched, then bending it to cover his eyes, he made, brusquely, a half turn and disappeared into the crowd.

7 MAY

For the first time since the start of all these matters I went back to Baoghal's. We deplored together the departure of Barnabé Pudge, that excellent Gaelist. Mrs. Baoghal left us alone during our lesson and nothing happened.

It's agreeable to feel respected. And Mève looked at me with devotion. She did not even dare to say to me: "Good day, Miss."

8 MAY

Actually, I am invited to a party at the Mac Adam's. It is Beatia who writes me a note, so nice, so nice, with a post-scriptum by Eva, charming, truly charming. I am in quite a state and all over the place. I know well that if I was not the daughter of the Vampire, I would not be invited, the proof is that they never did it before, the two bitches. All the same, it gives me pleasure. But I have one of those fits of nerves. It's weird. In any case, what an event. Happily. I have found it a little flat, existence, these times.

10 MAY

It was true. Joël's poem appeared in the *Sunday Dubliner*. It's a fantastic epic: *The Combat of the Asparagus with the Mussels*, a little in the style of Homer's *Batrachomyomachia*, Lewis Carroll's *Gulliver's Travels*, and of Vermot's *Ale Maniaque*.

Mammy read it, she found that it had neither tail nor what's it. But I do not think that she grasped the symbolism; this appeared to me to be of a culinary nature and concerned the respective virtues of the vegetable kingdom and the animal kingdom from the point of view of suction, but these are psychological notions that are beyond that old worn-out nut. In any case she was delighted. She made for Joël, as an indication of her delight, a carrageen tart, that she asked me to bring to him.

I fucked it, the tart, into the first sewer opening on the way, from fear that Joël would become dysenteric, and I bought one in York Street, in Jack Fath's, the fashionable fatteners.

I found Joël taking a siesta. The rain that has fallen the last few days had wiped clean his notice. Not one neighbor was there anymore to acclaim him. I woke him up gently and gave him the tart, which he would immediately have thrown out the window if I had not reassured him as to its origin. I also had a letter for him that he began to open with care, meticulous and futile.

He had a look about him that was quite barmy.

—It's awfully good, your poem, I said to him. We are proud of you at home.

—You will never guess how many I have made, of buttons, since I started this trade?

—Of course, Mammy did not understand very much.

—Seven dozen, of which twenty-three are without holes and two square.

—You are going to publish others?

—I want to make handles for pocketknives, now. The button has no future. Because of the zip fastener.

—You have no news of the vampire, by chance?

—No. Look, it's Abel Mac Adam who invites me to a party in his home. Who is this fool?

—You know, the son of the primitivist philosopher; me too, I'm going to it.

—You're going to dance, you?

—I've learned.

—He admires me, eh, this lad?

—Joël handed me the letter.

The Mac Adam son, indeed, found the poem to be "terrific," "stupendous," and "perfect"; he had been particularly touched by the "anacomic and satyric formulation of the loss of substance that the friction of things makes the self undergo."

—Wow, I said, how he expresses himself.

—You know him?

—We did a little physiology together.

—Hilarious.

—It's not what you think.

—Oh me, I don't give a feck. You do what you want with your little thing. We eat the tart?

—And Mrs. Killarney?

—She's walking the kid. We'll keep her a piece. Hold on, there is still some ouisqui in the corner. Say then, I take her with me, my old biddy?

—I don't know.

—It will be more fun.

—I don't know.

—There will be, perhaps, Tim.

—I don't know.

—And your Barnabé.

—No. He lives in Cork now.

—You sad?

—No.

—And what is he fecking around with in Cork?

—He has a hardware shop.

—No joke? That's not bad, hardware. It's not bad at all. If I were at it? I would make nails from ray teeth, screws from duck wishbones and tap nozzles from calf shinbones.

He emptied his glass.

—What do you think of that?

—You're going to publish another poem?

—Yes, that's an idea, hardware. Say, I'm going to uncork another bottle. I like to drink to my ideas.

—You should send it to Mary, your poem.

—That's yet another idea. That makes for another bottle. I also like to drink to the ideas of others. I should bring a load of bottles to Mac Adam's, because the people there will have at least a little brain.

—If you lived alone with Mammy, you wouldn't drink very often.

—That's true that. How you must get bored all on your own opposite her. Although, it's not Mrs. Killarney either who would provide opportunities. But I provide my own.

Suddenly, he focused on my legs:

—Say then, you must wear other stockings if you go to this party.

—They are my best pair.

—They're revolting. You will buy yourself new ones. Very good ones. Of silk. Sheer. Cloudy. And, behind, the seam must be completely straight, absolutely perpendicular to the line of the horizon. Show me, you. Look at that zigzag. It's disgusting. I bet that you are still one of those ones who roll their stockings above the knee. Yes? Lamentable! You will please me by buying a girdle for that day. By the way, have you received other fashion magazines from Paris? Yes? So you'll loan them to me. I like very much to keep myself up to date. And Presle. What has he been up to?

—He is going to make a tour here one of these days.

—That's great. I hope that he'll be able to slip some bottles of Ricard through the customs.

—Yes. Would I be able to arrive at the same time as you at the Mac Adams?

—If you like. Why? That intimidates you?

—Of course.

—You've never gone there, eh?

—No.

—It's because of Daddy that they invite us now.

—And because of your poem.

—That is also because of Daddy.

—In that case, it's also because of Bess.

—You know, after what you said the other day, I went to put some flowers on her grave.

I was just as amazed as when I learned that Mary appreciated the paternal spankings. It's peculiar, all the same, humanity.

11 MAY

After having counted my savings and re-read all the Parisian magazines in my possession, I went window-licking in the commercial streets of the city. I did not yet dare to buy anything. What is terrifying is that in certain shops, it seems, there are men to serve you. But what is it that they have to serve you with? I preferred not to enter. And then, girdles, they are really too expensive for me. And then, is it really necessary to wear one? *Votre Beauté* says: *It is not possible to devote too much care to the choice of a girdle which will, for the entire day, envelope your body.* It's pretty that word "envelope." It's just that, in one issue, they write: *Every woman should wear a girdle*, and in another: *The ideal would be that every woman is able to do without one.* As for me, I have the impression that I am sufficiently muscled to do without. I will buy myself, instead, shoes with high heels.

14 MAY

Finally I bought myself silk stockings, very sheer and smoke colored, a black suspender belt, panties of pink silk jersey, and cute court shoes of purple kid with lizard skin appliqués and five and a half centimeter Louis XV heels. As for a brassiere, that would really have been an unnecessary expense, given the robustness of my bust. I will have a dress of silk faille, with a pistachio-vanilla squared pattern and little puff sleeves.

15 MAY

I undressed in order to dress. I started with the stockings; they were so agreeable to the touch that I caressed my legs for a long time. Then I paid good attention that the rear seams were truly rectilinear when I put on my suspender belt. I looked at myself in a mirror and found myself to be very elegant and shapely. I would have been content to stay like that, so well it pleased me, but, for the first time that I went to a party, that would, perhaps, have been a little daring. The dress suits me well, the shoes did not hurt my feet too much. I had forgotten the panties of pink silk jersey; I put them on last.

I went down. Mammy exclaimed:

—How beautiful you are, it's a pity that your father couldn't see you like that, he would have been terribly proud of you.

I sent her to search for a taxi; which was imprudent because there was every chance that she would forget, on the way, why she went out. All the same, she came back after a quarter of an hour, I took my precautions once again before leaving, and I gave Joël's address to the driver. He immediately started the conversation with me.

—So, he said, you know the son of the vampire.

I answered him that he was my brother, he was very interested and, from threading gradually the needle, we almost made a head to tail.

We arrived at the cul-de-sac, I said to the fellow to wait, and I entered. One does not knock on the door when one enters a shop. Without a doubt, I didn't make much noise because I was able to discern in a corner, in the glimmer from an oil lamp that filtered through the small bones, primary material for the artisanal activities of my brother, I made out (I write) a corporeal bundle that was sighing rhythmically. As I am beginning to be more knowledgeable, I understood immediately that it involved two human beings in the process of the eventual procreation of a third human being. Scrutinizing more attentively the matter, I confirmed that their respective positions did not conform to standard practice, at least as I imagined it to be from results obtained from observations in the animal kingdom. I had, therefore, under my eyes, one of those variations to which, one day, Mary had made allusion, and which consisted of a turning over of the delegate of the feminine sex, which now found itself to be supine. In the present case, the said delegate, expressing itself in the voice of Mrs. Killarney, began to supplement her activity with a spoken commentary that was quite incoherent but the gist of which seemed to be that she was going to pass from life to death. However, the other person replied, while swearing Hell and damnation, that he was experiencing great pleasure; but I recognized neither the voice nor the style of my brother. I was witnessing, therefore, an adultery and even worse again, because Joël and Mrs. Killarney were not married.

Concluding that I was one too many, I retired on tippy-toes. Once outside, I selected a dark corner in which to relieve my emotion. I had not thought of the taxi driver, who was strolling around smoking a cigarette. Greatly interested, he approached me and, accompanying his words with a gesture, he proposed: "A drink," a pleasant old joke borrowed from the fine flower of the Norman spirit by the intermediation of the soldiers of General Humbert, in the course of the failed landing of the French of 1798; at least, that is the opinion of Michel Presle.

I was a little annoyed to be disturbed in this way, but I could not stop myself from bringing to a close that which I had started. At the same time, I was touched by the sympathetic movements of this good man, and I feared hurting him by not making him a polite gesture. I was truly embarrassed. Fortunately, the door of the shop opened and a man, of massive proportions and probably a butcher, came out and went off without having seen us. Mrs. Killarney's head came out and cried:

—Who's there?

—It's me, I replied. Sally. I come to get Joël.

—Something serious has happened? Who is this man?

—It's the taxi driver. We're invited to a party at the Mac Adam's.

—Eh well! Come in, Miss Mara. But I think he is not ready. He must be sleeping. An hour later, I succeeded in shoving Joël into the car with the help of Mrs Killarney. I asked her if she was coming.

—No, thank you. They're for the young, those sorts of things.

She banged the door shut and I gave to the driver the Mac Adam address. I had him stop in front of Aunt Patricia's house in order to profit, once more, from her facilities, because I was becoming more and more excited. When I came back down Joël and the driver had disappeared. I extracted them from a neighboring pub, but not without having absorbed three ouisquis to give me courage, and we arrived at our destination two hours late. It was I who paid the taxi with my last feoirlíns.

We were welcomed by a tremendous ovation. Joël did not delay in disappearing towards the bottles, while my girl-friends—and I noticed then that I did not lack for them—deluged me with questions, hugs, kisses, and compliments. I was very intimidated in spite of the ouisquis and I noticed that I was alone in having neither face powder nor lipstick. There was even Ignatia who had some of it on her nails, red.

When the enthusiasm aroused by our arrival had calmed a little, someone put a disk on the phonograph and some couples began to dance. It was a mazurka, which I had just learned: a gliding step, one leg back—the other forward, a turn, a glide, change leg again, a turn, a leap; six-time with eight movements. Throat tight, the beater beating, the tongue dry, I asked myself if I was going to be asked out. I was, not immediately, and by a boy that I had never seen.

When he put his arm around my waist and I felt his hand in the small of my back, my excitement was so intense that I almost fainted. Flashes flowed along my vertebral column, my eyes fluttered, a ball of fire roasted my intimities and I began with some steps of the gallop from the lancers' quadrille. We soon stumbled; my cavalier (oh!) gripped me more strongly to stop me falling; as a result the deepest depths of my being grew moist, and, leaning my head back, I became almost faint while my wandering feet, searching vainly the n-th movement of the x-th measure, only encountered the bruised toes of my cavalier (oh!).

—This is not working out? he asked me amicably.

—Aaah! I went.

—Would you not like a glass to settle you? he proposed to me.

—Good idea, I responded.

He released his hold and, taking me by the arm (like a young bride, oh!), he led me to the refreshments. Abel was busy with them, I chose a ouisqui, my cavalier (oh!) the same. After having knocked back a notable fraction of his glass, he asked me:

—You are really the daughter of the vampire?

—Seems so.

—My name is Steve.

—Mine is Sally.

—I have never seen you here.

—Perhaps not.

—*Bhfuil tú ag foghluim na Gaedhilge?*

—*Táim le tamall.*

—With Padraic Baoghal?

—Seems so.

—Me too. He is going to take me as a student in place of Barnabé Pudge. You know him?

—Do I know him! The hardware merchant?

—It's an occupation, said Steve.

—So, what do you do, you yourself?

—Vampirologist. I would like the hear you talk of your daddy, because I am interested in unpublished details and your father has marked out a fine career in the activity that I have adopted as the object of my erudition.

—Bugger off, I responded to that.

—Pardon?

—I said to you to go and have yourself buggered.

—Miss.

He inclined himself gracefully and went away. I remained, for a moment, alone.

Abel, who was pouring drinks, proposed refilling my glass, which I accepted immediately. I had noticed that he was keeping a respectful distance.

—You are afraid of me? I asked him, encouraged by a certain internal warmth, probably due to the ouisqui.

He mumbled some words, a bottle in his hand. I went up to him:

—Who is that dirty cad?

I showed him the one named Steve, by finger.

—A friend of Patricia. A student of vampirology.

—That's why I interest him?

—I . . . euh . . . I don't know.

I thought that the time had come to flirt. With whom, that was all the same to me, why not with this Abel who I barely knew. I tried then to remember something: "Where so, did I meet him the last time; we were sitting beside each other, if I remember well, where was that?" So I continued:

—And you, I do not interest you?

—Yes . . . yes . . . very much.

—It's not only Daddy who can be interesting. Don't you think?

—Yes . . . yes . . . certainly.

A new disk had just been put on, it was a Boston. I adore the Boston. I believe that I like it as much as herring with ginger, and the idea of dancing it with a man of agreeable physique excited my spinal marrow to the point where I could not control my words although I knew that I was pushing flirting beyond permissible limits.

—Let's dance to that, I proposed to Abel.

He looks around him with the look of a man who is drowning, then, not seeing any way out, he places the bottle on the table, and embracing me, we took off. I had understood that he was timid. Indeed, he continuously stepped on my toes. To give him confidence, I pressed myself against him, very strongly, and I did not delay in recalling under what circumstances I had come into contact with him the first time: of course, the last tea party of Mrs. Baoghal.

—Do you remember me? I murmured against his neck.

—Euh . . . yes . . . not here really, he whispered in a very emotional voice.

Not here, what? What is it that he wanted to insinuate? I would have asked him for explanations after this dance if it had not been interrupted by an incident that I was surprised had not already happened. The Boston was at its fifty-second measure (although I was flirting, I had counted them), when it was interrupted. With a heart-rending cry, Joël, in effect, had just fallen on, and begun to devour, the disk on which it was engraved. Some courageous individuals went to undertake the rescue of the innocent thing, but it was futile. From the second mouthful, my brother collapsed, ruining definitively all hopes of recovering the Boston, reduced to fragments. After having stayed immobile for a few moments, Joël began to make jackknife jumps while letting out loud, funereal cries. We made a circle around the poet, but his inspiration did not appear to take anything as a subject except the negation of the nearby furniture. Caïn Mac Adam, son of his father, and fearful for the furniture, dumbfounded my brother with a bottle broken on his head and asked me, politely, to take him *at home*. That which I did.

I was very sorry that my ball had been terminated so rapidly and I expressed my most lively regrets to Beatia. She promised to invite me again. Pelagia did the same.

18 MAY

After having slept for forty-eight hours, Joël returned home. His leaving made me sad. Although his presence only manifested itself through expiratory snoring—that, simultaneously emerged from his nostrils and through his teeth—it allowed me to bear that of my poor mother. And here I am again, alone with her.

20 MAY

I received a letter from Barnabé. As they say in French, it was a "chicken." In other words, a declaration of love. I read it to my poor mother to entertain her a little. We had a good laugh. But all the same, I cannot deny that it gave me a certain degree of pleasure.

22 MAY

A new letter, from Barnabé. To be handled with tongs, it was so ardent. That brought a little gaiety to our sad hearth.

27 MAY

I did not expect it. Pelagia has invited me to a party at her home. I do know if Joël is invited. Mammy gave me some feoirlíns so that I could buy face powder and lipstick. I found the bottle of perfume from Michel Presle that Athanase gave me. I will saturate myself with it on the day of the party.

I went to see Joël. It had rained all night, all of the day before, and all of that day as well. The lane was in a bad way. It was necessary to jump over the pools or to restrain oneself so as not to slip in the adjacent mud. At the back, the brother's shack seemed devoid of color. The breeze agitated awkwardly a broken shutter. I pushed open the door and, although it stank, entered. It stank copiously, skillfully, intensively. Incrustations of stink stalactited from the ceiling and stalagmited from the ground. In the half light, silence. I discovered Salomé, who was snoring softly. She looked to be all alone in the middle of piles of bones destined to be buttons. I made a tour of the shop, of the bedroom, of the kitchen, of the shithouse. There was nobody. No one except Salomé, all ashen, scrofulous, sleeping.

I went out and stayed for a time on the doorstep. The rain again began to dash into the pools and into the mud. It would perhaps be humane, and consequently, Irish, to take the kid and to place her with her grandmother, so that both of them would have a valid motive to put off snuffing it. But then, there was reason to hesitate; that could be the abduction of an infant. I tried to assess my degree of maturity in maternity. As I now knew myself, I was beginning to suspect that I would not pass away still a virgin and that I would not kick the bucket without having been bucked by a male, one at a minimum. In consequence of which I could foresee an insemination of what the papers call the womb, with, as a final conclusion, the production of a baby that I would have to nourish with milk products and whose, what the sports pages call, anus, I would have to wipe, while waiting for the time, when, having become adult, the kid would wipe himself without help, bite into beefsteaks, and consecrate a part of his winnings at the races to the maintenance of the old wreck that I would have become.

All of that was quite abstract. The hand of a man planted on my arse, that excited me. But then, from thread in needle and eel in girl, I should feel in me some excitement because, after some months, this excitement would make another me, this was what had not seemed obvious to me before, whilst millions of drops of water were drowning themselves in the quagmire of the alleyway.

I really believe that I would have ended up taking the brat, if the humid stumbles of a parcel of rags had not begun to propagate waves from pool to pool. Mrs. Killarney was returning *at home* peculiarly sloshed. She took a full quarter of an hour to arrive at my feet, having during the final stage caused a growing pool to overflow by means of a flaccid fall.

I did not help her raise herself up again. She managed it all alone. And recognized me without hesitation:

—Do come in, Miss Mara, do come in. There is news, there is news.

She charged in, straight in front of her, and, making a half pirouette, collapsed onto a pseudo piece of furniture that could claim to be a seat, crushing under her the wishbones of some macerated sparrows.

—A ouisqui, Miss Mara, she proposed. A ouisqui?

It was not to be refused.

—Do sit you down, Miss Mara, do sit you down. There is news, there is news.

I installed myself on a crate that was not too sticky, and swigged down my ouisqui to compensate for the density of the smell. Mrs. Killarney did the same.

—Eh well, she said, the news, here is the news, I'm going to tell it to you, the news. Your brother Joël, he is gone.

—To buy matches? I asked.

—No, to join the Foreign Legion of the French.

—That's certain, that?

—He swore it to me that he was going to do it.

—But why, Mrs. Killarney, would he join the Foreign Legion of the French?

—Because of desperation in love, Miss Mara.

—Love for whom?

—For me, certainly, Miss Mara. He imagines that I have been unfaithful to him, Miss Mara. You understand me?

—I get the picture.

—I say that to you although this is not something to be said in front a young girl, but, still, that is what he accuses me of. Is it not a shame to believe that of an honest woman like me? It must be that he is a swine. And he leaves me with an infant on my arms and all these bits and pieces, which horrify me. What is to become of me Miss Mara, what is to become of me?

The old cow began to snivel. I said to myself: "Joël must be a bollox, all the same. All the same."

All the same.

Salomé began to shriek.

I thought that they would be company for my poor fool of a mother, and I brought them back to the house. Mrs. Killarney can always do the cooking. Like before.

1 JUNE

What a pleasure to put on stockings, to daub oneself with rouge, and to fuck perfume in all one's little crannies! All lively, I arrived at Pelagia's house. I danced Tangos, Maxixes, and other fashionable stuff. We drank much, laughed much. My arse was felt a little and I sized up some young men. It was very nice. We finished up laughing with a general all-in. Timoléon took me home on his bike. We swerved around, it was hilarious.

I am delighted.

4 JUNE

A new letter from Barnabé. I read it to Mammy and Mrs. Killarney after the dinner to give them a little laugh. The dinner was quite reduced, I am annoyed, I felt that there being two more mouths to feed was no reason to omit the herring with ginger (which I adore); we were five not so long ago. Mammy said nothing in reply, but it was somewhat cool afterwards. Then, to distract them, I read them Barnabé's letter. The beginning was very interesting. He spoke about his new occupation, the hardware business, which is divided across four departments: heavy hardware, buildings hardware, marine hardware and household hardware, which includes gear for hunting and fishing. There was also the matter of the infinite variety of nails, which Barnabé listed in Irish: *tardhleóir, oidhearcas, shoilise*, etc., all words the significance of which I was unaware, not yet having started to learn technical vocabulary with Padraic Baoghal.

We launched ourselves into a series of conjectures as to the possible meanings of these words but our knowledge went no further than nail and tack, and, in French, I could see no further than the word *clou*.

—Ah! if Monsieur Presle were here, I sighed, he would give us the equivalents of all of them in thirty-six languages, including Laz and Ingoush.

—A really nice lad, Monsieur Presle, said Mammy.

—And so polite, added Mrs. Killarney. Not once did he

suggest coupling to me.

—He is the only one of us all who ever had a good influence on Joël, said Mammy.

—Are you making an insinuation, Mrs. Mara that I have had a bad one? asked Mrs. Killarney.

—Not very good, responded Mammy, not very good.

—How so? But I have made you a grandmother!

—I thank you for that.

—And you are not going to claim that it is because of me that he joined the Foreign Legion of the French?

—Yes. You were unfaithful to him, I said.

—You, said Mammy, no obscenities.

—But I did not deceive him!

—And the day when I came to collect him to go to a party?

Mrs. Killarney reflected:

—Ah, yes, the butcher.

—There, you see, said Mammy.

—So what, what of it?

—One can always deceive oneself, this proves it.

—An incident. That is not a reason to criticize my influence.

—It was the first time? I asked.

—That what?

—With the butcher?

—Oh! went Mrs. Killarney, I don't recognize you anymore, Miss Mara. Putting such crude questions . . .

—There I must admit, said Mammy, that you are going beyond permissible limits.

—Miss Mara, I am horribly shocked.

—Sally, I can't get over you!

—It's a shame, Miss Mara, to come out with such lascivious ideas in the presence of an honest woman.

—Sally, you are making your mother blush!

—I have never heard suggestions of such indecency.

—I did not realize that my daughter is a pornographer!

—Ah! my poor Mrs. Mara, the today's youth is so depraved.

—Yes, said Mammy, she only thinks of that.

—About what so? I asked.

—About bouc-ery, responded Mammy.

Mrs. Killarney turned towards me, raising her eyes to heaven.

—We should forgive her, she sighed.

—I forgive her, Mammy hurried to say.

—You're not so sharp, I replied.

—Now, Sally, you are not going to be insolent to her. I find Mrs. Killarney to be very intelligent given her social background.

—A ninny and a slut, I went.

—I don't need to hear this nonsense, groaned Mrs. Killarney as she poured out a good measure of ouisqui. And with all of that, we know nothing more about the nails.

—We have to resign ourselves, said Mammy.

—Ah! If Monsieur Presle was here, I sighed.

There was a ring at the door.

I go to see, and who was behind the door? Michel!

—I am just passing through Dublin. I leave this same evening for Cork.

I was so excited that my tongue tied.

—You are so beautiful, he said to me while patting my bottom. You are filling out. You're a pretty filly.

—Who is that? shouted Mammy.

—It's Monsieur Presle, I cried.

—When one talks of the wolf one sees its tail, screamed Mrs. Killarney.

—Do come in, bellowed Mammy.

—I cannot stay for long, Michel said to me. There is no question of my missing the train.

—You would like to drink some ouisqui, I suggested.

—Of course, my little one.

He even drank several of them. Mammy was delighted to see him again and Mrs. Killarney held him in high esteem. As for me, my heart was beating really strongly.

—So, Mother Mara, said Michel, your husband pulled quite a stunt.

—Don't talk to me about it. But, all the same, he was not so stupid as to let himself be caught.

—Any news of him?

—He never wrote much.

—And Mary? And Joël?

—Mary is a Post Office assistant in Gyleen.

—Why not.

—And Joël, he has joined your Foreign Legion.

—Was that really necessary?

—Absolutely not. An idea of his own.

—And just at the time when he was beginning to be a poet, I added.

—And this kid here?

—That is my granddaughter.

—You let that happen to you? Michel asked me, extremely surprised.

—Not likely, I responded.

I must have looked inane as I said that.

—It's mine, said Mrs. Killarney.

—Well!

—It's also Joël's, added Mammy.

—Well!

Michel turned to me again.

—You never told me of that. It's true that you did not write to me all that much.

—You neither, Monsieur Presle.

—That's true, that's true.

He sighed.

—I must be going.

Mammy and Mrs. Killarney protested, but he was completely decided.

—I cannot miss my train.

—Can I can accompany you to the station? I asked him, trembling.

—Of course, that would be nice.

The tram is direct as far as Kingsbridge. Terminus. We sat beside each other. Michel calmly planted his hand in my thigh.

—So, he went, you wear a suspender belt now?

—Sometimes, I responded, completely blushing.

—And you also wear rouge?

—Yess, I murmured.

—The country is changing.

—It's since I have been going to parties. I am invited because I am the daughter of the vampire. I know how to dance now.

—A true transformation. It suits you, not too badly.

He caressed me softly, while saying that. Of course that overwhelmed me and I began not to see straight.

—I really missed you, Monsieur Presle, I stuttered, I really missed you.

—Me too, my little one. And about the Irish, is that going well?

He let go of my thigh in order to put his arm around me. His hand reappeared, holding my left breast.

—You are making progress?

—Yess, Monsieur Presle.

—I do not doubt it. You were a good student of French. You are gifted with tongues.

—Yess, Monsieur Presle.

I could hold out no longer: I allowed my head to fall onto his shoulder while letting out a little moan.

—You think that I am going to kiss you, eh?

—Yess, Monsieur Presle. Because of the association of ideas.

—You are right.

And he kissed me. The first time that a man was kissing me! I closed my eyes and saw a magnificent firework display with Roman candles, Bengal fire, and everything. But alas! that evening the station did not seem to be so far away, and there was no bouquet.

Few people for the train to Cork. Michel was travelling first class, he had a compartment all to himself. He smoked a cigarette distractedly while telling me of his work; he was going to study an Anglo-Irish manuscript at the rectorate of Macroon. I encouraged him to go to see the uncle Mac Cullogh. He thanked me. A guard called out. The station filled with smoke. Michel tapped my bottom for the last time, as he said to me "Good girl" and mounted the carriage. He remained standing, hands in his pockets, smiling at me. I waved my handkerchief. The train moved off. Michel disappeared.

I left slowly and, indecisive, I remained a moment on the footpath looking vaguely at the blackish Liffey, and, beyond, the blank mass of the Phoenix Park. I was going to head towards the tram when someone hailed me.

It was Tim.

—Hello, Sally, would you not like it if I brought you home?

Of course he had his bike with him.

As I adore that, a trip on the pillion, I accepted.

5 JUNE

This evening, again, there was no herring with ginger as a starter. I groaned. Mammy looked down. Mrs. Killarney as well, without giving any explanation. I ask myself what they are up to.

I received a new invitation, to a party at the home of the Ex'Grégor O'Grégors, who, by the way, I do not know. From Pelagia. I immediately bought myself three new pairs of stockings, another suspender belt, two bottles of perfume, one for the hair and the other for the armpits, and a second pair of dancing shoes, without very high heels. They made me a bit too tall.

Hold on, I was going to forget, yesterday, Tim de-maidened me.

7 JUNE

Still no herring with ginger.

8 JUNE

I went to the party at the home of the Ex'Grégor O'Grégors. We drank a lot and danced galops, chahuts, and jigs. Arcadius O'Cear taught me some steps for the Shimmy and for the Charleston, sorts of American bourrées. Afterwards we went to rest in a little dark room and, as Tim wasn't there, I granted him my favors; but whether too tired, or because of too much drink, Arcadius was not able to take them.

9 JUNE

About yesterday evening and the other day, I am not fully aware of what happens.

11 JUNE

Another party. By chance I found myself alone with George O'Connan. As for him, he succeeded just as well as Tim. As, yet again, it all happened in darkness, there are still gaps in my sexual education that will need to be plugged. For that I will need full daylight. Now that the weather is good, I could perhaps practice my close encounters in the Phoenix Park.

12 JUNE

Still no herrings with ginger. I gave out to Mammy, who is lost for an answer.

14 JUNE

My last lesson with Baoghal. Like last year, he is going to spend some months in Italy. I must work with him for yet another year before being able to begin writing my novel, about which I have still no ideas, except the title, if that. I wished them a good journey, him and Mrs. Baoghal, who, naturally, was present during the conversation. During all of this time, I was asking myself if ever, one day, I would have a close encounter with Padraic Baoghal. It's just that he is so fucking old, thirty-five autumns at least. And then, I have no inclination at all . . .

When leaving, I do not know what overcame me, I leaned towards Mève and I whispered in her ear: "I love you." Then I fled, my heart clanging and my legs weak.

16 JUNE

Still no herring with ginger. Mammy is crazy.

18 JUNE

A letter from Barnabé. I no longer have the will, even, to read it to my little audience. I don't even know what's in it. I barely made an effort to make it out. The poor lad. The fool, as Tim said. I vaguely saw that he had met an eminent French linguist who was passing through Cork. And who had spoken of me. Presle, no doubt.

20 JUNE

A party at the home of the O'Connor O'Connor O. Again people that I did not know. I met some pals there, George, Tim, Arcadius. I tried an encounter with Padraic O'Gregor Mac Connan, but we were disturbed by the arrival of Pelagia. Then I wanted to see if Tim had good memories of me. Excellent ones. But, again, it all transpired in darkness.

21 JUNE

Mammy is suggesting that we spend our holidays with the uncle Mac Cullogh, along with Mrs. Killarney and the Salomé in nappies. To say that that brat is my niece! What can I do!

In any case, that says nothing at all to me. Now that I know what it's all about, I have no inclination to act as a support to the uncle or to the buck Barnabé. When I think about my ignorance of last year, it makes me shudder to the foundations of my being.

The Mac Cullogh farm? For me, no thanks.

22 JUNE

Not only is there no longer herring with ginger at home, there is not even carrageen tart. I cried with rage.

24 JUNE

After the lunch today, I felt quite peculiar. An immense nostalgia impregnated my little (immortal) soul, and I lay there, sprawled on a chair, legs apart, a hand hanging loosely between, saying to myself, with somber irony, that even a twit would very well meet my needs. I was looking dreamily at my whiskey, while softly clinking a piece of ice against its sides, when there was a ring.

I was so startled by it, that I sent myself into the air, or more exactly my glass, and spilled its contents on my dress. Nevertheless, I bounded towards the door, which I opened.

It was Michel Presle.

—You look quite disturbed, he said to me.

—Yess, no, I responded.

—What's going on with you? he asked me looking at my dress.

I sniggered stupidly.

—It's not what you think it is. Just a ouisqui. A ouisqui.

—Good, good. I am leaving my suitcase here, I will collect it shortly.

—You are leaving already?

—Yes. At five o'clock I am taking a little cargo boat to the Isle of Man. You should study Manx, he said to me, giving me a little slap on the arse.

I quivered and my mouth became completely dry. As I prepared myself to respond to his question, I noticed that Michel had already come in. I ran after him.

—A ouisqui? I proposed to him.

—You are alone in the house! Yes, a ouisqui, surely.

—No, Mammy is taking a little siesta. And Mrs. Killarney and Salomé are in the kitchen.

—Your life must be sad here, now that Joël and Mary are no longer here.

—A là là, Monsieur Presle, don't talk to me about it. All this shit for me! How shitty it is for me! Ah, fuck it!

—He looked at me smiling with even a little air of laughing at me.

—There is no need to laugh, I said, vexed.

—It's your language that makes me laugh.

—I do not speak French well? I thought that you were proud of me.

—Yes, but I have an apology to make to you. I notice that I have taught you big words.

—They exist, such, the big words?

—Any of my compatriots would be quite amazed to hear you.

—Like Athanase.

—Say that's true. You saw him. What do you think of him?

—That he is a bastard, a louser, and a cunt.

Michel continued to laugh at everything that I said. Finally, that really irritated me.

—What big words do I say?

—Eh well: "fuck," "shit," "cunt" for example. In France, a young girl does not use these words except among family or with friends.

—But you are a friend, Monsieur Presle.

—I hope so. So I am not reproaching you in any way. It's just a little piece of advice.

—I thank you, Monsieur Presle. And if you were nice you would make me a list of all of those words.

—That's it. It will begin with "amour" and end with "zeb." I will think about it.

—You're so sweet, Monsieur Presle.

—And even more so than you think, he said getting up to go and get his suitcase, because I have brought you a present.

—Oh, I went, pressing with joy my hands against my heart and closing my eyes so as to have a surprise.

—Michel put onto my knees a flat box that I opened, trembling. It contained a "Scandale" girdle. I let out a cry of happiness.

—Yes it's true that you are sweet, Monsieur Presle! I said. You will allow me to try it on?

—Please do.

I began to undress myself.

—So, you never wear a brassiere? remarked Michel.

—Is it that one must?

—No, no.

—My knickers, I wear them on top or underneath?

—Don't wear them at all.

I began to envelope (like the fashion magazine said) my body in the girdle, not without difficulty though. Then, as I attached my stockings, I glanced over at Monsieur Presle. All the same, his eyes had begun to pop out of his head.

It was at this moment that Mammy came in.

—So, Monsieur Presle, she exclaimed joyfully. I am very happy to see you.

—My respects Mrs. Mara, he said rising up, which allowed me to confirm, all the same, that not only his eyes had changed their state.

—It's a present from Monsieur Presle, I said to Mammy as I pulled at the girdle so that it molded me well.

—You spoil her too much, Monsieur Presle! You have been extravagant.

—Let's not talk about it.

—She's a fine girl, eh, my Sally!

—Superb.

I put on my dress again.

—Now, I must ask you to excuse me, said Michel. I have some errands in town.

—Is it that I can accompany you, Monsieur Presle?

—Well surely, well surely.

We took the tram for O'Connell Street. We were seated side by side with a little gap between us. Not much was said during the journey. Then Monsieur Presle went here, went there; as for me, I followed him like a little dog, I waited on him obediently when necessary. When he had finished, he asked me:

—What will we do now?

—Why don't we go to Phoenix Park, I proposed.

—What an idea!

—That would give me pleasure.

—But I have no more time.

—That would give me pleasure.

He looked at me.

—Why?

—That would give me pleasure.

He seemed to reflect, hesitate, to reflect again.

—No, definitely, I don't have the time.

I was really disappointed.

Afterwards he spoke to me about a lad from Dublin, some-body named Joyce, a pornographer who is obliged to have his books printed in Paris. Then he came back to the house to get his suitcase, and he went off. He kissed me nicely. As it should be done. But not more. Afterwards I was sad, sad, sad. I installed myself in front of a bottle of ouisqui, while waiting for dinner.

There was still no herring with ginger with the fucking dinner.

—I'm just about sick of this, I declared. I want herring with ginger, I do. Why do we never eat herring with ginger anymore?

Mammy began to cry.

—You would do better to explain to her, said Mrs. Killarney.

After many splutters, she gave me the reason: no more cash in the house. Before leaving, Daddy had swiped all that remained of the Sweepstake.

—The rotter, I murmured.

And added:

—So, there will never be herring with ginger again?

—Never.

—Nor carrageen tart?

—Nor carrageen tart.

That left me thoughtful.

A little later Mammy began by saying to Mrs. Killarney:

—Do you not think that it's a good occupation, hardware merchant?

—It has to be recognized that it brings in lots, said Mrs. Killarney.

On board the Saint Patrick.

At last I am going to get to know Paris. We left an hour ago; Barnabé is seasick and puking like a dog.

We were married this morning and we boarded towards the night. It was raining. The wind was blowing. The gangway was poorly lit. Barnabé was walking in front. It was laborious; all the time I was scared of falling into the water. Finally I did not advance at all. Then, Barnabé shouted to me:

—Sally, hold tight the rail!

I advanced my hand in the darkness, but I only found a rope, damp and cold. I understood that my conjugal life had just begun.

POSTFACE

Although first published anonymously as an apparent work of soft erotica written by a "real" Sally Mara, readers now see Sally's diary as a work by a man writing as a young woman (see Appendix for what early readers could have known about Sally Mara, the supposed author). Raymond Queneau tried hard to "be" Sally as he wrote it and perhaps enjoyed entering into the mind of an imaginary young Irish virgin obsessed with sex in the context of a dysfunctional family and a quasi-Joycean Dublin. Fundamentally, Queneau's "Sally," is not, as her name implies, a witty person (sally, pl. sallies: a witty remark, a rushing forth); she is funny because of her naivety, candor, pedantry, self-assurance, and, most importantly, by her idiosyncratic (mis)use of French; for her a newly learned language. However, quite frequently Queneau allows his mask to slip and "she" comes out with sophisticated uses of obscure verb tenses, unrealistically clever or obscure witticisms, and arcane references. The quite numerous extended entries for single days, many with long sections of dialogue, also subvert the diary format.

The foundations of *Journal intime* (I will continue to use this title here, it's shorter) are linguistic. Sally has learned her own, at times bizarrely sophisticated, version of French in a very short time (while her mischievous tutor, Michel Presle

210

was in Dublin, and "he learned Irish in no time") and she is quickly coming to grips with Irish, a difficult language. She wants to impress her beloved tutor, a polyglot, academic philologist, by writing her diary in French and a novel in Irish. But, most of all, the whole story floats in a complex linguistic context where characters sometimes use or seem to understand languages they do not know.

All of this allows Queneau, who was constantly fascinated by language and languages—with perhaps the greatest scope of any of his novels—to indulge in multi-layered humor that the original readers would have found well-nigh impossible to penetrate fully. He held that:

> A masterpiece is comparable to a bulb, of which some are content to peel the outer skin, while others, less numerous, dissect it layer by layer: in brief, a masterpiece is like an onion.

Although he hardly anticipated that *Journal intime* would be regarded as a masterpiece in the full sense of the word (he wrote much of it fast as he needed extra money, probably to help with an upcoming first visit to the US), it is actually a sophisticated work that has earned significant appreciation from commentators in more recent decades. Early readers seeking a work of conventional pulp fiction may have been left with mixed feelings. Its constant humor undermines persistent conventional attitudes to girls and women and especially to sex education; even potential prurient tendencies of readers are wickedly toyed with. The predisposition of criminals and their the families to excuse or minimize their crimes is also exposed. An objective of this translation is to expand appreciation of its merits.

In writing Sally's diary, Queneau adopted an approach to

the description of the environments of his characters equivalent to that used by James Joyce in *Ulysses*. A familiarity with the city of Dublin is frequently evident, and, although there are some unwarranted assumptions, the level and quantity of accurate geographic detail is surprising, particularly given that he never visited. He exhibits impressive knowledge of street networks, tramcar routes, and the National Gallery (many individual works in its collection are listed); even the presence of a cinema on Grafton Street. Joyce used reference works and enquiries to friends to refresh his memories of Dublin, while Queneau apparently used tourist guides and maps that he had obtained while reading *Ulysses*. However, he avoids the locations of the major events of Joyce's stories. Instead, the action is largely in the areas between Rialto, lower Rathmines and Kevin Street, around the Baoghal residence located somewhere near Upper O'Connell Street, the Phoenix Park, and from West Merrion Square to Grafton Street. There is also a clear reference to Finegans Wake (another drawing of male genitalia) and influences by the works of other Irish writers, including J.M. Synge's *The Playboy of the Western World*. All this is supplemented with references to contemporarily relevant personages such as the neo fascist General O'Duffy and the Blue Shirts, and the revered ascetic Matt Talbot. W.B. Yeats and his somewhat kindred spirits from earlier decades have been significantly adjusted and recast as Padraic Baoghal and friends.

During the nineteen thirties, and following his wife's example, Queneau underwent a long course of psychoanalysis and read many works on psychology and mental disorders by Freud and others, some repeatedly. These interests are evident in the varied psychological makeups of the characters in *Journal intime*, and they are also exploited to create darkly satirical or comical situations. Quite a number of the characters exhibit evidence of sadism, masochism or in the case of Joël, Sally's brother, of an apparent Oedipus complex displaced by an extra generation. John Mara, Sally's father is a classical psychopath. Mara family life is characterized by the drinking of enormous volumes of whiskey ('ouisqui'), large meals followed by gargantuan amounts of cheese, and disputes and fighting, but is punctuated by recitations, singing and shared hilarity. There are also moments of familial tenderness and, once, the mostly boorish Joël, her brother, sagely advises the younger Sally on good silk stockings and how to adjust their seams. Queneau's many detailed descriptions of Mrs. Baoghal's and, later, Sally's colorful dresses may have benefitted from feminine advice.

But Queneau's degree from the Sorbonne was in philosophy and he never lost interest in philosophical systems, eastern as well as western. Most of his novels have philosophical themes or sub-themes. His wartime novel, *Pierrot mon ami* (1942), is a Hegelian parable of uncertainty, a detective story without a crime or a criminal. *Les Fleurs bleues* confounds dreaming with living. *Journal intime* is infused with contradictions and exaggerations that induce a strong sense of unreality—or of the uncertainty of perceived reality. Inexplicably, a Freudian textbook on psychological complexes becomes *General Dourakine* a well known (in France) nineteen century children's storybook by the Contesse de Ségur and, one character, Aunt Cornelia mysteriously becomes Aunt Patricia. Was Mrs. Baoghal pregnant before her marriage? Did Joël really have sexual intercourse with the very young family servant Bess in the kitchen, twice? Sally's sordid encounter at the start of the book is an ecstatic experience. Male arousal is represented as spirituality. Intense passion is marked by "restraint." Ghastly murder and abuse lead not to infamy, but to fame and celebrity.

Whether by analogy with equivalent conditions in France or by accident, Queneau via Sally Mara has provided us with biting social satire of pre-war Irish society; a lower middle-class society where daughters often do not have jobs and families have servants. To an informed present day reader, quite a lot of the shocking aspects of the lifestyles and events described are not that far from common realities of that time, and even later: disgusting living conditions for the poor, corporal punishment, sexually predatory men, mistreatment of servants, an abusive father, and a mostly passive mother. The neglect and steady deterioration of Salomé, the new baby of Joël and the Mara family's first cook, Mrs. Killarney, is deeply disturbing. Bess, the young, orphan (?) girl hired as the family's replacement cook, is clearly terrified of John Mara, Sally's father, and his subsequent murder of her is truly horrifying. The heavy drinking and eating by the Mara family, including Sally's sister Mary who, initially, is just sixteen years old, is extreme. Ever relevant issues related to "consent" arise and there is uncertainty as to sexual orientation. Sally even uses (or coins?) the term "pansexual.

Sally is, in some ways, a cartoon figure (her more extreme actions have few consequences) and a quasi-superhero (her athletic feats of world record standard are unbelievable and her combative skills worthy of Batman's Robin). However, her somewhat screwball life seems broadly realistic, and, in Ireland at least, can now be seen as much more realistic than it could have been seen to be when *Journal intime* was first published in 1950. Sally (along with her sister Mary) has been kept ignorant of even the most basic facts of life, is regularly exposed to sexual harassment in the world outside as well as at home, and has very limited opportunities to understand (even statues are censored) or express her burgeoning sexuality. When relevant topics arise, her mother and even her aunt stubbornly refuse to explain; they seem to lack any inclination or even the language to do so. Explicit terms and frank speaking are reacted to with shock, strong disapproval and derision. What makes Sally interesting is that she struggles valiantly and comically against these limitations. She is determined to learn, is (nearly) always in control, startlingly forward and adventurous at times, and is able to repulse unwanted sexual advances (and there are quite a few) with terrible efficiency. She is also a diligent student of languages. She and Mary are methodical in their preliminary research into reproduction and male anatomy but, notably, the younger Mary who is apparently more astute and more ethical, eventually overtakes her with respect to sexual experience. Sally's boyfriend, Barnabé, is in love with her but is in thrall to Church strictures and chronically averse, not just to "action" but to any discussion of sexual matters. On reading their conversations, many, from older generations at least, may easily identify with Barnabé, or Sally, in recalling their own youthful senses of sinfulness, bashfulness, or frustration. Although, in the end Sally takes the easy option of an early, and probably passionless marriage, she does become, if posthumously, a multi-lingual, published, and republished author.

Some of the realistic and feminist aspects of *Journal intime*, written during the summer and autumn of 1949, may owe much to Simone de Beauvoir's revolutionary work *Le Deuxième Sexe*, which was published by Gallimard, the prestigious French publishers, as two volumes in June and November 1949. Extracts were available much earlier in Sartre's monthly journal *Les Temps modern*. Moreover, Queneau's position as a senior member of the reading committee at Gallimard would have given him access to both volumes of de Beauvoir's much-anticipated volumes long before their publications.

On 7 June 1949, at the end of a list of writing projects, Queneau wrote in his diary: "And the *Journal intime de Sally Mara* I am letting it drop." The manuscript of *Journal intime* consists of fourteen 24-leaf school copybooks, but only copybooks, numbers five to 14 are dated; number five was begun on 23 August, and number 14 was completed at 10.45 on 15 November. Date differences indicate that he wrote quickly during late August early September and October. Just copybooks numbers one, two, and four have substantial alterations that necessitated the removal and addition of many whole pages. Queneau was very busy over that summer and autumn. He was a member of the jury at the "legendary" first *Festival du film maudit* in Biarritz (27 July–8 August) and attended the Cannes film festival (6–26 September).

All of this indicates an initial start, restarts, doubts, uncertainty, delays, and substantial revisions that were followed by much greater sureness as to plot and significant events, which, combined with the skills of an experienced novelist, enabled a race to a timely finish. His diaries and other sources prove that he has familiar with *Le Deuxième Sexe* and the parallels between tropes and subthemes in *Journal intime* and issues raised in *Le Deuxième Sexe*, especially its second volume, *L'Éxperience vécu* are striking. The keeping by girls and young women of private diaries "into which they pour their souls," their ignorance of male anatomy, their observations of animal anatomy and copulations, their vulnerability when walking in the street, their struggles with emerging sexuality, their fascination with beauty magazines, are just some of these. Therefore, it is possible that *Le Deuxième Sexe* gave Queneau at least some of the inspiration he needed as to the tenor of the work and many of the ideas he needed to restart and quickly complete *Journal intime*. Could it be that, for its time, *Journal intime* was in efect a feminist work that, by the

way, was initially subversively aimed at purchasers of works
of pulp fiction.

Some look down on Queneau's Sally Mara works because they
are well known to have been written quickly but, as Queneau
wrote in 1951 to his young son Jean-Marie, in reference to
one of his most highly regarded novels:

> My novel is called *The Sunday of Life* and I hope that it is
> not too bad. I wrote it in 25 days, but it was simmering
> for 4 years.

So, for accomplished novelists writing fast can be writing
well, provided the research is done, sources (here including
a Dublin guide, a manual for learners of Irish, and detailed
information on early nineteen thirties films, women's magazines [the style and content of *Votre Beauté* are captured
impressively], perfumes etc.) are available and the basics of
the story to be written: voice, outline plot, personalities of the
most important characters are decided—many other aspects
can just develop and evolve smoothly as they write.

That the early pages of *Journal intime* are repetitive and
somewhat awkward or over-blown is probably a deliberate
indication that Sally is undertaking a new venture, not just
stretching her occasionally strange French vocabulary and
writing to impress Michel Presle, but struggling to achieve
what she in "her innocence," conceives as "intimacy." She
also tests her stylistic limits with poetical flourishes (echoing
Arthur Rimbaud according to the original and greatest great
fan of 'Sally Mara' and her works, Pierre David):

> . . . j'ai pris solennellement deux résolutions en ce jour
> d'aujourd'hui, tandis que la lune des nuits se balançait

lunairement immobile sous la sphère des cieux illuné, éclai-
rent de sa pâleur lunaire le navire où Michel se prélassait . . .

. . . I made two solemn resolutions on this day of days,
as the night-time moon was hanging moon-like and still
under the canopy of the moonlit sky, lighting with its pale
moonlight the ship on which Michel was floating off . . .

Of course, what we are getting is Queneau, while pretending to be Sally Mara, being the erudite, humorous, ironic
writer he always was. Accordingly, Sally surprisingly quickly,
becomes capable of playing with complexities and eccentricities associated with the French language. Some literary
devices survive quite well, such as switches from past tenses to
the present historic to heighten the drama in certain scenes.
For example, the comically horrifying great family contest
involving the fearful young Bess on Sally's nineteenth birthday, recounted on 17 April 1935.

> Joël intervened. In a melodramatic voice, saturated with
> booze, he declared that it is for the son to punish insults
> to his mother and, taking Bess by her arm, he pulls her
> from the paternal clutches. Daddy, grabbing the other arm,
> ripostes that it is for the husband to inflict abuse on anyone
> who covers his wife with sauce. Bess oscillates to the right
> and to the left. However, Mary gets up and declares that she
> is opposed to any chastisement; she takes hold of Bess by
> the waist and robs her from her persecutors. [And so on.]

Although there are elements of the story that may be over-
worked, e.g., recurring lists of apparently innocuous words—
some (if not all) with second sexual meanings—that continue
to shock an increasingly knowledgeable and experienced Sally,

there are many episodes that are laugh-out-loud, some perhaps because they may remind readers of their own youthful experiences. For example, Barnabé's subservience to conservative Catholic strictures and extreme reluctance to talk of sexual matters are illustrated hilariously by means of some prolonged dialogues. Aunt Cornelia/Patricia, although apparently worldly-wise, also manages to omit essential details relative to sex and reproduction as she lectures Sally colorfully and at some length on the perfidy of Padraic Baoghal.

Somewhat analogously to the young Gargantua's quasi-scientific search for the ideal arse-wipe, Sally periodically adopts a formalized laboratory notebook-like style as she laboriously extends her understanding of human reproduction. And there are her sporadic cogitations on the difficult challenges and decisions to be faced by her as a debutante author, which if droll or arcane, are also apposite. Also, Sally and Mary's drunken repetitiveness and exactitudes as they make their tortuous way home and meet Barnabé. While Mrs. Mara, Sally's mother, is periodically depicted as dimwitted, on some occasions, as when Mrs. Killarney claims to be pregnant by Joël (Sally's older brother), she displays a quick defensive shrewdness that could hardly be bettered. In preparatory notes for *Journal intime* Joël, Sally's brother, is named "James" and is clearly the archetypical young genius Irish writer who finally emigrates, in his case rather drastically, to join the French Foreign Legion. Always given to excessive drinking, "batters" and crazy ideas for making money, his addiction develops to the stage where he becomes a parody of the classic alcoholic, devising endless excuses for a celebratory tipple.

Inevitably, there are some more of less general references in *Journal intime* / *Sally Mara's Intimate Diary* that might be clear to French readers (some more so in 1950), but obscure to most Anglophone readers:

Page 5. Georges Dumézil (1898–1986) was a comparative philologist who studied proto-Indo-European religion and society, and was said to speak fluently over thirty languages.

Page 17. On 6 February 1934, a right-wing anti-parliamentary demonstration in front of the Chambre des députés in Paris became a riot leading to about thirty deaths and two thousand injured.

Page 50. Ricard pastis was first available in 1932.

Page 51. *Le Temps de Cerises* (Cherry Time) is a sad love song, its lyrics seen in France as a metaphoric representation of the failed 1870 Paris commune. That Mrs. Mara sang this song may indicate that she and her devilish husband, John Mara, (a non-nationalist) had much different political outlooks.

Page 51. *Votre Beauté* was conceived in the early 1930s by Eugène Schueller, founder of L'Oréal cosmetic group. It was the first women's magazine entirely dedicated to beauty care.

Page 78. The perfume Lanvin's *Scandal* (1931) was a leather chypre fragrance. *Missive* (1932) from Roger and Gallet was a feminine perfume. *Zibeline* (1928) by Weil was a floral aldehyde fragrance for women. *Guerlain's Vol de Nuit* (1933) was inspired by a novel by Antoine Saint Exupery. However, in mid twentieth century France, *Scandale* was also a widely and daringly advertised brand of women's high quality underwear, particularly girdles.

Page 85. Reading Mrs. Mara's advice to Mrs. Killarney to pray to St Boldo (best known in northern Italy), French readers may think of a common remedy for constipation, *Boldoflorine*. However, it may cause abortion.

Page 149. "Let the ribbons flutter," "laisser flotter les rubans," is from an old popular song and signifies "don't worry about it."

Page 164. Henri Desiré Landru (1869–1922) was guillo-
tined for the murders of ten women he had seduced and
embezzled in Paris between 1914 and 1919.

Page 180. Jacques Fath (1912–1954) was a Parisian designer
who helped shaped past World War haute couture before
his premature death.

Also, even Irish and especially other English speaking people may not be aware of the significance, and/or relevance,
of some references, including relating to the Irish language;
again in order from start of text:

Page 27. For the native and expert Irish speakers I have
asked, "Cuir amach do theanga" ("Put out your tongue.")
has no sexual connotations. See page 35 note.

Page 32. W.B. Yeats's mother (a Pollexfen) was from Sligo.

Page 35. In the text Mève's translation of "Cuir amach do
theanga" is represented as "Tire ta langue" but of course she
would have answered in English, "Put out your tongue."
But the phrase "Tirer la langue" ("to pull the tongue") can
mean "to do nothing." So, Mève seems to have understood
Cuir amach du theanga as "Stop." But what did Joël intend
in the first place? "Tirer la langue" can also mean "to fool
a person." So, Joël tricks the sex-obsessed Sally, and then
Sally, apparently callously, rejects the amorous Mève—but
Joël, according to Sally, knows no Irish and Mève no French.

Page 43. The film *Bombshell* (1933) starred Jean Harlow,
who thereafter became known as the 'Blonde Bombshell'.
She died in 1937, aged 26.

Page 47. Father Theobald Mathew (1790–1856) cam-
paigned against drunkenness. Matt Talbot (1856–1925), a
poor workingman, was known for his struggles with alco-
holism, piety and self-mortification.

Page 57. In James Joyce's *Finnegans Wake*, Shaun, a son of

Henry Chipenden Earwicker and Anna Livia Plurabelle (they have twin boys and a girl), while making a geometric diagram, "accidentally" draws a representation of his father's genitalia. The other son, Shem, is a postman.

Page 64. *Tarzan the Ape Man* (1932) starred Johnny Weismuller and Maureen O'Sullivan. *Tarzan and his Mate*, with the same lead actors, premiered in 1934.

Page 73. Until the nineteen fifties, most books in Irish were printed using a distinctive "gaelic" script with 18 letters, all equivalent to letters of a standard roman alphabet, but the "I" lacked a dot. The sounds of the consonants listed by Sally are subject to change (aspiration), and this was indicated by the addition of a "dot" on top. However, when ordinary Roman typefaces are used (now standard), aspiration is indicated by the addition of a following "h."

Page 81. *Is cuma dhom*, "It doesn't matter to me" or "It's not my business." *Ná bíodh eagla ort*, "Let not fear be on you" or "Don't be afraid."

Page 105. Irish language terms for units of currency: Feoirlín (farthing, a quarter penny), pingin (penny), raol (sixpence), scilling (shilling), flóirín (florin, two shillings), coróin (crown, five shillings), punt (pound).

Page. 124. Prepositional pronouns, single words that combine common prepositions with the full range of personal pronouns, are a characteristic feature of Irish, and learning them is a significant task for beginners.

Page 195. The words *tardhleóir, oidhearcas, shoillse* are all ranks and titles, "ambassador," "excellency," "majesty," respectively. This an arcane bilingual "joke," a play on registers that only a person with very good Irish could get.

Page 209. The *SS St. Patrick* (1,922 tons, 1930) served on the Rosslare to Fishguard route (a good option when traveling on to France from Dublin or from Cork) until sunk by German aircraft on 13 June 1941.

Both works initially signed "Sally Mara" (*Journal intime* is a sort of prequel to *On est toujours trop bon avec les femmes*) were long ignored or disdained by critics and by commentators on Queneau's writings. Nevertheless, although this changed only gradually, *Journal intime* has received less attention than *OETTBALF* (as Queneau sometimes referred to it), or Barbara Wright's translation, *We Always Treat Women Too Well*. Already in 1962 Jean Dubuffet (renowned painter and founder of the Art Brut movement), for one, was greatly impressed by *Journal intime* and, having read it, wrote immediately to Queneau to express his appreciation. Michel Lécureur, Queneau's biographer, quotes: "Dubuffet, whose talents as a writer are too frequently underrated, coined, one day, this neat phrase to resume Queneau's tone: 'You strike the light of the joy-of-life on the flint of despair. [. . .]'." Dubuffet continued:

Never read anything that was so profoundly hilarious. [. . .] Marvelous original ideas succeed each other on every line [. . .] I must tell you that [. . .] during the three or four days when I was reading your book, the street, life and the world seemed to me to be rejuvenated and enlivened by your colors: like a dazzling Irish jig that is both everywhere and marvellously heartening, a savoury sophisticated carnival, and irresistibly exciting.

Having yet more to say, Dubuffet, wrote again to Queneau on the same day: "You are one of the very few to take up the idea that humor can be a lever capable of toppling the foundations of the edifice [of conventionality]."

NOTES ON THE TRANSLATION

The US based academic, Madeleine Velguth (translator of Queneau's *Children of Clay* and of his autobiography in verse, *Chêne et chien*), wrote about the difficulties she experienced in translating some early sections of *Journal intime*, and possible solutions to them. She noted: "Not the least of the tasks confronting the translator [. . .] is [. . .] one of recognition: recognizing puns, many of them sexual in nature, recognizing 'fractured' proverbs and aphorisms, and finally, recognizing 'anglicisms' and awkward French." Influenced by this and the fact that no translation of *Journal intime* to English had yet been published, I used to believe that, because of the language-dependency and arcane nature of much of the humor, such a translation would be very difficult or practically impossible. Or perhaps more importantly, that it would be a subversion of the original linguistic context. Putting it succinctly, the translation of *Journal intime* to English creates a new foreground that corresponds to the formerly hidden linguistic background (English) and the formerly predominant French foreground disappears.

But, after some time I came to feel that an English translation, combined with a commentary that highlights the consequences of translation and thereby maintains the reader's awareness of the missing and additional linguistic layers, could even become a valid alternative version of the story. Ideally, *Journal intime* in a somewhat French-flavored English might also leave its readers with an appreciation of comic potentials peculiar to the French language, and so, perhaps, some desire to learn more of French culture and language. Understanding another language facilitates escaping from habitual social contexts and constraints, and writing in French Sally clearly luxuriates in playing with a language that is spoken in what, to "her," are exotic French social circles:

> What a beautiful language all the same, French, and what a pleasure it is for me, alone in my dressing gown before an Irish turf fire, to be able to play with delicious, exotic phrases that are used on the other side of the sea by dockers in Le Havre, drivers of hackney cabs, mustard makers in Dijon and crooks in Marseilles.

(Of course, in translation the risk is that "she" may just seem to be "playing with delicious exotic phrases" that are used by dockers in Dublin, and crooks in London.)

Some translations of novels from various languages even give a new text that may well have been originally written in English. Such a domestication approach can extend to bowdlerization. A vivid example of this relates to Proust's *A la recherche du temps perdu*, when Françoise, the devoted, gifted but headstrong cook and general servant of the narrator's family, declares (in the patois of her poor mother):

> Qui de cul d'un chien s'amourose,
> Il lui paraît une rose.

This, in the admired translation by C.K. Scott Moncrieff became a sort of nursery rhyme:

Snaps and snails and puppy-dog's tails,
And dirty sluts in plenty,
Smell sweeter than roses in young men's noses
When the heart is one-and-twenty.

The alternative, which may be termed *foreignization*, seeks to preserve the cultural norms of the source language. For *Journal intime*, in particular, a domestication approach could even result in the elimination of much of the dark and rough humor. Consequently, I have felt a constant need, with respect to the innumerable choices that had to be made in translating *Journal intime*, to preserve a certain degree of strangeness in Sally's writing and use of language. In general, I have translated her French somewhat literally, preserving tenses and sentence structures and using "vrai ami" English words where clarity could be maintained—and clarity was always a top priority. Sometimes the original syntax and word order are close to French as-it-is-spoken and I have tried to preserve this also. All of this gives the resulting English a degree of stiffness and a style that may sometimes be quirky or stilted but achieves, I hope, an appropriate tone and register—foreign, naive and, hopefully, still replete with meaning. The intention is to encourage readers always to be aware of the "journey" that the text has made: Sally's English (in Queneau's imagination) to Sally's French to the translator's English. Nevertheless, the language of lower middle-class Dublin is represented by the use of common terms such as "mammy" (for maman), "daddy" (papa), "bum" (tutu), "the brother," "courting," "slagging," "to cop on," "your fella," "that one," "the chancer," "the Missus" (when her servant Mève refers to "Madame" [Baogal]), "youse' for the plural of "you".

For lines and paragraphs of direct speech, I have preserved the common French editorial practice of starting lines of direct speech with an em-dash (—) and not separating with quotation marks the speech elements from the clarifications such as 'she said' etc. For example, rather than:

Mammy said suddenly, just like that:
"Look, there are no matches in the house."
"I will go out and buy a box," answered Daddy, calmly without raising his head.
"You will go out like that," asked Mammy, quietly.
"Yes, answered Daddy," calmly.
That was the last word I heard him say. He never came back.

Like this:

Mammy said suddenly, just like that:
—Look, there are no matches in the house.
—I will go out and buy a box, answered Daddy, calmly without raising his head.
—You will go out like that, asked Mammy, quietly.
—Yes, answered Daddy, calmly.
That was the last word I heard him say. He never came back.

In this style, basic rules of English syntax are sometimes violated by the inclusion of exclamation and question marks mid-sentence:

—You have killed him! she asked me.

Sally's writing is characterized, in particular, by misunderstandings of definitions and usages that generate sexual references, and the innocent use of strong language. Early on, she resolves:

Si parfois un mot me manque, je m'en fous. Je continue
droit devant moi.

If sometimes I am missing a word, I don't give a fuck. I go
straight ahead.

In the nineteen fifties and sixties, this, coming from a sup-
posedly well-educated young woman, would have taken
aback and/or amused French readers. So, a significant share
of Queneau's humor in *Journal intime* depends on a young
woman's innocent use of terms the equivalent of which she
would not consider using if she were "bien rangée" (well
brought up). So, in translation the use of blunt equivalents
is necessary to preserve the humor. After all, in Queneau's
most widely read novel, *Zazie dans le Metro*, the prepubescent
Zazie's frequent use of the expletive "mon cul" just had to
be translated as the disconcerting—especially coming from a
little girl—"my arse."

The reason for Sally's frequent and innocent use of French
coarse words is given very early on:

"Foutre, me disait [Michel Presle, mon prof de français],
est un des plus beaux mots de la langue française. Il signifie:
jeter, mais avec plus de vigourosité. "

"Fuck," [Michel Presle, my French tutor] told me, "is one of
the most beautiful words in the French language. It means:
to throw, but with extra vigorosity."

Towards the end of the story, while visiting again, Michel
Presle eventually becomes aware of the consequence of this
unconventional approach to teaching French, and, accepting
his responsibility, he gently tries to make amends:

—Your life must be sad here, now that Joël and Mary are no longer here.

—A là là, Monsieur Presle, don't talk to me about it. All this shit for me! How shitty it is for me! Ah, fuck it!

[. . .]

Michel continued to laugh at everything that I said. Finally, that really irritated me.

—What "big words" do I say?

—Eh well: "fuck," "shit," "cunt" for example. In France, a young girl does not use these words except among family or with friends.

—But you are a friend, Monsieur Presle.

—I hope so. So I am not reproaching you in any way. It's just a little piece of advice.

Translating coarse language and slang is complicated by cultural differences and temporal shifts. The verb 'foutre' with its English near-equivalent "fuck," is a good example. The etymology of "foutre" goes back to the Latin "futuere" (to copulate, a man with a woman). Its use in this sense is illustrated well by an excerpt from the *Goncourt Journal*:

Je suis ce soir, au chemin de fer, à côté d'un ouvrier complètement saoul, qui répète à tout moment : "Non, je ne la foutrais pas, quand on me donnerait tout Paris . . . oui, tout Paris, non, je ne la foutrais pas!" (*Goncourt, Journal,* 1872, P. 900).

I am on a train this evening, beside a workman who is completely drunk, who repeats continuously: "No I would not fuck her if they gave me the whole of Paris . . . yes, the whole of Paris, I would not fuck her."

Queneau also used "foutre" in its full original sense in *Le Chiendent* (1933) when the characters Étienne Marcel and Saturnin Belhôtel, felt obliged to make use of the basic service of a brothel:

> Mais les deux hommes bavardaient sans arrêt et se racontaient leurs souvenirs d'enfance. A la fin, Camélia vint les rappeler à l'ordre, on réclamait les dames ailleurs. Alors ils montèrent, foutirent et redescendirent continuer à boire.

> But the two men went on talking without a break, and were swapping reminiscences of their childhood. Finally, Camélia came to call them to order, the girls were wanted elsewhere. So they went up, fucked, and came down again and went on drinking.

However, while "foutre," and "fuck," are both intrinsically copulatory terms, other meanings and uses for both have existed for a very long time and have become dominant—their degree of vulgarity varying with the form of the word used, and tending to diminish with time. Some uses of "foutre" translate to "fuck" quite straightforwardly:

> "Foutre le camp" (1838) or "to fuck off."

> "On me foutrait en prison" (1909) or "I would be fucked into prison."

> "Ils se foutent de nous" (1936) or "they don't give a fuck about us."

Others may have no straight English equivalent involving the use of "fuck":

"En foutre plein la vue à quelqu'un" or "to amaze someone."

"Foutre son pied [quelque part]" or "[for] him/her to go [somewhere]."

The multiple associated uses for "foutre" and its derivatives have become so widespread and common that many French speakers who routinely use phrases like "je m'en fous" (I don't care) or "je fous le camp" (I am leaving) may no longer have any idea of the fundamental meaning of the verb. This has been facilitated in contemporary French by the use of "baiser" as the common term for "to have sexual intercourse.' (To avoid misunderstanding or offense, the verb "baiser," fundamentally meaning "to kiss" has been totally supplanted by others, particularly "s'embrasser.")

In contrast, "fuck" in English retains its sexual use, which may explain its popularity with comedians because of its continued edge and power to shock. Consequently and in general, depending on the context, "fuck" may not often be the appropriate choice when translating "foutre" and its derivatives to English. Some may hold that this should apply to translating all corresponding individual words and phrases in *Journal intime*.

I then thought that examination of translations of *Journal intime* to other languages—to German and Italian for example—might give some insights as to possible options with respect to English. In German, Sally's first use of "foutre," "foutre au feu" becomes "in den Ofen feuern" (to fling, sling into the fire) but, in explanation, this is followed repetitively by, in parentheses "foutre au feu" and "foutre." However, the next three "foutres" become "umhauen" (to chop, knock flying, bowl over) and the fourth is "feuern" again. Toward the end of the story, "Ah, foutre" becomes "Ach, es ist zum

Kotzen"! (the verb "kotzen" means "to puke,' so "Oh, it makes me puke") and "Der Laden stinkt mir" (literally "the shop stinks"). So, there is little consistency in the rendering of "foutre" and its variants into German, and even an expectation that the German reader understands the original French "foutre." In Italian, Sally's early "foutres" become "sbattere" ("to beat, throw, fuck") or sbatterglielo (fling). Towards the end, "Ah, foutre" is translated as "Ah, cazzo" (an equivalent of "Oh, fuck"; cazzo means "penis" etc.) and as "mi girano" (literally, "turn me around" or "I am getting annoyed"), Somewhat better, but as the story progresses continuity is lost. In conclusion, as determined by further enquiries, the diffi- culties with translating Sally's "foutres" to German or Italian seem to be related to their copulatory "f-words" ("ficken" and "fottere," respectively) not having wide ranges of common, more or less sanitized, metaphorical uses, unlike both "foutre" and even "fuck."

Perhaps because of the continuing harshness of "fuck," some choice has arisen in English with respect to attenuated f-words. 'Eff' as in "eff off" or the "effing boss" is, of course, simply "fuck" partially redacted. "Feck" has long been com- mon in Ireland and has been propagated by the popular televi- sion series *Father Ted*. A misspelling, such as "fug" (as Norman Mailer was obliged to use in *The Naked and the Dead*) or "fock," is another option. "To frig" sounds less harsh but it may not always be fully understood; basically it means "to fuck" or "to masturbate" (transitively or intransitively). In French the only common alternative f-word is "ficher" (to do, give, put), but in informal, especially younger company "ficher" may be regarded as excessively polite.

Umberto Eco wrote, as he mused on issues that might arise in translating detective novels: "Plot and story are so import- ant that a translation can be deemed satisfactory even though it shows scant respect for certain stylistic subtleties found in the original." The (opposite) lesson here for a translation of *Journal intime* is that taking only immediate contexts into account when translating phrases that include "foutre" ("con," "merde," etc.) and derivatives could undermine a significant thread of humor that continues for the entire story i.e., Sally's innocent use of very strong language. Consequently, giving priority to this theme, I have translated the equivalents of "En foutre plein la vue à quelqu'un" ("to amaze someone") as "to fuck over someone's impression or opinion," and 'foutre son pied [quelque part]" ([for] her to go [somewhere]) as "to fuck her feet [somewhere]." Correspondingly, when Sally is communing with her diary "foutre" always becomes "fuck", but when she is translating what was originally spoken in English I have avoided "fuck" and allowed the mores of that time and circumstances to influence the choice. For Joël's remarks while at home it is the still coarse "feck"; when Sally is seriously drunk and holding forth ("je m'en foutais royalement") it is "I could not give a royal shite"; and when she rejects Steve the vampirologist ("va te faire foutre") it is the literally quite accurate "bugger off." In doing this I have taken advantage of the greater flexibility of English with respect to still rude but attenuated f-words. It should be noted that such options were not available to Queneau writing in French.

Another issue in translating *Journal intime* is the occurrence throughout of Irish language words and phrases. Words, phrases, and even long passages in a second language are not unknown in novels. Leo Tolstoy's *War and Peace* (Russian with passages in French), Thomas Mann's *The Magic Mountain* (German and French) and Umberto Eco's *The Name of the Rose* (Italian and varieties of Latin) come to mind. The difference with the Irish words and phrases embedded in a 1950's

French novel is that Queneau would have had absolutely no expectation that readers (especially of the Scorpion edition) would understand them.

Understandably, some of these Irish interpolations are misspelt or incorrect because of errors by the printers or because of Queneau's limited knowledge of Irish, and I have corrected them in this work. Around the time he was writing *Journal intime*, Queneau listed in his own journal the many languages that he had studied, including Turkish at that time, but not Irish. In fact, as I discovered after a long search, he plucked words and phrases from a learning manual that had lists of useful words and phrases (Seàn O'Beirne's *Irish Self-Taught*, 1933). He could have acquired this as early as 1936, when he was translating the English translation of Maurice O'Sullivan's *Fiche Bliain ag Fàs* (1933) to give *Vingt ans de jeunesse* (1936). In some places Queneau cleverly used Irish to bury humor so deeply as to make its excavation very difficult if not impossible for "normal' readers. Taking a more straightforward example, Sally's lecherous teacher of Irish is Padraic Baoghal; "baoghal" (old spelling, now "baol") is an Irish word meaning "danger."

Translating a work as linguistically and humoristically as complex as *Journal intime* inevitably resulted on losses with respect to meaning and humor. The following notes are intended to compensate, particularly with respect to the use of *argot* (French slang words), but inevitable inadequately so. In order of place in text:

Page 15. "To innocents, full hands" is a literal translation of "Aux innocents, les mains pleines," roughly the equivalent of "Beginner's luck."

Page 53. "But they are so diverse and so contradictory that I can see neither their head nor tail," "ni queue ni tête," means literally "neither tail nor head," meaning "to be pointless" but there is also a double entendre. "Queue" can also mean "penis."

Page 65. "Bloody obvious, he couldn't stop himself." The original was "Question cousue de fil-à-la patte," which is an amalgam of two phrases, "cousu de fil blanc" (sewn with white thread) "a trick easily seen through" and "avoir un fil à la patte" (a [bird's] leg secured with a string) "to be unable to resist."

Page 65. It was probably "illico" ("right away" or "pronto") that "Sally" intended to write. Is this a covert recognition by Queneau that he is the author, "incognito"?

Page 74. "Wasteful," is here a reasonable equivalent to "dilapidée." This is the feminine past participle of the verb "dilapider" which means "to squander, waste, embezzle." Mrs. Killarney uses much strangely formal language during this scene.

Page 89. In French, for verbs in the perfect tense (passé composé) using être, the past participle of the verb should agree in gender and number with the subject of the sentence. For example: il est parti (he left, went away), elle est partie, ils sont partis, elles sont parties. However, conventionally, for mixed groups the rule (nowadays frequently challenged, like here by "Sally" in "1934") is that even one male makes the whole group grammatically "male." Hence, for Sally, Mary, the nanny goat, Betty, and the uncle (the sole male), it is "nous sommes partis," not "parties."

Page 109. Originally, "bouquiner"; it's what a bookish person does. But for "Sally" it derives from "bouc" (billy goat), so, "to copulate." Marcel Proust has the promiscuous Odette de Crécy (impishly) say to the very bookish Charles Swan "Comme cela doit être amusant de bouquiner . . ."

Page 123. "she had worms in her nose," "elle avait des vers dans le nez." "Tirer les vers du nez à quelqu'un" means "to worm a secret out of someone." Surgical psychoanalysis?

Page 135. "shaking I know not what" or "à branler je ne sais quoi"; the reflexive form of "branler" (to shake), "se branler," means "to masturbate."

Page 143. "Impasse" is the common French term for "no through road." The English equivalent "cul-de-sac" means "bottom of the bag," as "cul" means "bottom" or "arse."

Page 153. "sing-song." "Turlutaine," means words repeated endlessly; "la turlurette," is "the chorus of song"; and "turlute" is argot for "fellation."

Page 159. "it is evident men prefer the buttonhole and women the knot," or "il est évident que l'homme préfère la boutonnière et la femme le nœud." "Boutonnière," (a "button-hole" or a "flower on a lapel") can also mean "knife wound" or "slash," and "bouton" ("button") can mean "clitoris"; while "le nœd," ("the knot") can mean "the glans penis."

Page 161. "rozzer," "argousin," a slang term for "policeman."

Page 172. "Pour une fois que je m'étais payé un pinte de bon sang." "For the one time that I had a good time / a really good laugh." A very, very dark "joke" with a long build up!

Page 180. "L'asperge" (the asparagus) can mean "the penis" and "la moule" (the mussel) "the vulva." The ancient epic *Batrachomyomachia*, (*The battle of Frogs and Mice*) is a parody of Homer's *Iliad*. Of course, Gulliver's Travels is by Jonathan Swift not Lewis Carroll. The *Almanach Vermot* is an annual humorous publication initiated in 1886.

Page 185. It seems that Sally and the taxi driver became quite friendly as they talked together. In the text it is, "il a été très intéressé et, de fil en aiguille, on a presque fait un tête-à-queue. Fil en aiguille" (thread in needle) can mean "to recount in order without omitting the least detail."

"Tête-à-queue" (head to tail) may be a play on "*tete-à-tête*," noting that "queue" can mean "penis."

Page 189. "Va te faire foutre," a strong insult which means, literally, "go (and) have yourself fucked." Earlier, Sally had addressed Steve as "vous" but insults may be given extra force by use of the familiar pronoun "tu/te." When Sally repeats the rejection, she says more formally: "Je vous ai dit d'aller vous faire foutre."

Page 193. "But then, from thread in needle and eel in girl, . . ." "Mais que, de fil en aiguille et d'anguille in fille, . . ." Here the French internal rhyming and wordplay are impossible to render with any justice; translating components: "de fil en aiguille (gradually), "fil" (thread) and "fille" (girl); "aiguille" (needle, aiguiller: to copulate) and "anguille" (eel, penis).

Page 196 /197. "bouc-ery" "Un équarrisseur" is a "knacker," i.e. a person who disposes of dead animals. But nowadays, especially in Ireland, this term has negative connotations, so I used "butcher." Also, here "équarrissage" is used to indicate "that," i.e. sexual activity, but I have used "bouc-ery" in reference to the etymology of both "boucher" and "butcher," both derived from "a seller of goat meat." However, it is almost as difficult to imagine a woman like Mrs. Mara actually using "knackery" ("équarrissage" in the original) as using "bouc-ery" with the meaning inferred in this context.

Page 201. "Tim de-maidened me," "Tim m'a dépucelée." From "pucelle," maiden; figuratively "Tim deflowered me."

Page 206. ". . . a bastard, a louser, and a cunt," ". . . un salaud, un dégueulasse et un con."

Finally, an admission, I consciously departed from the published text once, toward the end of Sally's entry for the

eventful 7 March 1935 (Page 132) when Mève demonstrates
graphically the depth of her feelings for her employer, Padraic
Baoghal. Endemic or extreme mistreatment of domestic servants is a significant theme in *Journal intime*: Mrs. Killarney
is casually violated by Joël, Bess lives in fear and is eventually
murdered and desecrated, Mève is treated as a thief by Mrs
Baoghal and, whatever the reason, she detests Padraic Baogal.
In this scene Baoghal has been knocked unconscious by Sally
and the task is to revive him. In the manuscript and in the
proofs it is simply "Legs apart, Mève placed herself above his
head." However, in the published text Mève asks "—Will I
empty a teapot on his coffeepot (head)?" In both versions,
Sally replies "—No, cold water would be preferable." Later,
when Sally recounts this event to Mary and her mother this
"made Mammy double up to the extent that she nearly suffocated." Whatever Queneau's motivation for replacing Mève's
(wordless) suggestion, this restoration simultaneously sup-
ports an important subtheme and makes sense of Mrs Mara's
extreme reaction.

APPENDIX: Sally Mara as Known to Early Readers of *Journal Intime*

These two pieces contain as much information as readers of her *Journal Intime* could have had about Sally Mara when it was first published in 1950. Some readers may have already read "her" 1947 novel *On est toujours trop bon avec les femmes*. The name of Raymond Queneau did not feature in either work.

1947: From *On est toujours trop bon avec les femmes.*

Introduction

One never knows what people have in their minds. One might know someone for twenty years, if they become a writer it is always a surprise. During different visits that I made to Ireland between 1932 and 1939, I met Sally Mara several times. At first a young girl, who was unremarkable except for her date of birth: Easter Monday 1916. Then I saw her among the group associated with Padraic Baoghal, the poet. Timid and barely pretty, she married, while still very young, a hardware dealer from Cork, a rather nice town.

When I returned to Ireland after an absence of seven years, Padraic Baoghal gave me a sealed package; it was the novel that we present today to the French public. Sally Mara had died quietly and unexpectedly from some disease in 1943. She entrusted me with the task of translating to French a manuscript that she knew to be un-publishable in its original language.

After having read (not without some surprise) Sally's work, I visited her husband. The hardware merchant of Cork, who had increased greatly in weight since the death of his wife, remembered the book only vaguely; he had no objection to it being published beyond the borders of Éire.

Everyone will judge *We always treat women too well* as it pleases them. I do not believe that one should see political or historical intentions in the free and easy way events are recounted: it was not quite like this, it seems, that the insurrection in Dublin took place on Easter Monday 1916.

Michel Presle
November 1947

1949: Advance Notice of Publication
An upcoming novel!

SALLY MARA
Author of "On est toujours trop bon avec les femmes."
50,000 copies sold
INTIMATE DIARY

Sally Mara died on the first of May 1943 in Cork (Ireland). Her French teacher translated in 1947 her novel *On est toujours trop bon avec les femmes*, which was a success in bookshops and won the first Prix du Tabou. The press were unanimous.

Combat wrote: "A success"; *Franc-Tireur*, "Gripping, makes your hair stand on end"; *France-Dimanche*, "An hilarious drama"; *La Gazette des Lettres*, "A masterpiece of comicalness and humor"; *Samedi-Soir*, "Under full sails to enormous sales"; *Carrefour*, "It's idiotic."

After two years of hesitation the hardware merchant of Cork, her husband, conveyed to us the personal diary of Sally that he had found behind some bottles of Ricard pastis. He sent us a long letter upholding the memory of his wife and he finished it with these words: "Innocence has its limits but that of Sally had none."

A 260 page volume . . . . .246 fr.

120 copies on fine paper . . . . . 800 fr.

LES ÉDITIONS DU SCORPION, 1 RUE LOBINEAU, PARIS (6c) — ODÉon 59-68

Acknowledgements

For me, this translation project has been both an educational and a pleasurable exercise, but one that could not have reached its present state without the help, advice and suggestions for improvements of others. All remaining inadequacies and errors are mine and mine alone.

First of all, Madeleine Velguth (University of Wisconsin Milwaukee), a prize-winning translator of works by Raymond Queneau, was a crucial support to the project from the beginning and an invaluable source of expertise and advice. Suzanne Bagoly, director of the 'Centre de Documentation Raymond Queneau' at the Bibliothèque de Verviers, Belgium was unstinting in her support during and after my visit. The staff at Bibliothèque Armand Salacrou, Le Havre were also helpful and courteous when I visited to examine manuscripts and printer's proofs. As for more general sources and references, I am indebted to the Librarian and staff of the James Hardiman Library, National University of Ireland Galway. The early encouragement and advice of Adrian Frazier, Paul Gosling, Padraic de Bhaldraithe, and Anis Memon bolstered my courage to proceed and persevere. The friendship, entertaining letters, support and encouragement of Jean-Marie Queneau, who unfortunately died just last year, was invaluable and touched me to the core. Temporally near last, but certainly not least, Mairéad Byrne's penetrating review of the translation and accessory texts and helped to make this a much better work.

Finally, I will always remember the mirth of my old school friend Séamus O'Callaghan as I read excerpts to him. Most of us then were Barnabés.

Bibliography

Manuscripts and Printer's Proofs

Manuscript of *Journal intime de Sally Mara* (14 school copybooks). Bibliothèque Armand Salacrou, Le Havre, France.

Printers proofs of *Œuvres de Sally Mara*. 1. *On est toujours trop bon avec les femmes*. 2. *Journal intime*. Bibliothèque Armand Salacrou, Le Havre, France

Preparatory notes for *Journal intime de Sally Mara*. Centre de Documentation Raymond Queneau (CDRQ), Bibliothéque Communale, Verviers, Belgium.

Dictionaries and Language manuals

François Caradec, Jean-Bernard Pouy, *Dictionnaire du français argotique et populaire* (Paris: Larousse, 2009).

Patrick S Dinneen, *Foclóir Gaedhilge agus bearla: - Irish-English Dictionary* (Dublin: Irish Texts Society, 1934).

Claude Duneton with Sylvie Clavel, *Le Bouquet des Expressions imagées: Encyclopédie thématique des locutions figurées de la langue française* (Paris: Éditions du Seuil, 1990).

Seán O'Beirne B.A., *Irish Self-Taught* (London: E. Marlborough & Co. Ltd., 1933).

Niall Ó Dónail, *Irish–English dictionary* (Dublin: Oifig an tSoláthair, 1977).

Some other Works and Sources

Roger Chauviré, *L'Irlande* (Paris: Henri Didier, 1936).

Pierre David, *Dictionaire des personnages de Raymond Queneau* (Limoges: PULIM, 1994).

Simone de Beauvoir, *Le deuxième sexe, tomes* I et II (Paris: Gallimard 1949).

James Patrick Gosling, *Raymond Queneau's Dubliners: Bewildered by Excess of Love* (Newcastle, UK: Cambridge Scholars Publishing, 2019).

James Patrick Gosling, *Queneau irlandais : Les œuvres complètes de Sally Mara* (Dijon, France: Essais, Éditions universitaire de Dijon, 2022).

Michel Lécureur, *Raymond Queneau: Biographie* (Paris: Les Belles Lettres / Archimbaud, 2002).

Finlay Muirhead ed, *Ireland*, London: Ernest Benn (Paris: Librairie Hachette, The Blue Guides, 1932).

O'Súilleabháin, Muiris, *Fiche Blian ag Fás*, an tríú heagrán (1933; Má Nuad: An Sagart Má Nuad, 1981).

Jean-Yves Pouilloux, *Les Œuvres Completes de Sally Mara: Notice*, pp. 1719–37, in Raymond Queneau, *Œuvres Complètes – Romans*, tome II (*Œuvres Complètes, III*) (Paris: Gallimard, 2006).

Anne-Isabelle Queneau, *Album Raymond Queneau* (Paris: Gallimard, 2002).

Raymond Queneau, *Le Chiendent* (Paris: Gallimard, 1933).

(Raymond Queneau) Sally Mara, *Journal Intime* (Paris: Éditions du Scorpion, 1950).

Raymond Queneau, translated by Eugen Helmlé, *Das intime Tegebuch der Sally Mara*, (Frankfurt am Main, Fischer Taschenbuch Verlag, 1984)

Raymond Queneau, translated by Leonelle Prato Caruso, *Il diario intimo di Sally Mara* (Milano, Feltrinelli, 1991).

Raymond Queneau, *Les Œuvres Complète de Sally Mara* (Paris: Gallimard, 1962).

Raymond Queneau (ed. by Anne-Isabelle Queneau), *Journaux – 1914–1965* (Paris: Gallimard, 1996).

A Rivoallan, *Littérature Irlandaise Contemporaine* (Paris: Libraire Hachette, 1939).

Printed in the USA
CPSIA information can be obtained
at www.ICGtesting.com
JSHW080928280723
45552JS00003B/4